THE
SHADOW WORLD

BY

HAMLIN GARLAND

FOREWORD

This book is a faithful record, so far as I can make it, of the most marvellous phenomena which have come under my observation during the last sixteen or seventeen years. I have used my notes made immediately after the sittings and also my reports to the American Psychical Society of which I was at one time a director as the basis of my story. For literary purposes I have substituted fictitious names for real names, and imaginary characters for the actual individuals concerned; but I have not allowed these necessary expedients to interfere with the precise truth of the account.

For example, *Miller*, an imaginary chemist, has been put in the place of a scientist much older than thirty-five, in whose library the inexplicable "third sitting" took place. *Fowler*, also, is not intended to depict an individual. The man in whose shoes he stands is one of the most widely read and deeply experienced spiritists I have ever known, and I have sincerely tried to present through *Fowler* the argument which his prototype might have used. Pg iv *Mrs. Quigg*, *Miss Brush,Howard*, the *Camerons*, and most of the others, are purely imaginary. The places in which the sittings took place are not indicated, for the reason that I do not wish to involve any unwilling witnesses.

In the case of the psychics, they are, of course, delineated exactly as they appeared to me, although I have concealed their real names and places of residence. *Mrs. Smiley*, whose admirable patience under investigation makes her an almost ideal subject, is the chief figure among my "mediums," and I have tried to give her attitude toward us and toward her faith as she expressed it in our sittings, although the conversation is necessarily a mixture of imagination and memory. *Mrs. Hartley* is a very real and vigorous character—a professional psychic, it is true, but a woman of intelligence and power. Those in private life I have guarded with scrupulous care, and I am sure that none of them, either private or professional, will feel that I have wilfully misrepresented what took place. My aim throughout has been to deal directly and simply with the facts involved.

I have not attempted to be profound or mystical or even scientific, but I have tried to present clearly, simply, and as nearly without bias as possible, an account of what I have seen and heard. The weight of evidence seems, at the moment, to be on the side of the biologists; but I am willing to Pg v reopen the case at any time, although I am, above all, a man of the open air, of the plains and the mountains, and do not intend to identify myself with any branch of metapsychical research. It is probable, therefore, that this is my one and final contribution to the study of *the shadow world.*

HAMLIN GARLAND.

CHICAGO, *July, 1908.*

THE SHADOW WORLD

I

A hush fell over the dinner-table, and every ear was open and inclined as Cameron, the host, continued: "No, I wouldn't say that. There are some things that are pretty well established—telepathy, for instance."

"I don't believe even in telepathy," asserted Mrs. Quigg, a very positive journalist who sat at his right. "I think even *that* is mere coincidence."

Several voices rose in a chorus of protest. "Oh no! Telepathy is real. Why, I've had experiences—"

"There you go!" replied Mrs. Quigg, still in the heat of her opposition. "You will all tell the same story. Your friend was dying in Bombay or Vienna, and his spirit appeared to you, *à la Journal of Psychic Research*, with a message, at the exact hour, computing difference in time which no one ever does , and so on. I know that kind of thing—but that isn't telepathy."

"What is telepathy, then?" asked little Miss Brush, who paints miniatures.

"I can't describe a thing that doesn't exist," replied Mrs. Quigg. "The word means feeling at a distance, does it not, professor?"

Harris, a teacher of English, who seldom took a serious view of anything, answered, "I should call it a long-distance touch."

"Do you believe in hypnotism, Dr. Miller?" asked Miss Brush, quietly addressing her neighbor, a young scientist whose specialty was chemistry.

"No," replied he; "I don't believe in a single one of these supernatural forces."

"You mean you don't believe in anything you have not seen yourself," said I.

To this Miller slowly replied: "I believe in Vienna, which I have never seen, but I don't believe in a Vienna doctor who claims to be able to hypnotize a man so that he can smile while his leg is being taken off."

"Oh, that's a fact," stated Brierly, the portrait-painter; "that happens every day in our hospitals here in New York City."

"Have you ever seen it done?" asked Miller, bristling with opposition.

"No."

"Well," asserted Miller, "I wouldn't believe it even if I saw the operation performed."

Pg 5

"You don't believe in any mystery unless it is familiar," said I, warming to the contest.

"I certainly do not believe in these childish mysteries," responded Miller, "and it is strange to me that men like Sir Oliver Lodge and Sir William Crookes should believe in slate-writing and levitation and all the rest of that hocus-pocus."

"Nevertheless, hypnotism is a fact," insisted Brierly. "You must have some faith in the big books on the subject filled with proof. Think of the tests—"

"I don't call it a test to stick pins into a person's tongue," said Mrs. Quigg. "We newspaper people all know that there are in the hypnotic business what they call 'horses'—that is to say, wretched men and boys, women sometimes, who have trained themselves so that they can hold hot pennies, eat red pepper, and do other 'stunts'—we've had their confessions times enough."

"Yes, but their confessions are never quite complete," retorted young Howard. "When I was in college I had one of these 'horses' appeal to me for help. He was out of a job, and I told him I'd blow him to the supper of his life if he would render up the secrets of his trade. He took my offer, but jarred me by confessing that the professor really could hypnotize him. He had to make believe only part of the time. His 'stunts' were mostly real."

Pg 6

"It's the same way with mediums," said I. "I have had a good deal of experience with them, and I've come to the conclusion that they all, even the most untrustworthy of them, start with at least some small basis of abnormal power. Is it not rather suggestive that the number of practising mediums does not materially increase? If it were a mere matter of deception, would there not be thousands at the trade? As a matter of fact, there are not fifty advertising mediums in New York at this moment, though of course the number is kept down by the feeling that it is a bit disreputable to have these powers."

"You're too easy on them," said Howard. "I never saw one that wasn't a cheap skate."

Again I protested. "Don't be hasty. There are nice ones. My own mother had this power in her youth, so my father tells me. Her people were living in Wisconsin at the time when this psychic force developed in her, and the settlers from many miles around came to see her 'perform.' An uncle, when a boy of four, did automatic writing, and one of my aunts recently wrote to me, in relation to my book *The Tyranny of the Dark*, that for two years beginning when she was about seventeen these powers of darkness made her life a hell. It won't do to be hasty in condemning the mediums wholesale. There are many decent people who are possessed by strange forces, but are Pg 7 shy of confessing their abnormalities. Ask your family physician. He will tell you that he always has at least one patient who is troubled by occult powers."

"Medical men call it 'hysteria,'" said Harris.

"Which doesn't explain anything," I answered. "Many apparently healthy people possess the more elementary of these powers—often without knowing it."

"We are all telepathic in some degree," declared Brierly.

"Perhaps all the so-called messages from the dead come from living minds," I suggested—"I mean the minds of those about us. Dr. Reed, a friend of mine, once arranged to go with a patient to have a test sitting with a very celebrated psychic who claimed to be able to read sealed letters. Just before the appointed day, Reed's patient died suddenly of heart-disease, leaving a sealed letter on his desk. The doctor, fully alive to the singular opportunity, put the letter in his pocket and hastened to the medium. The magician took it in his hand and pondered. At last he said: 'This was written by a man now in the spirit world. I cannot sense it. There isn't a medium in the world who can read it, but if you will send it to any person anywhere on the planet and have it read and resealed, I will tell you what is in it. I cannot get Pg 8 the words unless some mind in the earth-plane has absorbed them.'"

Harris spoke first. "That would seem to prove a sort of universal mind reservoir, wouldn't it?"

"That is the way my friend figured it. But isn't that a staggering hypothesis? I have never had a sealed letter read, but the psychic research people seem to have absolutely proved psychometry to be a fact. After you read Myers you are ready to believe anything—or nothing."

The hostess rose. "Suppose we go into the library and have more ghost stories. Come, Mr. Garland, we can't leave you men here to talk yourselves out on these interesting subjects. You must let us all hear what you have to say."

In more or less jocose mood the company trooped out to the library, where a fire was glowing in the grate and easy-chairs abounded. The younger people, bringing cushions, placed themselves beside the hearth, while I took a seat near Mrs. Cameron and Harris.

"There!" said Miss Brush, with a gurgle of delight. "This is more like the proper light and surroundings for creepy tales. Please go on, Mr. Garland. You said you'd had a good deal of experience—tell us all about it. I always think of you as a trailer, a man of the plains. How did you happen to get into this shadow world?"

"It came about while I was living in Boston. Pg 9 It was in 1891, or possibly 1892. A friend, the editor of the *Arena*, asked me to become a member of the American Psychical Society, which he was helping to form. He wished me to go on the Board of Directors, because, as he said, I was 'young, a keen observer, and without emotional bias'—by which he meant that I had not been bereaved."

"Quite right; the loss of a child or a wife weakens even the best of us illogical," commented Harris. "No man who is mourning a relative has any business to be calling himself an investigator of spiritualism."

"Well, the upshot was, I joined the society, became a member of the Executive Board, was made a special committee on 'physical phenomena'—that is to say, slate-writing, levitation, and the like—and set to work. It was like entering a new, vague, and mysterious world. The first case I investigated brought out one of the most fundamental of these facts, which is, that this shadow world lies very close to the sunny, so-called normal day. The secretary of the society had already begun to receive calls for help. A mechanic had written from South Boston asking us to see his wife's automatic writing, and a farmer had come down from Concord to tell us of a haunted house and the mysterious rappings on its walls. Almost in a day I was made aware of the illusory side of life."

Pg 10

"Why illusory?" asked Brierly.

"Let us call it that for the present," I answered. "Among those who wrote to us was a woman from Lowell whose daughter had developed strange powers. Her account, so straightforward and so precise, determined us to investigate the case. Therefore, our secretary a young clergyman and I took the train for Lowell one autumn afternoon. We found Mrs. Jones living in a small, old-fashioned frame house standing hard against the sidewalk, and through the parlor windows, while we awaited the psychic, I watched an endless line of derby hats as the town's mechanics plodded by—incessant reminders of the practical, hard-headed world that filled the street. This was, indeed, a typical case. In half an hour we were all sitting about the table in a dim light, while the sweet-voiced mother was talking with 'Charley,' her 'poltergeist'—"

"What is that, please?" asked Mrs. Quigg.

"The word means a rollicking spirit who throws things about. I did not value what happened at this sitting, for the conditions were all the psychic's own. By-the-way, she was a large, blond, strapping girl of twenty or so—one of the mill-hands—not in the least the sickly, morbid creature I had expected to see. As I say, the conditions were such as to make what took place of no scientific value, and I turned in no report upon it; but it was all very curious."

Pg 11

"What happened? Don't skip," bade Mrs. Cameron.

"Oh, the table rapped and heaved and slid about. A chair crawled to my lap and at last to the top of the table, apparently of its own motion. A little rocking-chair moved to and fro precisely as if some one were sitting in it, and so on. It was all unconvincing at the time, but as I look back upon it now, after years of experience, I am inclined to think part of it at least was genuine. And this brings me to say to Mrs. Quigg, and to any other doubter, that you have only to step aside into silence and shadow and wait for a moment—and the bewildering will happen, or you will imagine it to happen. I will agree to furnish from this company a medium that will astonish even our materialistic friend Miller."

There was a loud outcry: "What do you mean? Explain yourself!"

"I am perfectly certain that if this company will sit as I direct for twenty-one days at the same hour, in the same room, under the same conditions, phenomena will develop which will not merely amaze but scare some of you; and as for you, Mrs. Quigg, you who are so certain that nothing ever happens, you will be the first to turn pale with awe."

"Try me! I am wild to be 'shown.'"

Harris was not so boastful. "You mean, of Pg 12 course, that some of these highly cultured ladies would develop hysteria?"

"I am not naming the condition; I only say that I have seen some very hard-headed and self-contained people cut strange capers. The trance and 'impersonation' usually come first."

"Let's do it!" cried out Miss Brush. "It would be such fun!"

"You'd be the first to 'go off,'" said I, banteringly.

Harris agreed. "She is neuropathic."

"I propose we start a psychic society here and now," said Cameron. "I'll be president, Mrs. Quigg secretary, and Garland can be the director of the awful rites. Miss Brush, you shall be the 'mejum.'"

"Oh no, no!" she cried, "please let some one else be it."

This amused me, but I seized upon Cameron's notion. "I accept the arrangement provided you do not hold me responsible for any ill effects," I said. "It's ticklish business. There are many who hold the whole process diabolic."

"Is the house ready for the question?" asked Cameron.

"Ay, ay!" shouted every one present.

"The society is formed," announced Cameron. "As president, I suggest a sitting right now. How about it, Garland?"

Pg 13

"Certainly!" I answered, "for I have an itching in my thumbs that tells me something witching this way comes."

The guests rose in a flutter of pleased excitement.

"How do we go at it?" asked Mrs. Cameron.

"The first requisite is a small table—"

"Why a table?" asked Mrs. Quigg.

"The theory is that it helps to concentrate the minds of the sitters, and it will also furnish a convenient place to rest our hands. Anyhow, all the great investigators began this way," I replied, pacifically. "We may also require a pencil and a pad."

Miller was on his dignity. "I decline to sit at a table in that foolish way. I shall look on in lonely grandeur."

The others were eager to "sit in," as young Howard called it, and soon nine of us were seated about an oblong mahogany table. Brierly was very serious, Miss Brush ecstatic, and Mrs. Harris rather nervous.

I was careful to prepare them all for failure. "This is only a trial sitting, you know, merely to get our hands in," I warned.

"Must we keep still?"

"Oh no! You may talk, if you do so quietly. Please touch fingers, so as to make a complete circuit. I don't think it really necessary, but it Pg 14 sometimes helps to produce the proper mental state; singing softly also tends to harmonize the 'conditions,' as the professionals say. Don't argue and don't be too eager. Lean back and rest. Take a passive attitude toward the whole problem. I find the whole process very restful. Harris, will you turn down the lights before—"

"There!" said Miller, "the hocus-pocus begins. Why not perform in the light?"

"Subdued light will bring the proper negative and inward condition sooner," I replied, taking a malicious delight in his disgust. "Now will some one sing 'Annie Laurie,' or any other sweet, low song? Let us get into genial, receptive mood. Miller, you and your fellow-doubters please retire to the far end of the room."

In a voice that trembled a little, Mrs. Harris started the dear old melody, and all joined in, producing a soft and lulling chorus.

At the end of the song I asked, matter-of-factly: "Are the conditions right? Are we sitting right?"

Mrs. Quigg sharply queried, "Whom are you talking to?"

"The 'guides,'" I answered.

"The 'guides'!" she exclaimed. "Do you believe in the guides?"

"I believe in the *belief* of the guides," was my cryptic rejoinder. "Sing again, please."

I really had no faith in the conditions of the Pg 15 circle, but for the joke of it I kept my sitters in place for nearly an hour by dint of pretending to hear creakings and to feel throbbings, until at last little Miss Brush became very deeply concerned. "I feel them, too," she declared. "Did some one blow on my hands? I felt a cold wave."

Harris got up abruptly. "I'll join the doubters," said he. "This tomfoolery is too idiotic for me."

Cameron followed, and Mrs. Quigg also rose. "I'll go with you," she said, decidedly. I was willing to quit, too, but Mrs. Harris and Miss Brush pleaded with me to continue.

"Close up the circle, then. Probably Harris was the hoodoo. Things will happen now," I said, briskly, though still without any faith in the experiment.

Hardly had Harris left the table when a shudder passed over Mrs. Harris, her head lifted, and her eyes closed.

"What's the matter, Dolly?" whispered Mrs. Cameron. "Do you feel faint?"

"Don't be alarmed! Mrs. Harris is only passing into a sleep. Not a word, Harris!" I said, warningly. "Please move farther away."

In the dusky light the faces of all the women looked suddenly blanched and strange as the entranced woman seized upon the table with her hands, shaking it hard from side to side. The table seemed to wake to diabolic energy under her palms. This Pg 16 was an unexpected development, and I was almost as much surprised as the others were.

"Sing again," I commanded, softly.

As they sang, Mrs. Harris withdrew her hands from the table and sat rigidly erect, yet with a peaceful look upon her face. "She does it well," I thought. "I didn't think it in the quiet little lady." At length one hand lifted and dropped limply upon the table. "It wants to write," said I. "Where is the pad? I have a pencil."

As I put a pencil under the hand, it was seized in a very singular way, and almost instantly Mrs. Cameron gasped, "That's very strange!"

"Hush!" said I. "Wait!"

Holding the pencil clumsily as a crippled person might do, the hand crept over the paper, and at last, after writing several lines, stopped and lay laxly open. I passed the pad to Brierly. "Read it aloud," I said.

He took it to the light and read:

"Sara, be not sceptical. Believe and you will be happier. Life is only the minutest segment of the great circle.

MARTIN."

"My father!" exclaimed Mrs. Cameron. "Let me see the writing." Brierly handed the pad to her. She stared upon it in awe and wonder. "It is his exact signature—and Dolly held the pen just Pg 17 as he did—he was paralyzed toward the last—and could only write by holding his pen that way."

"Look! it's moving again," I exclaimed.

The hand caught up the pencil, and, holding it between the thumb and forefinger in a peculiar way, began moving it in the air. Brierly, who sat opposite, translated these movements. "She is drawing, free-hand, in the air. She is sketching the outline of a boat. See how she measures and plumbs her lines! Are you addressing me?" he asked of Mrs. Harris.

The sleeper nodded.

"Can't you write?" I asked. "Can't you speak?"

A low gurgle in the throat was the only answer at the moment, but after a few trials a husky whisper began to be heard. "I will try," she said, and suddenly began to chuckle, rolling upon one hip and throwing one foot over the other like a man taking an easy attitude. She now held the pencil as if it were a cigarette, laughing again with such generous tone that the other women recoiled. Then she spoke, huskily. "You know—San Remo—Sands," came brokenly from her lips.

"Sands?" queried the painter; "who is Sands?"

"Sands—San Remo—boats."

The painter was puzzled. "I don't remember any Sands at San Remo. It must be some student I knew in Paris. Is that what you mean?"

Pg 18

Mrs. Harris violently nodded. As abruptly as it came, this action left her, and then slowly, imperceptibly, her expression changed, a look of ineffable maternal sweetness came into her face; she seemed to cradle a tiny babe upon her arm. At last she sighed, "Oh, the pity of it, the pity of it!"

For a minute we sat in silence, so compelling were her gestures and her tone. At last I asked, "Has any one here lost a little child?"

Mrs. Cameron spoke, hesitatingly, "Yes—I lost a little baby—years ago."

"She is addressing you—perhaps."

Mrs. Harris did not respond to this suggestion, but changed into an impersonation of a rollicking girl of rather common fibre. "Hello, Sally!" she cried out, and Mrs. Cameron stared at her in blank dismay as she asked, "Are you talking to me?"

"You bet I am, you old bag o' wool. Remember Geny? Remember the night on the door-step? Ooo! but it was cold! *You* were to blame."

"What is she talking about?" I asked, seeing that Mrs. Cameron was reluctant to answer this challenge.

"She seems to be impersonating an old class-mate of mine at college—"

"That's what!" broke in the voice.

Mrs. Cameron went on, "Her name was Eugenia Hull—"

"Is yet," laughed the voice. "Same old sport. Pg 19 Couldn't find any man good enough. You didn't like me, but no matter; I want to tell you that you're in danger of fire. Don't play with fire. Be careful of fire—"

Again a calm blankness fell upon the psychic's delicate and sensitive face, and the hand once more slowly closed upon the pencil.

"My father again!" exclaimed Mrs. Cameron. "How could Dolly have known that he held his pen in just that way? She never saw him."

"Do not place too much value on such performances," I cautioned. "She has probably heard you describe it. Or she might have taken it out of your subconscious mind."

The pencil dropped. The hand lifted. The form of the sleeper expanded with power. Her face took on benignity and lofty serenity. She rose slowly, impressively, and with her hand upraised in a peculiar gesture, laid a blessing upon the head of her hostess. There was so much of sweetness and tolerance in her face, so much of dignity and power in every movement that I was moved to applaud the actress. As we all sat thus, deeply impressed by her towering attitude, Mrs. Cameron whispered: "Why, it is Bishop Blank! That is exactly the way he held his hand—his robe!"

"Is it the bishop?" I asked.

The psychic bowed and in solemn answer spoke. Pg 20 "Tell James all will yet be well," she said, and, making the sign of blessing once more, sank back into her chair.

Meanwhile the irreverent ribalds in the far end of the room were disturbing the solemnity of all this communion with the shades, and at my suggestion we went up-stairs to Mrs. Cameron's own sitting-room, where we could be quiet. Seizing a moment when Mrs. Harris was free from the "influence," I woke her and told her what we were about to do. She followed Mrs. Cameron readily, although she seemed a little dazed, and five of us continued the sitting, with Mrs. Quigg and Cameron looking on with perfectly evident doubt of our psychic's sincerity. Harris was rigidly excluded.

In the quiet of this room Mrs. Harris passed almost immediately into trance—or what seemed like a trance—and ran swiftly over all her former impersonations. Voice succeeded voice, almost without pause. The sweet mother with the child, the painter of San Remo, the jovial and slangy girl, the commanding and majestic figure of the bishop—all returned repeatedly, in bewildering mixture, dropping away, one after the other, with disappointing suddenness. And yet each time the messages grew a little more definite, a little more coherent, until at last they all cleared up, and this *in opposition to our thought, to our first interpretations.* It developed that the painter was Pg 21 not named "Sands," but "Felipi," and that he was only trying to tell Brierly that to succeed he should paint rocks and sands and old boats at San Remo. "Pauline," the woman who had seemed to hold a babe, was a friend of Mrs. Cameron's who had died in childbirth. And then swiftly, unaccountably, all these gentle or genial influences were scattered as if by something hellish, something diabolic. The face of the sweet little woman became fiendish in line. Her lips snarled, her hands clawed like those of a cat, and out of her mouth came a hoarse imprecation. "I'll tear your heart out!" she snarled. "I'll kill you soul and body—I'll rip you limb from limb!" We all recoiled in amazement and wonder. It was as if our friend had suddenly gone insane.

I confess to a feeling of profound astonishment. I had never met Mrs. Harris before, but as she was an intimate friend of Mrs. Cameron, and quite evidently a woman of culture, I could not think her so practised a joker as to be "putting all this on."

While still we sat in silence, another voice uttered a wail of infinite terror and despair. "I didn't do it! *Don't* kill me! It was not *my* work." And then, still more horrible to hear, a sound like the gurgling of blood came from the psychic's lips, mixed with babbled, frantic, incoherent words. I had a perfectly definite impression that she was Pg 22 impersonating some one with his throat cut. Her grimaces were disgusting and terrifying. The women shivered with horror. A few seconds later and her face changed; the hideous mask became white, expressing rigid, exalted terror. Her arms were drawn back as if tied at the elbow behind her back. Her head was uplifted, and in a low, monotonous, hushed voice she prayed: "Lord Jesus, receive—"

A gasping, gurgling cry cut short her prayer, and, with tongue protruding from her mouth, she presented such a picture of a strangling woman that a sudden clear conception of what it all meant came to me. "She's impersonating a woman on the scaffold," I explained. "She has shown us a murder, and now she is depicting an execution. Is it Mrs. R., of Vermont?" I asked.

She nodded slowly. "Save me!" she whispered.

"Waken her, please. Don't let her do that any more," pleaded Mrs. Cameron, in poignant distress.

Thereupon I called out, sharply: "That is enough! Wake! *Wake!*"

In answer to my command she ceased to groan; her face smoothed out, and with a bewildered smile she opened her eyes. "What are you saying? Have I been asleep?"

"You have, indeed," I replied, "and you've disclosed a deal of dubious family history. How do you feel?"

"I feel very funny around my neck," she answered, wonderingly. "What have you been doing to me?" She rubbed her throat. "My neck feels as if it had a band round it, and my tongue seems swollen. What have you been about?"

I held up a warning hand to the others. "You went off into a quiet little trance, that's all. I was mistaken. Either you are a psychic or you should have been an actress."

As we stood thus confronting one another, Mrs. Cameron came between us, saying, "Do you know, Pauline came and talked with me—"

At the word *Pauline* the spell seemed to fall again over the bright spirit of Mrs. Harris. Her eyelids drooped, her limbs lost their power, and she sank into her chair as before, a helpless victim, apparently, to the hidden forces. For a moment I was at a loss. I could not believe that she was deceiving us, but it was possible that she was deceiving herself. "In either case, she must be brought out of this," I decided, and, putting my hands on her shoulders, I said: "If there is any 'control' here, let them stop this. We want no more of it. Stop it!"

My command was again obeyed, and the psychic slowly came back to herself, and as she did so I said, warningly, to Mrs. Cameron: "Do not utter another word of this in Mrs. Harris's presence. She seems to be extremely sensitive to hypnotic Pg 24 influence, and I think she had better go out into the air at once."

In rather subdued mood we went below to rejoin the frankly contemptuous members of the party.

"Well, what luck?" cried Howard.

"You all look rather solemn," said Harris. "What about it? Dolly, what have you been doing?"

Mrs. Cameron described the sitting as wonderful, but Mrs. Harris only smiled vaguely, and I said: "Your wife seemed to go into a trance and impersonate a number of individuals. She shows all the signs of a real sensitive."

Harris, who had been studying his wife with half-humorous intentness, now took command. "If you've been shamming, you need discipline; and if you haven't, you need a doctor. I think we'll go home and have it out," he added, and shortly after led her away. "Some nice cool air is what we need," he said at the door.

No sooner were the Harrises out of the door than the women of the party fell upon me.

"What do you think of it, Mr. Garland?" asked Mrs. Cameron.

"If Mrs. Harris were not your friend, and if I had not seen other performances of the same sort, I should instantly say that she was having her joke with us. But I have seen too much of this sort of thing to take it altogether lightly. That's the way Pg 25 this investigating goes. One thing corroborates another. 'Impersonation' in the case of a public medium may mean nothing—on the part of a psychic like your friend Mrs. Harris it means a very great deal. In support of this, let me tell you of a similar case. I have a friend, a perfectly trustworthy woman, and of keen intelligence, whose 'stunt,' as she laughingly calls it, is to impersonate nameless and suffering spirits who have been hurled into outer darkness by reason of their own misdeeds or by some singular chance of their taking off. My friend seems to be able in some way to free these poor 'earth-bound souls' and send them flying upward to some heaven. It's all very creepy," I added, warningly.

"Oh, delightful! Let it be *very* creepy," called Mrs. Quigg.

"To begin with, my friend is as keen-eyed, as level-headed as any woman I know—the last person in the world to be taken for a 'sensitive.' I had never suspected it in her; but one night she laughingly admitted having been 'in the work' at one time, and I begged for a sitting. We were dining at her house—Jack Ross, a Miss Wilcox, and I, all intimate friends of hers, and she consented. After sitting a few minutes she turned to me and said: 'My "guide" is here. Be sure to keep near me; don't let me fall.' She still spoke smilingly, but I could see she was in earnest.

Pg 26

"'You see,' she explained, 'I seem to leave the body and to withdraw a little distance above my chair. From this height I survey my material self, which seems to be animated by an entirely alien influence. Sometimes my body is moved by these forces to rise and walk about the room. In such cases it is necessary for some friend to follow close behind me, for between the going of "the spirit" and the return of my "astral self" there lies an appreciable interval when my body is as limp as an empty sack. I came very near having a bad fall once.'

"'I understand,' said I. 'I'll keep an eye on you.'

"In a few moments a change came over her face. She sank into a curious negative state between trance and reverie. Her lips parted, and a soft voice came from them. She spoke to Miss Wilcox, who sat opposite her: 'Sister—I am very happy. I am surrounded by children. It is beautiful here in the happy valley—warm and golden—and oh, the merry children!'

"Miss Wilcox was deeply moved by this message and for a moment could not reply. At length she recovered her voice and asked, 'Are you speaking to me?'

"'Yes. I am worried about mother. She is sick. Go to her. She needs help. Good-bye!' The smile faded; my friend's face resumed its impersonal calm.

Pg 27

"'Did you recognize the spirit?' I asked.

"Miss Wilcox hesitated, but at last said: 'My sister was active in the work of caring for orphan children. But that proves nothing. Anna may have known it—there is no test in this. It may be only mind-reading.'

"'You are quite right,' I replied. 'But the message concerning your mother can be tested, can it not?'

"At this moment the face of the psychic squared, and a deep, slow voice came pulsing forth. 'Why do you wilfully blind your eyes? The truth will prevail. Mystery is all about you. Why doubt that which would comfort you?'

"'Who are you?' I inquired.

"'I am Theodore Parker, the psychic's control,' was the answer.

"Soon after this my friend opened her eyes and smiled. 'Do you know what you've said?' I asked. 'Yes, I always have a dim notion of what is going on,' she answered, 'but why I am moved to speak and act as I do I don't know. It is just the same when I write automatically. I know when I do it, but I can't see the connection between my own mind and the writing. It is as if one lobe of my brain kept watch over the action of the other.'

"She now passed into another period of immobility and so sat for a long time. Suddenly her face hardened, became coarse, common, vicious in line. Pg 28 Flinging out her hand, she struck me in the breast. 'What do you want of me?' she demanded, in the voice of a harridan. 'What are you all doing here? You're a nice lot of fools.'

"'Who are you?' I asked.

"'You know who I am,' she answered, with a hoarse laugh. 'A sweet bunch you are! Where's Jim?'

"'Does any one recognize this "party"?' I asked. 'Ross, this must be one of your set.'

"Ross laughed, and the 'influence,' thrusting her face close to his, blurted out, menacingly: 'Don't know me, hey? Well, here I am. I wanted a show, and they let me in. What you going to do about it?'

"'I reckon you lit in the wrong door-yard,' I replied; 'nobody knows you here. Skiddoo!'

"She made an ugly face at me, and struck at me with her claw-like hand. 'I'd like to smash you!'

"'Good-bye,' said I. 'Get out!' And she was gone.

"Before a word could be spoken, a look of hopeless, heart-piercing woe came over my friend's face. She began to moan and wring her hands most piteously. 'Oh, where am I?' she wailed. 'It is so cold, so cold! So cold and dark! Won't somebody help me? Oh, help me!'

"I gently asked: 'Who are you? Can't you tell us your name?'

Pg 29

"'Oh, I don't know, I can't tell,' moaned the voice. 'It's all so dark and cold and lonely. Please tell me where I am. I've lost my name. All is so dark and cold. Oh, pity me! Let me come in. Let me feel your light. I'm freezing! Oh, pity me. I'm so lonely. It's so dark.'

"'Come in,' I said. 'We will help you.'

"The hands of the psychic crept timidly up my arm and touched my cheek. 'Thank you! Thank you! Oh, the cheer! Oh, the light!' she cried, ecstatically. 'I see! I know! Good-bye!' And with a sigh of ecstasy the voice ceased.

"I can hardly express to you the vivid and yet sombre impression this made upon me. It was as if a chilled and weary bird, having winged its way from the winter's midnight into a warm room, had been heartened and invigorated, had rushed away confident and swift to the sun-lands of the South.

"One by one other 'earth-bound souls' who, from one cause or another, were 'unable to find their way upward,' came into our ken like chilled and desperate bats condemned to whirl in endless outer darkness and silence—poor, abortive, anomalous shadows, whose voices pleaded piteously for release. Nameless, agonized, bewildered, they clung like moths to the light of our psychic.

"Some of them appeared to be suffering all the terrors of the damned, and as they moaned and Pg 30 pleaded for light, the lovely face of my friend was convulsed with agony and her hands fluttered about like wounded birds. Singular conception! Wonderful power of suggestion!

"At length, with a glad cry, the last of these blind souls saw, sighed with happiness, and seemed to vanish upward, as if into some unfathomable, fourth-dimension heaven. Then the sweet first spirit, the woman with the glad children, returned to say to Miss Wilcox, 'Be happy—George *is* coming back to you.'

"After she passed, my friend opened her eyes as before, clearly, smilingly, and said, 'Have you had enough?'

"'Plenty,' said I. 'You nearly took my eye out in your dramatic fervor. I must say your ghosts are most unhappy creatures.'

"She became very serious. 'Please don't think that these spirits are my affinities. My work is purely philanthropic, so Theodore Parker used to tell mother. It was my duty, he said, to comfort the cheerless, to liberate the earth-bound, and so I had to have these poor creatures waiting around. That's why I gave it up. It got to be too dreadful. We never could tell what would come next. Murderers and barnburners and every other accursed spirit seemed to be privileged to come into my poor empty house and abuse it, although Parker and his band promised to protect me. I stopped it. I will not sit Pg 31 again,' she said, firmly. 'I don't like it. It would be bad enough to be dominated by one's dead friends, or the dead friends of one's friends, but to be helpless in the hands of all the demons and suicides and miscreants of the other world is intolerable. And if I am not dominated by dead people, I fear I am acting in response to the minds of vicious living people, and I don't like that. It's a dreadful feeling—can't you see it is?—this being open to every wandering gust of passion. I wouldn't let any one of my children be controlled for the world. Don't ask me to sit again, and please don't let my friends know of my "gift."'

"Of course we promised, but the effect of that sitting I shall not soon forget. By-the-way, Miss Wilcox 'phoned and proved the truth of her message. Her mother really was ill and in need of her."

As I closed this story, Cameron said: "Garland, you tell that as if you believed in it."

"I certainly do believe in my friend. It's no joke with her. She is quite certain that she is controlled by those 'on the other side,' and that to submit is to lose so much of her own individuality. You may call it hysteria, somnambulism, hypnotism, anything you like, but that certain people are moved subconsciously to impersonate the dead I am quite ready to believe. However, 'impersonation' is the least convincing from my point of Pg 32 view of all the phases of mediumship. I have paid very little attention to it in the course of my investigation. It has no value as evidence. You are still in the tattered fringes of 'spiritism,' even when you have seen all that impersonation can show you."

"Well, what do you suggest as the proper method for the society?"

"As I told you at beginning, I have had a great deal of experience with these elusive 'facts,' and it chances that a practised though non-professional psychic with whom I have held many baffling sittings, is in the city. I may be able to induce her to sit for us."

"Oh, do, do!" cried Mrs. Cameron and Miss Brush together.

"Who is she?" asked Miller.

"I'll tell you more about her—next time," I said, tantalizingly. "She is very puzzling, I assure you. When and where shall we meet?"

"Here," said Cameron, promptly. "I'm getting interested. Bring on your marvels."

"Yes," said Miller, and his mouth shut like a steel trap. "Bring on your faker. It won't take us long to expose her little game."

"Bigger scientific bigots than you have been conquered," I retorted. "All right. I'll see what I can do. We'll meet one week from to-day."

"Yes," said Cameron; "come for dinner."

Pg 33

As I was going out, Mrs. Quigg detained me. "If it had been anybody but nice little Mrs. Harris, I should say that you had made this all up between you. As it is, I guess I'll have to admit that there is something in thought transference and hypnotism. *You were her control.*"

"That will serve for one evening," I retorted. "I'll make you doubt the existence of matter before we finish this series of sittings." And with this we parted.

Pg 34

II

I was a little late at Cameron's dinner-party, and no sooner had I shown my face inside the door than a chorus of excited inquiry arose.

"Where is the medium?" demanded Cameron.

"Don't tell us you haven't got her!" exclaimed Mrs. Quigg.

"I haven't her in my pocket, but she has promised to appear a little later," I replied, serenely.

"Why didn't you bring her to dinner?" asked Mrs. Cameron.

"Well, she seemed a little shy, and, besides, I was quite sure you would all want to discuss her, and so—"

"Yes, do tell us about her. Who is she? Does she perform for a living? What kind of a person are we to expect?" volleyed Miss Brush.

To this I replied: "She is a native of the Middle West—Ohio, I believe. No, she does not do this for a living; in fact, she makes no charge for her services. She is very gentle and lady-like, and much interested, naturally, in converting you to spiritualism; for, like most psychics, she believes Pg 35 in spirits. She says her 'controls' have especially urged her to give me sittings. I am highly flattered to think the spirit folk should consider me so particularly valuable to their cause. Seriously, I hope you will appreciate the wonderful concessions Mrs. Smiley is making in thus putting herself into our hands with the almost certain result of being discredited by some of us. I believe she really is doing it from a sense of duty, and is entitled to be treated fairly."

"Has she been in the business long?" asked Mrs. Quigg, with lurking sarcasm.

"Ever since she was about ten years old, I believe, but she sits only 'to spread the glad tidings.'"

"Is she married?"

"Yes, and has a devoted husband, and a nice little American village home. I know, for she sent me a photograph of it. She has two children 'in the other world.' Please don't think all mediums the ignorant and vicious harpies which the newspapers make them out to be. I know several who are very nice, serious-minded women."

At this point dinner was announced, and the dining-room became the field of a hot verbal warfare. The members of the society were all present excepting Mrs. Harris, who had been greatly upset by her own performance. Bart Brierly, the painter, was there to defend the mystery of life against our scientific friend Miller, whose conception of the Pg 36 universe was very definite indeed. Mrs. Quigg supported Miller. Young Howard was everywhere in the lists, and his raillery afforded Cameron a great deal of amusement.

I contented myself with listening for the first half-hour, but at last took occasion to say to Miller: "Like all violent opponents of the metapsychical, you know very little of the subject you are discussing. To sustain this contention, let me ask if you have ever read the account of Sir William Crookes's experiments with psychic force?"

Miller confessed that he had not. "I have avoided doing so, for I respect Crookes as a chemist," he added.

I continued: "Crookes began by pooh-poohing the whole subject of spiritualism, very much as you do, Miller; but after three years of rigid investigation, he was forced to announce himself convinced of the truth of many of the so-called spirit phenomena. It is instructive to recall that when he was willing to hazard his scientific reputation on a report of this character to the Royal Society, of which he was a member, his paper was thrown out. The secretary refused even to enter it upon the files of the institution."

"I know about that," replied Miller, "and I consider the secretary justified. To his thinking, Crookes had lost his head."

"No matter what he thought," I replied. "Any Pg 37 paper by a man of Crookes's standing, with his knowledge of chemistry and of life, and his long training in exact observation, should have been considered. The action of the secretary was due simply to prejudice, and many of those who voted to ignore that report are to-day more than half convinced that Sir William has been justified. Each of his experiments has been repeated and his findings verified by scientific men of Europe. It is a pleasure to add that our own Smithsonian Institution published two of his speculative papers some years ago. So it goes—the heresy of to-day is the orthodoxy of to-morrow."

"Didn't Crookes afterward repudiate that early report?" asked Miller.

"On the contrary, in 1898, upon being elected to the presidency of the British Association for the Advancement of Science, he said I think I can recall almost his exact words : 'No incident in my scientific career is more widely known than the part I took in certain psychic researches. Thirty years have passed since I published an account of experiments tending to show that outside our scientific knowledge there exists a force exercised by intelligences differing from the ordinary intelligence common to mortals. This fact in my life is well understood by those who honored me with the invitation to become your president. Perhaps among my audience some may feel curious as to whether I Pg 38 shall speak out or be silent. I elect to speak, although briefly. I have nothing to retract. I adhere to my published statements. Indeed, I might add much thereto.' And when you realize that this includes his astounding experience with 'Katie King,' his words become tremendous in their significance."

"What was the 'Katie King' experience?" asked Mrs. Cameron. "I never heard of it."

"It is a long and very interesting story, but in substance it is this: While in a condition of contemptuous disbelief as to the alleged phenomena of spiritualism, Sir William chanced to witness a séance wherein a young girl named Florence Cook was the medium. Her doings so puzzled and interested him that he went again and again to see her. Dissatisfied with the conditions under which the wonders took place, he asked Miss Cook to come to his house and sit for him and his friends. This she did. She was a mere girl at the time, about seventeen years of age, and yet she baffled this great chemist and all his assistants. You sometimes hear people say, 'Yes, but he was in his dotage.' He was not. He was in his early prime. He brought to bear all his thirty years' training in exact observation, and all the mechanical and electrical appliances he could devise, without once detecting anything deceitful."

"Even in the 'Katie King' episode?" asked Harris.

Pg 39

"Even Katie stood the test. But before going into that, let me tell you some of his other experiments. He says among other amazing things that he has seen a chair move on its own account, without contact with a medium. He saw Daniel Home—another medium with whom he had sittings—raised by invisible power completely from the floor of the room. 'Under rigid test condition,' he writes, 'I have seen a solid, self-luminous body the size of an egg float noiselessly about the room!' But wait! I will quote from my notes his exact words." Here I produced my note-book, and read as follows: "'I have seen a luminous cloud floating upward toward a picture. Under the strictest test conditions, I have more than once had a solid, self-luminous, crystalline body placed in my hand by a hand which did not belong to any person in the room. *In the light*, I have seen a luminous cloud hover over a heliotrope on a side-table, break a sprig off, and carry it to a lady; and on some occasions I have seen a similar luminous cloud condense to the form of a hand and carry small objects about. During a séance in full light, a beautifully formed small hand rose up from an opening in a dining-table and gave me a flower. This occurred in the light in my own room, while I was holding the medium's hands and feet. I have retained one of these perfectly life-like and graceful spirit hands in my own, firmly resolved not to let it Pg 40 escape, but it gradually seemed to resolve itself into vapor, and faded in that manner from my grasp.'"

"Oh, come now," shouted Howard, "you're joking! Crookes couldn't have written that."

I continued to read: "'Under satisfactory test conditions, I have seen phantom forms and faces—a phantom form came from the corner of the room, took an accordion in its hand, and glided about the room playing the instrument.'"

As I paused, Harris said: "Was all that in his report to the Royal Society?"

"It was."

"Well, I don't wonder they thought he was crazy. The whole statement is preposterous."

"But that is not all," I hastened to say. "Under rigid conditions scales were depressed without contact, and a flower, separating itself from a bouquet, passed through a solid table."

Miller made a gesture of angry disgust. "To save the reputation of a really great scientist, don't quote any more of that insane dreaming."

"I didn't know any one but campers in 'Lily Dale' could be so bug-house," added Howard.

I went on. "Crookes might have induced his brother scientists at least to listen to his report had he stopped with this. But he proceeded to say that he had witnessed the magic birth of a sentient, palpable, intelligent human being, who walked about in his household, conversing freely, while Pg 41 the medium, from whom the spirit form sprang, lay in the cabinet like one dead. It was his account of this 'spirit,' who called herself 'Katie King,' that caused the whole scientific world to jeer at the great chemist as a man gone mad."

"We have a right to draw the line between Crookes the chemist and Crookes the befuddled dupe," insisted Miller.

Mrs. Cameron drew a long breath. "Do you mean to say that this 'Katie King' phantom actually *talked* with the people in the room? Does Sir William Crookes say that?"

"Yes. Over and over again he declares that 'Katie King' appeared as real as any one else in his house. He becomes quite lyrical in description of her beauty. She was like a pearl in her purity. Her flesh seemed a sublimation of ordinary human flesh. And the grace of her manner was so extraordinary that Lady Crookes and all who saw her became deeply enamoured of her. She allowed some of them to kiss her, and Crookes himself was permitted to grasp her hand and walk up and down the room with her."

"How was she dressed?" asked Mrs. Brush.

"There! Now we are getting at the essentials," I exclaimed. "Usually in white with a turban."

"Did she look like the medium?"

"She was utterly unlike Miss Cook in several physical details. She was half a head taller, her Pg 42 face was broader, her ears had not been pierced, and she was free from certain facial scars that Miss Cook bore; and once when Miss Cook was suffering from a severe cold, Sir William tested 'Katie King's' lungs and found them in perfect health. On several occasions he and several of his friends, among them eminent scientists, saw 'Katie' and the medium together, and at last succeeded in photographing them both on the same plate, although never with Miss Cook's face exposed, because of the danger, to one in a trance, from the shock of a flash-light."

"I don't take any stock in that excuse," said Howard. "But go on, I like this."

"For months the great chemist brought all his skill to bear on Miss Cook's mediumship without detecting any fraud or finding any solution of the mystery. The sittings, which took place in his own library, were under his own conditions, and he had the assistance of several young and clever physicists, and yet he could not convict Miss Cook of double-dealing. The story of the final séance, when 'Katie King' announced her departure, is as affecting as a scene in a play. She had said that her real name was 'Annie Morgan,' but that in the spirit world she was known as 'Katie King.' She came, she said, to do a certain work, and now, after three years, that work was done, and she must return to the spirit world."

Pg 43

"What was that work?"

"To convince the world of the spirit life, I imagine. 'When the time came for "Katie" to take her farewell,' writes Crookes, 'I asked that she would let me see the last of her. Accordingly when she had called each of the company up to her and had spoken a few words in private, she gave some general directions for the future guidance and protection of Miss Cook. From these, which were taken down in shorthand, I quote the following: "Mr. Crookes has done very well throughout, and I leave Florrie the medium , with the greatest confidence, in his hands." Having concluded her directions, "Katie" invited me into the cabinet with her, and allowed me to remain until the end.'"

"Touching confidence!" interrupted Harris.

"'After closing the curtain she conversed with me for some time, and then walked across to where Miss Cook was lying senseless on the floor. Stooping over her, "Katie" touched her and said: "Wake up, Florrie, wake up! I must leave you now."

"'Miss Cook then woke, and tearfully entreated "Katie" to stay a little time longer.

"'"My dear, I can't; my work is done. God bless you," "Katie" replied, and then continued speaking to Miss Cook for several minutes. For several minutes the two were conversing with each other, till at last Miss Cook's tears prevented her Pg 44 speaking. Following "Katie's" instructions, I then came forward to support Miss Cook, who was falling onto the floor, sobbing hysterically. I looked round, but the white-robed "Katie" had gone, never to return to the earth-plane.'"

I glanced about the table at my silent listeners, and added: "Could anything be more dramatic than this sad farewell? Evidently the fourth dimension is both near and very far."

All the women were deeply impressed with this story, but to Miller it was as idle as the blowing of the wind. "The man was duped. It is absolutely impossible to think that he was not grossly deceived."

"Wait a moment," said I. "I defy you or any man to remain unchanged by it. The world is just catching up to this brave pioneer. At that time there were very few scientific men in the metapsychical field. Sir William stood almost alone. But public sentiment changed rapidly as the years passed. The English Society for Psychical Research was formed, and one by one Wallace, Lodge, and other scientific men were convinced of the truth of these phenomena. In Europe, as early as 1853, the work was taken up in the true scientific spirit, and Professor Marc Thury and the Count de Gasparin completely demonstrated the fact of telekinesis; and at about the same time that the Dialectical Society was getting into action, Flammarion, the astronomer, took Pg 45 up his study of the subject. But it was not until 1891 that anything like Crookes's searching analysis was made of a medium. This important sitting—a sitting which marks an epoch in science—took place in Milan, and was attended, among others, by Lombroso and Richet. For the first time, so far as is known, a flash-light photograph was taken of a table floating in the air."

At this moment the bell rang, and Mrs. Cameron exclaimed: "There! that may be your wonder-worker."

I looked at my watch. "I shouldn't wonder. She is a prompt little person."

III

We trooped into the sitting-room, where Mrs. Smiley, a plain little woman with a sweet mouth and bright black eyes, was awaiting us. She was perceptibly abashed by the keen glances that the men directed upon her, but her manners were those of one natively thoughtful and refined. She made an excellent impression on every one.

"Did you bring your magic horn, Mrs. Smiley?" I asked, to relieve her embarrassment.

"Oh yes!" she answered, brightly. "I carry that just as a fiddler carries his fiddle—ready for a tune at any moment."

She brought a large package from the foot of the sofa and gave it to me. I took it, but turned it over to Miller. "Here, open this parcel yourself, Mr. Scientist. I want you to be satisfied as to its character."

Miller undid the package as cautiously as if it were an infernal machine. As the paper opened and fell away, a short, truncated cone of tin was disclosed, with another smaller one loosely held within it. The two sections, when adjusted, made Pg 47 a plain megaphone, about twenty-four inches in length and some five inches in diameter at the larger end.

"What do you do with that?" asked Mrs. Cameron.

In a perfectly matter-of-fact way Mrs. Smiley replied: "Many of the spirit voices are very faint, and cannot be heard without this horn. I am what they call a 'trumpet medium,'" she added, in further explanation.

"Do you mean to say spirits speak through that horn?"

"Yes. That is my 'phone.'"

The ladies looked at one another, and Harris said: "Isn't it rather absurd to expect an immaterial mouth to speak through a tin tube, like the grocer's boy?"

She smiled composedly. "I suppose it seems so to you, but to me it just happens."

I set briskly to work arranging the library for the circle. In the middle of the room I placed a plain oaken table, which had been procured specially for the sitting. On this I stood the tin horn, upright on its larger end; beside it I laid a pad, a pencil, and a small slate.

"Mrs. Smiley, you are to sit here," I said, drawing an arm-chair to the end of the table nearest the wall. She took her seat submissively; and looking around upon my fellow-members with a full Pg 48 knowledge of what was in their minds, I remarked: "If all goes well to-night, this little woman, alone and unaided, except by this megaphone, will utterly confound you. We have had many sittings. We understand each other perfectly. I am going to treat her as if she were an unconscious trickster. I am going to use every effort to discover how she accomplishes these mysterious results, and Miller is to be notably remorseless. We are going to concede for the present the dim light required. I don't like this, but Mrs. Smiley is giving us every other condition, and as this is but a trial sitting, we grant it." I turned to Miller. "The theory is that light acts in direct opposition to the psychic force, weakening it unaccountably. Nevertheless, darkness is not absolutely essential. Maxwell secured many convincing movements in the light, and no doubt we shall be able to do so later."

"Who is Maxwell?" asked Miss Brush.

"Dr. Joseph Maxwell, Deputy Attorney-General of the Court of Appeals at Bordeaux and Doctor of Medicine. He is a noted experimenter with psychic forces. Indeed, he has the power himself. Now, Mrs. Smiley, I wish to begin my tests by tying your wrists to the arms of your chair. May I do so?"

"Certainly," she cheerfully answered. "You may padlock me, or put me in an iron cage, if you please. I leave it all to you."

Pg 49

"Well, there is a certain virtue in knotting a silk thread, for the reason that it is almost impossible to untie, even in the light, and to break it, we will agree, invalidates the sitting. For to-night we will use the thread. Miller, will you watch me?"

"With the greatest pleasure in the world," he answered, "and as a scientist I am going to treat you as a possible confederate."

"Very good. Let each watch the other."

Beneath the gaze of the smiling company, I took from my pocket a spool of strong silk twist, and proceeded to fasten the psychic's wrists. Each arm was tied separately in such wise that she was unable to bring her hands together, and could not raise her wrists an inch from the chair. Next, with the aid of Mrs. Cameron, I looped a long piece of tape about Mrs. Smiley's ankles, knotted it to the rungs of the chair at the back, and nailed the loose ends to the floor. I then drew chalk marks on the floor about the chair legs, in order that any movement of the chair, no matter how slight, might show. Finally, I pushed the table about two feet away from the psychic's utmost reach.

"With this arrangement we ought to be able to detect any considerable movement on your part," I said to my prisoner; "at any rate, I think we can keep you from jumping upon the table. Miller, you are to sit at her left; I will keep watch and ward at her right; the others of the society may Pg 50 take seats as they please—only the tradition is that the sexes should alternate. Cameron, please lock both doors and keep the keys in your pocket."

As soon as we were all seated and Cameron had locked the doors, I asked him to turn down the light, which he did, grumbling: "I don't like this part of it."

"Neither do I, but at a first sitting we must not expect too much. I am sure we shall be able to have more light later on. And now, while we are all getting into a harmonious frame of mind, suppose we ask Mrs. Smiley to tell us a little about herself. Where were you born, Mrs. Smiley?"

She replied, very simply and candidly: "I was born near Cincinnati. My father was a spiritualist early in the 'craze,' as it was called, and I was about nine when I became a medium. At first we did not know that I was the psychic. Demons seemed to take possession of our house, and for a few weeks nothing movable was safe. After awhile my father became sure that I was the cause of these disturbances, because everywhere I went raps were heard: the movement of small objects near where I sat made me an object of aversion or of actual terror to my school-mates. So finally my father asked me to sit. I didn't want to do so at first, but he told me it was my duty. They used to tie me in every way and experiment with me. It was very wearisome to me, but I submitted, and Pg 51 I have been devoted to the work ever since. After my father and mother died I gave up all opposition to my gift, and now it is a great comfort to me; for now I get messages from my father and my little daughter almost every day."

"Do they speak to you directly?" I asked.

"Yes. Sometimes clairaudiently, but generally through this cone when I sit in the dark."

"What do you mean by speaking?" asked Howard. "Do you mean they sound like actual people?"

"Just as real as you or any one," she answered.

I was waiting to say: "Don't be in haste; you will all know from actual experience what she means by voices."

"Have you ever seen these forces at work?" asked Harris.

"No; not the way you mean. I had a terrible shock once that cured me of being too curious. I was holding an accordion under a table by its bellows end, as Home used to do, and while the playing was going on I just believed if I looked under the table I could see something. So I lifted the cover and peeped under. I didn't know any more for a long time. When I came to my father was bathing my face and rubbing my hands. I never tried to 'peek' after that."

"Do you mean that they did this to punish you for your peeping?"

Pg 52

"Yes. They don't like to have you look directly at them when they are at work."

"Why?"

"I don't know. I never was punished again. I didn't need it."

"Would 'they' bat me if I were to peek?" asked Howard.

"They might not; but they refuse to 'work' while any one is looking."

"All that is suspicious."

"I know it is, but that is the way they act."

"You believe 'they' are spirits?"

"I *know* they are," she repeated. "If I didn't, I would be desolate. I have been sitting now for over thirty years, and these friendly voices are a part of my life. They comfort me more than I can tell."

She gave this account of herself with an air of quiet conviction that deeply impressed the circle, and at the end of her little speech I added: "She has agreed to put herself into our hands for a series of experiments, and if her health does not fail I think we shall be able to rival the doings of Florence Cook and Daniel Home, whose mediumships were the basis of Crookes's report. Now let each one of you spread his hands, or her hands, upon the table, just touching the little fingers, in order that a complete circuit may be established. Miller and I will make connection with our psychic."

Pg 53

"It all seems childish folly, but we'll do it," said Harris.

"What may we expect to happen first, Mrs. Smiley?" asked Mrs. Cameron, after we were in position.

"I don't know," she answered, frankly. "I have very little control over these forces. Often, when I am most anxious, nothing happens. Please don't expect much of anything to-night: my first sittings in a new place are seldom very good, and so much depends upon those who make up the circle. I never sit without a fear that my power has gone never to come back."

I helped her out in explanation: "The honest medium does not advertise to perform regularly, for the reason that this force, whatever it is, seems to lie almost wholly outside the will. Flammarion says 'it may be set down as a rule that all professional mediums cheat.' That is putting it pretty strong; but it seems true that the condition which leads to these phenomena is a very subtle physical and mental adjustment, and that the slightest distraction or mental unrest defeats everything. If the medium is paid for her work she is too eager to serve, and everything tempts her to deceive. Furthermore, it has been proved that the psychic is in the very nature of the case *extremely liable to suggestion*, and the combined wills of the sitters focussed on one desired phenomena becomes an Pg 54 almost irresistible force to certain psychics. On the other hand, the best observers say that the most striking proofs of spiritualism lies in the fact that the most amazing phenomena come in opposition to the will of both the psychic and the sitters. We may not secure a single movement to-night, and, indeed, we may have two or three barren sittings, but I am confident that in the end you will be satisfied. I am going to attempt to put Mrs. Smiley to sleep now, and when she is in her trance we can discuss her methods freely."

I began to hum a low, monotonous tune, and one by one the others joined in the refrain; soon the psychic's breath became labored, and in the pauses of the song she moaned. At length she drew her hands as far away from Miller's and mine as the threads would permit, thus breaking the circuit.

"She is in trance," I reported. "Now we have nothing to do but wait. You may say anything you please, or tell stories or sing songs, only don't argue. We will remain as we are for a while, and if the 'guides' are dissatisfied, they will order a change. Generally speaking, the 'controls' are very notional, and when we get into full communication with 'them' the entire present arrangement may be broken up. The theory is that all success is due to the co-operation of those 'on the other side.'"

Pg 55

"It looks to me like a plain case of hypnotism from this side," remarked Harris.

"Aren't there any fixed rules to the game?" asked Howard.

"After many years' exhaustive study of these antic spirits approaching them always from the naturalistic side , Maxwell deduces certain helpful rules: 'Use a small room,' he says, 'and have it warm. Medium and sitters must not have cold hands or feet.'"

"I can understand the psychic having cold feet now and then," interjected Harris.

"Maxwell finds dry air and clear weather most favorable; rainy and windy weather often cause failures. There seems to be some connection with the electrical condition of the atmosphere. After proving that a white light deters phenomena, he uses green, violet, or yellow screens for his lamps. 'Any kind of a table will do for the raps, or for levitation,' he says, 'but one with a double top seems to give best results.' His sitters use wooden chairs with cane seats, and my own experience is that a bare floor helps. He especially directs that the guide be consulted—'let the phenomena come as spontaneously as possible,' he adds."

"Does he find this sandwiching of the sexes helpful?"

"Yes. He says six or eight people, men and women alternating, make the best circle. 'Take Pg 56 things seriously, but not solemnly,' he advises. 'Don't argue; address the "control," and follow his advice. Avoid confusion by electing a director and asking for only one thing at a time. Keep the same people in the group for at least six sittings. Sit in a circle and touch hands. Be patient and good-tempered. A worried, irritated, sullen medium is a poor instrument. Finally'—and this is most important—'don't overwork the medium.' And with this important statement he ends: '*I am persuaded of the absolute harmlessness of these experiments, provided they are properly conducted.*'"

"I am glad to know that," said Mrs. Quigg. "After seeing Mrs. Harris's trance, I was in doubt."

"Maxwell's hints are extremely valuable to me," I continued, "for they confirm my own methods, some of which I had to learn by tedious experience. If I had known, for instance, the folly of allowing everybody to quiz the psychic, I might have been spared many hours of tiresome sitting. Maxwell is, indeed, an ideal investigator—he has made a great advance in methods, and his conclusions, though tentative, are most suggestive. No unprejudiced reader can finish his book,*Metapsychical Phenomena*, without feeling that its author is a brave and fearless writer, as well as a cautious and sane reasoner. His published experience throws a flood of light on mediums and their puzzling peculiarities."

Pg 57

"But it seems to me those rules give the medium and his 'guides' the free hand," said Miller, discontentedly.

"By no means," I retorted. "Maxwell plainly says, 'Where the "control" is insisting upon something which I do not like, I politely resist, and end by getting my own way.' Note the 'politely.' In short, he recognizes that a genuine medium is a very precious instrument, and he does not begin by clubbing him—or her—into submission. For all their wondrous powers, the people who possess these powers are very weak. They are not allowed to make anything more than a living out of the practise of the magic, and they live under the threat of having the power withdrawn. They are helpless in the face of a challenge to produce the phenomena, and yet the hidden forces are themselves helpless without them—"

"Is the table throbbing?" asked Brierly.

"I don't feel it."

"Have you ever had any convincing evidence of this psychic force—such as movement of objects without contact?" asked Harris.

"Yes. I have had a table rise at least twenty inches from the floor in the full light, with no one present but the medium and myself, and while our finger-tips alone touched the top. It felt as if it were floating in a thick and resilient liquid, and when I pressed upon it, it oscillated, in a curious Pg 58 way, as if the power were applied from below and in the centre of the table. The psychic was a young girl, and I am certain played no trick. I could see her feet on the floor, and her finger-tips were, like mine, on the top of the table. This was the clearest test of levitation I ever had, but the lifting of a pencil in independent writing is the same thing in effect."

"I see you have acquired all the 'patter,'" remarked Miller.

"Oh, yes indeed; all the 'patter,' and some of the guile. For instance, when I want to use 'those who have passed on' I do so, and when I don't I invent means to deceive them."

Mrs. Quigg caught me up on that. "Can you deceive 'them'?"

"I don't know that I do, really; but, at any rate, 'they' are not always mind-readers—that I have proved very conclusively. In all my experience I have never had any satisfactory evidence of the clairvoyance of these manifesting intelligences."

"I thought 'they' could read one's every thought."

"I do not find that 'they' can read so much as *one* of my thoughts, and I would not invest a dollar on their recommendations. Seldom does so much as a familiar name come up in my sittings, and no message of any intimate sort has ever come from the shadow world for me. The messages are Pg 59 intelligent, but below rather than above the average. 'They' always seem very fallible, very human to me, and nothing 'they' do startles me. I have no patience with those who make much of the morbid side of this business. To me it is neither 'theism' nor 'diabolism,' and is neither destruction of an old religion or the basis of a new one—But all this verges on the controversial, and is not good for our psychic. Let's sing some good old tune, like 'Suwanee River' or 'Lily Dale.' We must keep to the genial side of conversation. Spread your hands wide on the table and be as comfortable as you can. We may have to wait a long time now, all on Miller's account."

"Because he is a sceptic?"

"No; because he's belligerent," I answered. "It doesn't matter whether you believe or not if you do not stir up controversy. Miller's 'suggestion' is adverse to the serenity of the psychic, that's all. The old-time sleepy back-parlor logic has no weight with me. Maxwell and Flammarion are my guides."

For four hours we sat thus, and nothing happened. How I kept them at it I do not now understand, but they stayed. We sang, joked, told stories, gossiped in desperate effort to kill time, and not one rap, tap, or crackle came to guide us or to give indication of the presence of any unusual power. Part of the time Mrs. Smiley was Pg 60 awake and sorely grieved at her failure. She understood very well the position in which I seemed to stand. To Miller I was a dupe, the victim of a trickster. He himself afterward confessed that at the time he almost regretted his preternatural acuteness, and was ready to take himself away in order to let the show go on. But he didn't, and from time to time I encouraged our psychic by saying: "Never mind, Mrs. Smiley, there are other evenings to come. We will not despair."

At last she sank into profound sleep, and at exactly twelve o'clock I heard a faint tapping on top of the piano, just behind Miller. "Hooray, here they are!" I exclaimed, with vast relief. "What is the matter?" I asked of "the presence." "Aren't we sitting right?"

"*No,*" was the answer, by means of one decided tap.

"Am I right?"

"*No,*" answered the taps.

I may explain at this point that in the accepted code of signals one tap means "*No,*" three taps mean "*Yes,*" and two taps, "*Don't know,*" "*Will try,*" or any other doubtful state of mind. One has, of course, to guess at the precise meaning; but one may confirm one's interpretation by putting it in the form of a question that can be answered by "*Yes*" or "*No.*"

"Shall I change with Miller?" I asked.

Three brisk taps made affirmative answer.

Pg 61

I exchanged places with Miller, but did not again touch Mrs. Smiley's hand. Immediately thereafter the sound of soft drumming came from the piano at a point entirely out of reach of the psychic, and at my request the drummer kept time to my whistling. After some minutes of this foolery "the force" left the piano abruptly, as if with a leap, and dropped to the middle of the table. A light, fumbling noise followed, and I called out: "Is every hand in the circle accounted for?"

While the members of the group were, in turn, assuring me of this, a small bell on the table was taken up and rung, and the table itself was shoved powerfully toward the circle and away from the psychic. I assure you, my sitters were profoundly interested now, and some of the women were startled. A sharp, pecking sound came upon the cone. I called attention to the fact that this took place at least six feet from the psychic, and a moment later, with intent to detect her in any movement, I leaned far forward so that my head came close to her breast. I could not discern the slightest motion; I could not even hear her breathe. All this, while very impressive to me, was referred by the others to trickery on Mrs. Smiley's part.

At my request, the drumming on the cone kept time to "Dixey" and "Yankee Doodle," and at length I said to "the spirit": "You must have liked topical songs when you were on the earth-plane."

Pg 62

Instantly *the cone was swept violently from the table, and a deep, jovial, strong whisper came from the horn to me.* "*I do now,*" was the amazing answer.

"Who are you?" I asked.

"*Wilbur Thompson.*"

"Oh, it is you, is it? Well, I am glad you've found a voice; I felt rather helpless up to this moment. Are we sitting right?"

"*All right.*"

"What are you going to do for us to-night? Can you raise the table?"

"*I'll try,*" he whispered again.

"Are there other 'spirits' here?"

"*Yes; many.*"

"Can't 'they' write their names on the pad?"

There was a moment's silence, and then the sound of writing began in the middle of the table. When this had finished, I said, "Did you succeed?"

Again the cone rose, and another whisper, a fainter voice, answered: "*Yes, but the writing is very miserable.*"

The rest of the sitters were silent with amazement till Miller said, in a tone of disgust: "That is of no value. It is so easy for Howard, or some one else, to break the circle and write or speak through the cone."

"Yes, we'll have to trust one another for to-night," I admitted.

Pg 63

The psychic now began to twist and moan and struggle, choking, gasping in such evident suffering that Mrs. Cameron cried out: "Mr. Garland, don't you hear? She is ill! Let me go to her!"

"Don't be alarmed," I replied. "This struggle almost always precedes her strongest manifestations. It seems cruel to say so, but, remember, Mrs. Smiley has been through these paroxysms hundreds of times. It appears very painful and exhausting, but she has assured me that 'they' take care of her. She suffers almost no ill effects from her trance."

Miller, living up to his character as remorseless scientist, remarked: "I'd like to control her hands. Shall I try?"

"Not now, not till the 'guides' consent to it," I replied. "It is said to be dangerous to the psychic to touch her unexpectedly."

"I can understand that it might be inconvenient," remarked Harris, with biting brevity.

Again we sat in expectant silence until several of the group became restless. "What is she about now?" asked Cameron, wearily.

"She is in dead trance, apparently. Please be patient a little while longer. Are you still with us, 'Wilbur'?"

I was delighted to hear the three taps that answer "*Yes.*"

"Will you be able to do something more for us?"

Tap, tap, tap—given apparently with the pencil.

Pg 64

I observed: "From a strictly scientific standpoint, the movement of that pencil, provided it can be proved to have taken place without the agency of any known form of force, is as important as the fall of a mountain. It heralds a new day in science. Is every hand accounted for?" Each answered, "*Yes.*" At this moment there was a rustling at the base of the cone. "Listen! 'they' are at work with the horn."

The cone rocked slowly on its base, and at last leaped over the shoulders of the sitters and fell with a crash to the floor. "Mercy on us!" gasped Mrs. Cameron.

"Don't touch it! Don't move!" I called out. "Everybody clasp hands now. Here is a chance for a fine test. 'Wilbur,' can you put the cone back on the table?"

Tap, tap, answered "Wilbur." The two taps were given slowly, and I understood them to mean "*Don't know*" or "*Will try.*"

"Miller," I said, impressively, "unless some one of our circle is betraying us, we are having as good a demonstration as we could expect, barring the absence of light. Be watchful. 'Wilbur,' we're trusting to you now. Let's see what you can do."

As I spoke, the horn, with a ringing scrape, left the carpet, and a moment later bumped down upon Mrs. Quigg's head. "Oh!" she shrieked, "it hit me!"

Pg 65

Almost immediately a breathy chuckle came from the horn: "*Ha, ha! That shook you up a little, I reckon.*"

The other women were frozen with horror. "Don't let it touch me," pleaded Miss Brush.

And Mrs. Quigg, much shaken, called out: "Frank Howard, are you doing this?"

He was highly indignant. "Certainly not. Are you not holding one hand and Miss Brush the other? I am in-no-cent; I swear it!"

I commented on their dialogue severely. "See how you all treat an event that is wonderful enough to convulse the National Academy of Science. I do not believe the psychic's hands have moved an inch, and yet, unless some one of you is false to his trust, the miraculous has happened—Are you there, 'Wilbur?'" I queried of the mystic presence.

The cone swung toward me, and "Wilbur" answered: "*I am, old horse.*"

"Well, Wilbur, there are two bigoted scientific people here to-night, and I want you to put them to everlasting rout."

"*I'll do it, don't you worry*," replied the voice, and the cone dropped with a bang on the table, again making everybody jump.

"*That brought the goose-flesh!*" remarked "Wilbur," with humorous satisfaction.

I took a malicious delight in the mystification of my fellows. "Go down and shake up young Pg 66 Howard at the foot of the table," I suggested. "He is a little in the conjuring line himself."

Almost instantly Howard cried out: "The blooming thing is touching me on the ear!"

"Observe," called I, in the tone of a man exhibiting some kind of trained animal, "the cone is now at least six feet from the psychic's utmost reach. How do you account for that, Miller?"

"The boy lied," said Miller, curtly.

Howard was offended. "I'll take that out of you, old chap, when we meet in the street. I am telling the square-toed truth. I am not doing a thing but hold two very scared ladies' hands."

"Oh, come now!" I interposed. "If we are to be so 'tarnal suspicious of one another, we might just as well give up the sitting. If each of us must be padlocked, proof of any phenomenon is impossible."

A firmer hand now seemed to grasp the cone, and a deep whisper that was almost a tone came from it. "*You are right*," this new personality said, with measured and precise utterance. "*We come with the best tests of a supremely important revelation; we come as scientists from our side of the line; and you scoff, and take it all as a piece of folly, as an entertainment. Is this just? No, it is unworthy men of science.*"

"You are entirely justified in your indignation," I responded. "But who are you?"

"*My name on the earth-plane was Mitchell.*"

"I am glad to make your acquaintance, 'Mr. Mitchell,' and your rebuke is deserved. I, for one, mean to proceed in this matter seriously. What can you do for us to-night?"

"*Be very patient. Carry this investigation forward, and this psychic will astonish the world. Do not abuse her; do not tax her beyond her strength.*" He spoke with the precise and rather pedantic accent of an old gentleman nurtured on the classics, and produced upon me a distinct impression of age and serious demeanor utterly different from the rollicking, not too refined "Wilbur."

"I will see that she is treated fairly, 'Mr. Mitchell,' but of course this is not a rigid test. Will you be able to permit conditions more convincing?"

"*Yes, very much more convincing,*" he replied, slowly and ponderously, "*but do not worry the instrument to-night. Narrow your circle; be harmonious, and not too eager, and you will be abundantly rewarded.*"

"Won't you tell me who you were on the earth-plane?"

"*I was a friend of the father of the instrument,*" he answered.

The horn returned to the table quietly, and young Howard was the first to speak. "That is a fine piece of ventriloquism, any way you look Pg 68 at it," said he. "It is a nice trick to give that peculiar tinny sound to a whisper."

"So far as I can judge, so far as my sense of hearing goes and I have kept my ear close to the psychic's face , Mrs. Smiley has not moved, nor uttered a sound. What is your verdict, Mr. Cocksure Scientist?"

For the first time Miller's voice indicated some slight hesitation. "I haven't been able to *detect* any movement on the part of the psychic," he replied, "but of course I can't answer for the rest of the company. The performance has no scientific value. In the dark, deceit is easy. Harris may be the ventriloquist."

"Why not accuse the arch-conspirator of us all, our director?" exclaimed Mrs. Quigg.

"You flatter me," I responded. "If I could produce those voices I would go on the vaudeville stage to-morrow. I give you my word I am acting in entire good faith. I am quite as eager for the truth as any of you.—But, hark! the cone is on the wing again."

The megaphone was indeed moving, as if a weak, unskilled hand were struggling with it, and at last it swung feebly into the air, and a whisper that was hardly more than a breath was directed toward Mrs. Quigg: "*Daughter!*"

"Are you speaking to me?" she asked, in a voice that trembled a little.

The answer was but a sibilant sigh: "*Yes.*"

"Who are you?"

"Mother."

The answer was so faint that no one save Mrs. Quigg could distinguish the word. Almost at the same moment I caught the sound of other moving lips in the air just before me. "Who is it?" I asked. Like a little, hopeless sigh the answer came: *"Jessie."* This was the name of my younger sister. Then the cone dropped as though falling from exhausted hands, and I had no further message from this "spirit."

As we waited breathlessly the clear, silver-sweet voice of a little girl was heard by every one at the table. *"Good-evening, everybody. I am Maud; I came with my mamma. I have come to ask you to be very kind to her."*

"I am very glad to hear you, 'Maud,'" I answered. "Are there other spirits present?"

"Yes, many, many spirits. My grandpa is here; he is treating my mamma so that she will not be sick. Some one is here to see you, but is too weak to speak. My grandpa says 'we are trusting you.'"

With astonishing clearness this voice created in my mind not as light would create it the vision of a self-contained, womanly little girl, whose voice and accent formed a curious silvery replica of the psychic's, and yet I could not say that the psychic's vocal organs gave out these words. At last she said Pg 70 *"Good-bye,"* and the cone was softly laid upon the table.

All of this was performed in profound silence. There was no sound in the cone, except that of the voice, no rustle of garments, no grasp of fingers on the tin; and though I leaned far over, and once more placed my ear close to the psychic's lips, I could not trace the slightest movement connecting her with the movements on the table. I had the conviction at the moment that she sat in a death-like trance at my side.

A few moments later the cone was jammed together and thrown upon the floor—a movement, I had learned to know, that announced that the sitting was ended.

While the sitters still waited, I said: "Now, Cameron, you may turn on the gas, but do so very slowly. Mrs. Smiley seems in deep sleep, and we are warned not to startle her."

When the light became strong enough to see a form, we found our psychic sitting limply, her head drooping sidewise, her eyes closed, her face white and calm. The cone was lying not far from her chair, separated into two parts. The threads that bound her to her seat were to all appearance precisely as at the beginning of the sitting, except that they were deeply sunk into the flesh of her wrists. Her chair had not moved a hair's-breadth from the chalk-marks on the floor.

Pg 71

A moment later she opened her eyes, and, smiling rather wanly, asked of me: "Did anything happen?"

"Oh yes, a great deal. 'Wilbur' came, and 'Maud,' and 'Mr. Mitchell.'"

"I am very glad," she answered, with a faint, happy smile.

Mrs. Cameron bent to her pityingly. "How do you feel?"

"Very numb, but I'll be all right in a very short time. My wrists hurt; your thread is very tight. My arms always swell. Please give me a drink of water."

As I held the glass to her lips I was conscience-smitten to think that for five hours she had been sitting in this constrained position—a martyr to science; but I deferred the moment of her release till Miller had examined every bond. I used a small pair of scissors to cut the thread out of the deep furrows in her wrist, and it took a quarter of an hour of chafing to restore her arms to their normal condition, all of which had a convincing effect upon the doubters.

Miss Brush was indignant. "I think it is a shame the way you have treated your psychic."

"Oh, this is nothing," responded Mrs. Smiley. "I'd be unhappy and uneasy if you didn't tie me. I'm like the old man's chickens you've heard the story? : he had moved so much that the chickens, Pg 72 whenever they saw him put a cover on his wagon, would lie down and cross their feet to be tied."

After Mrs. Cameron had taken Mrs. Smiley to the dining-room for a cup of tea, the rest of us remained staring at one another.

"Now, which of us did that?" I asked.

"So far as the psychic was concerned, I don't see how she could have had any hand in it," said Miller. "But, then, it was all in the dark."

I had to admit that this diminished the value of the experiment. "But now listen," I said: "as we all seem to be suspicious of one another, I propose that we resort to a process of elimination. I shall take 'Mitchell's' advice and narrow the circle. Howard, you are a suspect. You are ruled out of the next sitting."

"Oh no," protested Howard. "That isn't fair. I did nothing, I swear!"

"You admit being a prestidigitator?"

"Yes, but I had nothing to do with this performance."

"Nevertheless, so far as conclusive proof is concerned, your presence in the circle invalidates it. Now I propose that Mrs. Smiley go to Miller's house, with no one present but Mr. and Mrs. Cameron and Mr. and Mrs. Miller. If we secure these same phenomena under Miller's conditions, we will then readmit one by one the entire membership of the society."

Pg 73

Mrs. Quigg resented being left out, and I pretended surprise.

"I thought from what you had said that these 'dark shows' were of no value?"

"The next one ought to have decided value if Professor Miller has any share in the test," she answered, quickly. "I believe in him."

"And not in me? That's a nice thing to say."

"I mean in his method. He is a cold, calm, merciless scientist. You're a man of imagination."

"Thank you," said I. "My critics would take issue with you there. However, if we get anywhere in this campaign we must begin with the smallest possible circle and slowly enlarge it. We hope also to increase the amount of light."

After some further argument, Cameron settled the matter by saying: "Garland is right; and, to show my own scientific temper, I rule Mrs. Cameron and myself out of the next sitting. That will put the whole problem up to Miller and Garland."

Miller and I walked away to the club together, pondering deeply on the implications of the night's performance.

"I don't see how it was done," Miller repeated. "Certainly she did not rise from her chair, not for an instant, and yet to believe that she did not have a hand in what took place is to admit the impossible. You have had other sittings with her, haven't you? You believe in her?"

Pg 74

"Yes, I think she is sincere, but possibly self-deceived. The fact that she is willing to put herself into our hands in this way is most convincing."

"There is nothing of the trickster about her appearance, and yet I wish she had permitted us to hold her hands to-night."

"Miller," said I, earnestly, "if you'll go with me into this experimentation with an open mind, I'll convince you that Crookes and Flammarion are the true scientists. It is the fashion to smile at Flammarion as a romantic astronomer, but I can't see *now* that he is lacking in patience and caution. For all his rather fervid utterances, he keeps his head and goes on patiently investigating. He has had more experience than even Crookes or Lombroso. For forty years he has been searching the dark for these strange forces, and yet he says: 'We create in these séances an imaginary being; we speak to it, and in its replies it almost always reflects the mentality of the experimenter. Spirits have taught us nothing. They have not led science forward a single step.... I must say that if there are spirits, or beings independent of us, in action, they know no more than we do about the other world's.' And yet as regards the physical facts of mediumship, he sustains all the investigators. 'These phenomena exist,' he says."

"Candidly, Garland, what is your own belief?" asked Miller, a few moment's later.

Pg 75

I evaded him. "I have seen enough to make me believe in Zöllner's fourth dimension, but I don't. My mind is so constructed that such wonders as we have seen to-night produce very little effect on me. They are as normal to me now as the popping of corn or the roasting of potatoes. As I say, I have demonstrated certain of these physical doings. But as for belief— well, that is not a matter of the will, but of evidence, and the evidence is not yet sufficient to bring me to any definite conclusion; in fact, in the broad day, and especially the second day after I have been through one of these astounding experiences, I begin to doubt my senses. Richet speaks of this curious recession of belief, and admits his own inability to retain the conviction that, at the moment of the phenomenon, was complete. 'No sooner is the sitting over than my doubts come swarming back upon me,' he says. 'The real world which surrounds us, with its prejudices, its schemes of habitual opinions, holds us in so strong a grasp that we can scarcely free ourselves completely. Certainty does not follow on demonstration, but on habit.' And in that saying you have my own mental limitations admirably put."

Miller plodded along by my side in silence for a few minutes, and then asked, abruptly: "What is the real reason that you keep up the fiction of the 'guide' when you don't believe in him?"

"For the reason that I think Mrs. Smiley honest in her faith, and that to be polite to the 'guides' is one of the first requisites of a successful sitting. Suppose the whole action to be terrestrial. Suppose each successful sitting to be, as Flammarion suggests, nothing but a subtle adjustment of our 'collective consciousness' to hers. Can't you see how necessary it is that we should proceed with her full consent? After an immense experience, following closely Crookes, de Rochas, Lodge, Richet, Duclaux, Lombroso, and Ochorowicz, Maxwell says: 'I believe in these phenomena, but I see no need to attribute them to any supernatural intervention. I am inclined to think they are produced by some force within ourselves—'"

"Just what does he mean by that?"

"I can't precisely explain. It's harder to understand than the spirit hypothesis. He himself admits this, and goes on to say that while he is certain that we are in the presence of an unknown force, he is convinced that the phenomena will ultimately be found orderly, like all other facts of nature. 'Therefore, in the critical state of research, the scientific problem, it seems to me, is not whether spiritism be true or false, but whether metapsychical phenomena are real or imaginary. Some future Newton will discover a more complete formula than ours,' he prophesies. 'Every natural fact should be studied, and if it be real, incorporated in the Pg 77 patrimony of knowledge.' He then adds, with the true scientist's humble acknowledgment of the infinite reach of the undiscovered universe: 'Our knowledge is very limited and our experience young.'"

"That is good talk," said Miller in reply, "but the question is, Does he really experiment in that condition of mind? An astronomer with his eye to a telescope is a highly specialized and competent being. An astronomer listening to whispers in the dark may be as simple and credulous as a child."

"I grant all that. But I see in it the greater reason why men like yourself should take up the investigation of these illusive and disturbing problems. These phenomena, as Flammarion says, introduce us into uncharted seas, and we need the most cautious and clearest-sighted scientists in this world as pilots. Will you be one of them?"

"You flatter me. As a matter of fact, I'm a very poor sailor," he answered, with a smile.

IV

If there is any one thing true in these manifestations of "spirit power," it is that the psychic is the agent for their production. Actively or passively, consciously or unconsciously, she completes the formula—her "odic force" is the final chemical which permits precipitation. Sometimes her will to produce, her wish to serve, hinders rather than helps. Often when she is most persistent nothing happens. Sometimes an aching foot or a disturbing thought cuts off all phenomena. For the best results, apparently, the psychic should be confident, easy of mind, and not too anxious to please.

I approached this sitting at Miller's house with some fear that it might end in disappointment to him and be a source of chagrin to Mrs. Smiley. The house was strange, our attitude intensely critical, and she was very anxious to succeed. It would be remarkable, indeed, if under these conditions she were able to meet us half-way. As we walked up the street together I did my best to reassure her.

Pg 79

"You may trust me fully, Mrs. Smiley," said I; "and Miller, though an inexorable scientist, is a gentleman. I am sure he will not insist on any experiment which will injure your health or give you needless pain. This is but our second sitting, and I, for one, do not expect you to be at your best."

"I *hope* we will have good work," she replied, earnestly, "but it is always harder to sit for tests. Tell me about Mrs. Miller. Is she nice? Will I like her?"

"She is very gentle and considerate; you will like her at once. I am sure she will be a help to you."

Her voice was very sincere as she said: "You don't know how anxiously I watch the make-up of my circle. It isn't because I am afraid of sceptics; I have no fear of those who do not believe; but each person brings such diverse influences, and these influences conflict and worry me, and then nothing takes place. I don't want to disappoint you and your friends, and that may hinder me."

The Millers occupied a modest little house far up-town, and were suburban, almost rural, in their manner of living. The chemist himself met us at the door, and, after greeting us cordially, ushered us into his library, which was a small room at the back of the hall. I observed that it had only one door and two windows, rather high up in the east wall—an excellent place for our sitting.

"So this is the den of inquisition," I began; and Pg 80 turning to Mrs. Smiley, I added: "I hope you are not chilled by it."

"Not a bit," she answered, cheerily.

As Mrs. Miller, a quiet little woman not so far removed from Mrs. Smiley's own type , entered the door and greeted us both, the psychic's face lighted up with pleasure. This argued well for our experiment.

I could see that Miller had made careful preparation along the lines of my suggestion. A plain old table was standing lengthwise of the room, the windows were hung with shawls, and a worn hickory chair stood with arms wide-spread to seize its victim. After surveying the room, Mrs. Smiley turned to me with a note of satisfaction in her voice, and said: "I like this room and this furniture; I feel the right associations here. The air is full of spirit power."

"I am glad your mind is at ease," said I, "for I am anxious for a very conclusive sitting. You tell 'Mitchell' that Miller is decidedly worth converting. I want 'Wilbur' to do his best, for I intend to tighten the bonds on you to-night."

She fearlessly faced me. "I am in your hands, Mr. Garland; do as you like. Mr. Mitchell told me this morning that he would yet convince you of the reality of the spirit world. He is assembling all the forces at his command, and will certainly do everything in his power."

Pg 81

"I am delighted to get that assurance," I responded.

"You are to sit here," said Miller, indicating the hickory chair, which he had placed near the north wall.

She took her seat meekly, placing her hands resignedly on the wings of the chair. "I like this chair," she said, with a smile; "it is so old-fashioned."

"Now," said I, "I am going to ask Mrs. Miller to fasten this long tape about your ankles. We mean to take every precaution in order that you may not involuntarily or subconsciously move your limbs."

Under close scrutiny, Mrs. Miller secured each foot in such wise that the knots came in the middle of the tape, and to make untying them absolutely impossible, I drew the two ends of the long ribbon back under the psychic's chair and tacked them securely to the shelf of a bookcase about two feet from the hind legs. To loosen them was entirely out of our victim's power.

Miller then unreeled a spool of silk twist, and this I tied squarely to the arm of the chair at a point about six feet from the loose end which I intended to hold. I knotted the silk about the psychic's wrists, drawing it to a hard knot each time, and gave the spool to Miller, while retaining the loose end of the thread in my own hands. The Pg 82 psychic could neither touch the tips of her fingers together nor lift her arms an inch from the chair. She was as secure as if bound with a rope, but as an extra precaution I passed the thread beneath the chair-arm and pulled it taut. "This will enable us to feel the lightest movement of her hands," I said to Miller, who had copied my device. "Are you satisfied with the conditions?"

He answered, with some reservation: "They will do. I would like to have light, but that I suppose is impossible."

"No, not impossible," replied Mrs. Smiley, "but the work is always weaker in the light; the voices are stronger in the dark."

Mrs. Miller took her seat exactly opposite Mrs. Smiley. I was at her right. Miller, after turning out the gas, sat opposite me and at the psychic's left.

At first the room was black as ink, but by degrees I from my position, opposite the window was able to perceive a faint glow of light through the curtain. Mrs. Smiley's back was near a wall of books, and, the room being narrow, Miller's chair pretty well filled the space between the table and the window behind it. The action of a confederate was excluded by reason of the bolted door. To enter the room by the window was impossible, for the reason that the slightest noise could be heard and the least movement of the curtain would Pg 83 admit the light. Barring the darkness, conditions were all of our own making.

However, we were hardly settled in place when Miller was moved to further precaution. "Mrs. Smiley, I would like to pin over your dress a newspaper, so that any slightest movement of your knees or feet could be heard. Do you object?"

"Not at all," she instantly replied. "I am sure my guides will do anything they can to meet your wishes. You may nail my dress to the floor if you wish."

Miller turned on the light, and together we pinned a large, crisp newspaper over her knees and tacked it securely to the floor in front of her feet. The corners where the pins were inserted were well out of the reach of her tethered hands.

Again the lights were lowered, and at my direction Miller placed his right hand on the psychic's left and touched fingers with Mrs. Miller. I did the same, thus connecting the circle. In this way we sat quietly conversing for some time.

"I want to make it quite plain to you," I said to them all, "that I am trying to follow Crookes's advice, which is to strip away all romance and all superstitious religious ideas from this subject. I am insisting on the normal character of these phenomena. Whatever happens to-night, Mrs. Miller, please do not be alarmed. There is nothing inherently uncanny or unwholesome in these Pg 84 phenomena. No one knows better than your husband the essential mystery of the simplest fact. Materialization, for example, is unusual; but if it happens it cannot be supernatural. Nothing is supernatural. Am I right, Miller?"

"We explain each mystery by a deeper mystery," he replied.

"All depends upon the point of view. I am interested in these obscure phases of human life. If they are real they are natural. To me the spiritistic 'demonstrations' are intensely human and absorbingly interesting as dramatic material, and yet I hope I am sufficiently the scientist to be alive to the significance of these telekinetic happenings, and enough of the realist to remain critical in the midst of the wildest carnival of the invisible forces."

"Don't you believe in them?" asked Mrs. Miller, with a note of surprise in her voice.

I replied, cautiously: "I am at this moment convinced of the reality of*some* of these phenomena by reason of my own experiments; but leaving one side my personal investigation, I must believe that Crookes, Maxwell, and Flammarion are competent witnesses. As to spiritualism—well, that is another matter."

"But where does all this lead to if not to spiritualism?" asked Mrs. Miller.

"As to the exact country, no one knows," I answered; "but the best of our experimenters are Pg 85 agreed that the gate opens upon a new field of science. These powers seem to be in advance of us and not a survival, and they may prove of value in the evolution of the race. That is why I want to enlist men like your husband in the work. Mediumship needs just such critical attention as his. Nothing like Maxwell or Richet's thoroughness of method has ever been used by an American physicist, so far as I know. On the contrary, our leading scientific men seem to have let the subject severely alone."

"Why?" asked Mrs. Smiley.

"Partly because of inherited prejudice, and partly because of their allegiance to opposing theories; and finally, I suspect, because they are connected with institutions that would not sanction such work. You can imagine how the physical department of a denominational college would investigate spirit phenomena! It was much the same way in England during the early part of last century, but they are far in advance of us now. The first notable step in the right direction was taken—as perhaps you may know—in 1869, by the Dialectical Society of London, which appointed a committee to look into the subject of spiritualism, with the expectation, no doubt, of being able to stop the spread of the delusion.

"The investigations which followed were under the especial charge of Alfred Russel Wallace; Pg 86 Cromwell Varley, chief of Electrical Engineers and Telegraphers; and Professor Morgan, president of the Mathematical Society. This committee, after careful investigation, reported voluminously to this effect: 'The phenomena exist.... There is a force capable of moving heavy bodies without material contact, which force is in some unknown way dependent upon the presence of human beings.'"

"Which was a long way from saying that spiritism was true," remarked Miller.

"It certainly was sufficiently vague, you would think, to be harmless; but several of the committee refused to join in even this cautious report, insisting that the conclusions ought to be verified by some other scientist. They suggested Sir William Crookes, who was at this time in the early prime of his life and a renowned chemist—just the man for the work. This suggestion was acted upon by Crookes a little later, and his report on this 'psychic force' had a good deal to do with the formation of the now famous Society for Psychical Research."

"I'd hate to be held responsible for that," said Miller, with humorous intent—"of all the collections of 'hants' and witches."

"On the Continent scientific observation had already begun. Count Agénor de Gasparin, of Valleyeres, was one of the first to take up this problem of telekinesis in the modern spirit. He made Pg 87 a long and complicated study of table-tipping in 1853, and published his conclusions in two large volumes in Paris a year later. His experiments were careful and searching, and drew the line squarely between the supernatural and the natural. He said, positively, 'The agency is not supernatural; it is physical, and determined by the will of the sitters,' and may be called the Charles Darwin of the subject. A year later Professor Marc Thury, of Geneva, added his testimony. He also said: 'The phenomena exist, and are mainly due to an unknown fluid, or force, which rushes from the organism of certain people.' To this force he gave the name 'psyscode.' The spirit hypothesis, he was inclined to think, was not impossible or even absurd. He used *absurd* in the scientific sense, of course."

"It is the most natural thing in the world to me," said Mrs. Smiley. "I would be desolate without it."

"Some ten years later Flammarion, the renowned French astronomer, began his studies of these unknown forces, and for a long time fought the battle alone in France as Sir William Crookes endured the brunt of the assault in England."

Miller here interposed with a covert sneer in his voice: "Yes, but Flammarion has always had the reputation of being more of the romancer than of the astronomer."

Pg 88

"You scientists do him an injustice," I answered, with some heat, "just as you have all been ignorantly contemptuous of Crookes. I confess I used to share in some small degree your estimate of Flammarion; but if you will read his latest book with attention and with candor, you cannot but be impressed with his wide experience and his patient, persistent search for the truth. I am persuaded that he has been a genuine pioneer all along. I cannot see but that he has examined very critically the scores of psychics who have come under his observation, and his reports are painstaking and cautious. His work must be considered by every student of this subject. It won't do to neglect the words of a man who has seen so much.—But here we go along lines of controversy when we should be sitting in quiet harmony. Let us defer our discussion until after our séance. Have patience, and I believe we can duplicate, if not surpass, the marvellous doings of even Richet and Lombroso. We may be able some day to take flash-light photographs of the cone while it is floating in the air."

"Has that ever been done?" asked Mrs. Miller.

"Oh yes; Flammarion secured photos of a table floating in the air. These pictures show conclusively that the psychic had nothing to do with it—at least, not in any ordinary way. Richet succeeded in fixing the apparition of a helmeted soldier on several plates. Crookes photographed 'Katie King' Pg 89 and her medium once or twice, and Fontenay has succeeded in getting clear-cut images of the 'spirit' hands which play round the head of Paladino. But it must be confessed that in Crookes's pictures there is a lack of finality in the negatives. He never succeeded in getting the faces of both 'Katie' and Miss Cook at the same time—and Richet's photographs have a made-up look."

Passing abruptly to a low, humming song, I made the attempt to put our psychic to sleep. In a few minutes her hands became cold and began to flutter. At last she threw my fingers away as if she found them scorching hot. Miller's hand was similarly repulsed. She then seemed to pass into quiet sleep, and I said: "Withdraw a little, Miller, but keep your silk thread taut."

Almost immediately faint raps came upon the table, and I asked: "Are you there, 'Mitchell'?"

Tap, tap, tap—"*Yes.*"

"Are we sitting right?"

Tap, tap, tap—"*Yes,*" answered the force, in a grave and deliberate way.

"As to these raps," I remarked, "they are easily simulated, but they have been absolutely proven by several of our best investigators. They have been obtained on a sheet of paper held in the air, on pencils, on a strip of cloth, on an open umbrella—under every possible condition. Maxwell secured them by pinching his own ear or by squeezing the Pg 90 arm of his neighbor. I have heard them on a man's shirt-front. They are the first manifestations of intelligent spirit power, and may be regarded in the light of established fact."

"I wouldn't be hasty about admitting even that," remarked Miller. "In the dark—or in the light—these obscure sounds may seem very ghostly, and yet be due to purely physical causes."

We sat in silence for a few moments, and at last I asked: "Is any spirit present?"

Almost immediately a childish voice came from the direction of the psychic, apparently issuing from her lips. "*Mr. Mitchell would like to have you tie the threads to the legs of the table.*"

"Are you 'Maud?'" I asked.

"*Yes, I am Maudie,*" she answered. "*Mr. Mitchell wants to try some experiment. He wishes you to tie the threads to the legs of the table.*"

I confess I didn't like the looks of this, but as a compromise measure I was willing to grant it. "If you don't object, Miller, we will do as the guides desire."

He hesitated. "It weakens our test. I don't understand the reason for the demand."

"I suggest we yield the point for the present. Perhaps 'they' will permit us to resume the thread a little later. I have found that by apparently meeting the forces half-way at the beginning we often get concessions later which will be of greater value than the tests we have ourselves devised."

Pg 91

Accordingly, I tied my end of the silk twist to the table leg at a distance of about twenty-six inches from the utmost reach of the psychic's hands. Miller did the same with his end. We then resumed our seats, and waited for over an hour.

During this time the psychic was absolutely silent and apparently in deep trance, and I was beginning to feel both disappointed and chagrined. Miller's tone was a bit irritating. I knew exactly what was in his mind. "I've fixed her now," he was exultantly saying to himself. "She can't do a thing; even her request to have the threads tied to the table does not avail her. Accustomed to have everything her own way, she fails the first time any real restraint is applied to her."

I was quite at the end of my confident expectancy, when the psychic began to stir uneasily and "Maudie" spoke complaining of the thread on her mother's right wrist. "*It's so tight it stops the blood,*" she said. "*Please loosen the thread a little. You may turn up the light,*" added the little voice.

While Miller gave me a light, I loosened the thread on her right wrist, which was very tight; but I tied a second thread about her arm in such wise that I would surely know at the end of the sitting if it had been disturbed. The table, I observed at the time, was more than two feet from her finger-tips. I called Miller's attention to this, Pg 92 and said: "She can't possibly untie these threads, and if she breaks them the sitting is invalidated."

Soon after the light was turned out "Maudie" requested that we all move away from Mrs. Smiley, down to the lower end of the table; and although Miller thought this permitted too much liberty of action on the part of the medium, I urged consent. "There are other sittings coming," I repeated once more.

Mrs. Smiley fell again into deep sleep, but nothing took place for a long time. During this period of waiting I told stories of my experience and the curious folk I had met in search for the true explanation of these singular phenomena.

"Have you ever witnessed any materializations?" asked Mrs. Miller.

"Yes; but none of it was of the sort that I could swear to. I mean that it seemed to me to be either downright trickery or subconscious actions on the part of the psychic, and yet I've seen some very puzzling phantoms. I am persuaded that a great deal of what is called 'fraud' arises from the suggestibility of the psychics. Lombroso speaks of this 'fixed idea' of the mediums, and their persistent, almost insane, attempt to produce the phenomena desired by the circle. You can understand how this would be if there is anything at all in hypnotism. Sometimes it all seems to belong to the realm of hypnotic visions. One medium helps another to build up Pg 93 this unreal world. Early in my career as an investigator I went to Onset Bay, where in July of each year all the spiritualists and 'mejums' of New England used to gather do yet, I believe , and I shall never forget the singular assemblage of 'slate-writers,' 'spirit artists,' 'spirit photographers,' 'palmists,' and 'psychometrists' whose signs lined the street and pointed along the paths of the camp.

"In its way it was as dramatic a contrast of light and shade, of the real and the unreal, as this otherwise prosaic republic can show. There under the vivid summer sun, beside the glittering sea, men and women met to commune on the incommunicable, to question the voiceless, and to embrace the intangible. It was, indeed, such a revelation of human credulity as might well have overpowered a young novelist. From the warm, pine-scented afternoon air I crept into one of these tiny cabins, and sat with my hands upon a closed slate in order to receive a message from Lincoln or Cæsar; I slipped beneath the shelter of a tent to have a sealed letter read by a commonplace person with an Indian accent; and I sat at night in dark little parlors to watch weak men and weeping women embrace very badly designed effigies of their lost darlings."

"Isn't it incredible? Can you imagine any reasonable person believing such things?" asked Miller.

"Millions do," I replied.

Pg 94

"Please go on," entreated Mrs. Miller. "What happened to you?"

"Nothing really worth reporting upon. In that day of utter credulity no tests were possible, but immediately after my return to Boston I had my first entirely satisfactory test of the occult. I went with Mrs. Rose, one of our members, to sit for 'independent slate-writing'—that is to say, writing on the inner surfaces of closed slates. Up to this moment I was profoundly sceptical, but I could not doubt the reality of what happened. I took my own slates—the ordinary hinged school slates; but whether they were my own or not made no difference really, for the final test which I demanded was such that any prepared slates were useless. I'm not going into tiresome detail. I only say that while sitting at the table with both Mrs. Rose's hands and my own resting upon the slates *I dictated* certain lines to be drawn upon the inside of the slates."

Miller's voice expressed growing interest. "And this was done?"

"It was done. I had in mind the test which Alfred Russel Wallace had used in a similar case. He dictated several words to be written while holding the slates securely in his own hands. In this instance I asked for the word 'Constantinople' to be written. The psychic smiled, shrugged her shoulders, and replied: 'I'll try, but I don't Pg 95 believe they can spell it.' 'Draw a straight line, then,' said I. 'I'll be content with a single line an inch long.' She laughingly retorted: 'It's hard to draw a straight line.' 'Very well, draw a crooked line. Draw a zigzag—like a stroke of lightning. Draw it in yellow. Draw a circle.' She said no more, but became silent, and we waited without change of position. Remember that I was holding the slate during all this talk. It did not leave my hands."

"What were the conditions? Was it light?" asked Miller.

"It was about two o'clock of an afternoon, and we sat in the bay-window of the parlor. It was perfectly light. No one moved. The psychic sat opposite us, leaning back in a thoughtful pose. Her hands lay in her lap, and she seemed to be merely waiting. At last a tapping came upon the slate, and she brightened up. 'It is done!' she called, exultingly. I opened the slates myself, and *there, drawn in yellow crayon, was a small circle with a zigzag yellow line crossing it exactly as I had dictated,* and under Mrs. Rose's hands in the corner of the slate was a gayly colored bunch of pansies. There were messages also, but I paid very little attention to them. The production of that circle under those conditions overshadowed everything else. It was a definite and complete answer to my doubt. It was, in fact, a 'miracle.' I recall going Pg 96 directly to a meeting of the society and reporting upon this sitting. You will find the bald statement of my experiment in the minutes of the secretary."

Miller was silent for a moment, then asked: "You're sure it was done after you took the slates in hand?"

"I am as certain of it as I am of anything."

"How do you account for it? Of course it was a trick."

"Trickery can't account for that yellow line. The messages could have been written beforehand, but no trick of prepared slates can account for my dictated design. I have had other cases of slate-writing which were almost as inexplicable, and Crookes and Wallace and Zöllner, as you remember, were quite convinced by evidence thus secured. Crookes *saw* the pencil at work. I have never witnessed the writing, but I have heard it at work under my hands and I have felt it under my feet. I have had writing on ten separate pages in a closed Manila-pad held between my hands."

Miller seemed to be impressed by these statements. "I have always considered slate-writing a cheap trick, but I don't quite see how that was done—always providing your memory is not at fault."

"I would not place much dependence on my present recollection," I frankly responded, "but I reported on the case at once while my mind was Pg 97 most accurate as to details. Speaking further of these tricks, if you choose to call them such, I have had several failures, where the failure meant as much as a success. I have held two slates with a psychic while we were both standing when the creaking and scratching and grinding went on between my hands. I give you my word I was convinced at the moment of holding between my palms a sentient force. I felt as Franklin must have felt when he played with the lightning in the bottle at the tail of his kite. Once I heard the writing going on in a half-opened slate, but I did not see the pencil in motion. Some of these cases of 'direct-writing' are the most convincing of all my experiences. People ask me why I didn't talk with the spirits about heaven and angels. I was not interested in their religious notions. I kept to this one line—I wanted to see a particle of matter move from A to B without a known push or pull. I paid very little attention to 'trance-mediums' like Mrs. Piper; and although I saw a great deal of what is called 'mind-reading' and 'thought-transference,' I did not permit the cart to get before the horse. 'Independent slate-writing' interested me, for the reason that I could put the clamps on it. Materialization, on the contrary, is so staged and arranged for that to prove its genuineness seems impossible at present; but slate-writing under your hand is a different matter."

Pg 98

"I'd like to have it under *my* hand," said Miller, grimly.

"You can have it if you'll go after it," I retorted, "and you can have it hard."

Mrs. Miller was deeply interested. "Tell us more. Have you had other messages written in that wonderful way?"

"Yes, many of them. One of the most curious examples of this kind I have ever seen came to me in Chicago. It was a 'new one,' as Howard would say. Old Mr. MacVicker told me one day that there was a woman on the West Side who had a trick of producing independent slate-writing beneath the stem of a goblet of water—"

"Why under a goblet of water?" interrupted Miller.

"As a test. You see, nearly every one who goes to a psychic wants first of all to witness a miracle. Each seeker demands that his particular message shall come hard—that is to say, under conditions impossible to the living. His reasoning is like this: 'The dead are free from the limitations of our life, therefore they should manifest themselves to us as befits their wider knowledge of the laws of the universe, and especially is it their business to outdo the most skilful conjurer! Hence each man insists on locked slates and sealed letters. These the poor psychics are forced to grant. To be just to them, I must say that I have found most mediums fairly Pg 99 willing to meet any reasonable test; in fact, many of them seem perfectly confident of the inscrutable, and venture upon what seems to be the impossible with amazing imperturbability. All they ask is to be treated like human beings. They are seldom afraid of results. Sometimes they bully the forces sadly, and make them work when they don't want to.

"Well, this particular psychic ushered me into her back parlor which was flooded with sunlight , and asked me to be seated at a small table covered with a strip of cloth. She was a comfortable, plump person, evidently from Kansas, in manner somewhat like the humorous wife of a prosperous village carpenter. I remember that we were rather sympathetic on various political questions. After some remarks on populism and other weighty matters, she filled a goblet with water, and, placing it upon a slate, passed it under the table with her right hand, asking me to put my hand beneath hers."

"There it is!" said Miller, with infinite scorn. "Always in the dark or under the table. No wonder Emerson called it 'a rat-hole philosophy.'"

"Suppose it's all the work of an 'astral' who can't abide the light?" I suggested.

"I know the theory, but I can't allow it."

"Why not? You permit the photographer his dark-room."

Then, with malicious delight in his petulance, I Pg 100 calmly continued: "I put my left hand beneath hers and my right upon the table. I could see her left hand lying in her lap, and as she turned sidewise to the table I was able to keep in view both of her feet. We held the slate so that the top of the goblet lightly touched the under side of the stand. The psychic was all accounted for, except the hand which was resting outspread on the under side of the slate. We sat for several minutes in this way, while she explained that 'they' would probably take words out of our conversation as a test, if I desired it. 'I am here to be shown,' I replied. She laughed at me, and on two different occasions brought the slate from beneath the table with writing under the stem of the goblet. This was all very well, but I said: 'A better test would be to have them write words that I dictate.'

"'I will ask them,' she said. She seemed to listen as if to voices inaudible to me, and at last said: 'They will try it.'

"Again we placed the goblet of water on the clean slate under the table, and while holding it as before, I said: 'Now ask them to write the name "William Dean Howells."'

"Almost immediately there was a decided movement of the slate—or so it seemed to me. A power seemed to wake on the slate, not through the psychic's hand, but independent of it. I heard plainly the scratching of a pencil, at the same time that the Pg 101 psychic's left hand and both of her feet were in full view, and at the same time that her hand was outspread, apparently motionless, upon the under side of the slate. In a few moments the scratching paused, and the psychic, with an embarrassed smile, said: 'They don't know how to spell the middle name.'"

"That is to say, *she* was the one who could not spell the name," said Miller.

"That's what I thought at the time, but I helped her out, and a moment later a decided tapping on the top of the table announced the completion of the task.

"As she slowly drew the slate out from under the table I was alert to see what had happened. The glass remained in the middle of the slate as before, with the water undiminished, and under the glass and confining itself to the circle of the stem were the words:

written as though acknowledging the barrier of the glass where its edge rested upon the slate."

Pg 102

"Wonderful!" exclaimed Mrs. Miller.

"Are you sure the writing was there as she drew the slate out?" queried Miller.

"Yes, I saw the writing as she was removing the goblet; and while with her left hand she drew a little circle around the outer edge of the stem I read the words. Now to say that the psychic wrote this with her finger-nail on the bottom of the slate and then turned the slate over is to me absurd. The glass of water prevented that. And yet she did it in some occult way. The transaction remains unexplained to me. I am perfectly sure she willed it, but *how* she caused the writing—the physical change—is quite another problem. Zöllner I believe it was secured the print of feet on the inside of a closed slate, and reasoned that only on the theory of a fourth dimension could such phenomena be explained. That reminds me of a sitting I once had with a young man wherein, to utterly confound us, the invisible hands removed his undershirt while his coat-sleeves were nailed to the chair."

"Oh, come now, you don't expect us to believe a miracle like that, even on your serious statement?" remarked Miller.

"I certainly do not," I responded, readily. "I wouldn't believe it on any one's statement. That is the discouraging thing about this whole business; you can't convince any one by any amount of Pg 103 evidence. A man will stand out against Zöllner, Crookes, Lodge, and Myers, discounting all the rest of the great investigators, and then crumple up like a caterpillar at the first touch of The Invisible Hand when it comes to him directly. This same young man gave me the most convincing demonstrations of materialized forms I have ever seen. In his own little home, under the simplest conditions, he commanded forth from a little bedroom a figure which was unmistakably not a mechanism. A lamp was burning in the room, and the young fellow was perfectly visible at the same moment as the phantom which stood and bowed three times."

"What did it look like?"

"It looked like a man's figure swathed in some white drapery. I could not see the face, but it was certainly not a 'dummy.' But come, let us see what the forces can do for us here to-night. I think we will need 'Annie Laurie' to clear the air of debate."

Mrs. Miller began the song, and we all joined in softly.

"Our newspaper is a trusty watch-dog," remarked Miller, significantly.

As he spoke the psychic began to toss and writhe and moan pitifully. Her suffering mounted to a paroxysm at last; then silence fell for a minute or two—absolute stillness; and in this hush the table Pg 104 took life, rose, and slid away toward us as if shoved by a powerful hand.

"So far as my hearing goes, the psychic does not move," I said. "Barring the light, this is a very good demonstration of movement without control. Every movement of the table our way removes it farther from the reach of the psychic."

"I hear nothing from the paper," confessed Miller, "and yet the table is certainly moving."

"I can believe this, because I have proved these movements without contact. In this case Mrs. Smiley cannot reach the table with her knees and her feet secured by tape nailed to the bookcase. You cannot believe she has gotten out of her skin. The newspaper is still on guard, and has uttered no alarm."

"It is very perplexing," Miller admitted; "but anything can happen in the dark."

"I admit it is very easy to deceive our senses, but the silk thread is not to be fooled."

Three times the table was urged in the same direction, each paroxysm of suffering, of moaning, of struggle, on the part of the psychic, being followed a few seconds later by absolute silence. It was in these moments of profound sepulchral hush that the heavy table lurched along the floor. It was a strange and startling fact.

"Why are you doing this?" I asked of the forces. "As a test?"

Pg 105

"*Yes,*" the raps replied.

"How do you account for it, Miller?" I asked, with challenge in my voice. "My conviction is that we are confronting a case of telekinesis—not as convincing as Flammarion's, but still inexplicable. If that table has moved an inch, it is the same as if it had moved a foot. You should feel rewarded."

Miller did not reply; and even as he pondered the megaphone, which had been standing on the top of the table, began to rock on its base, and a pencil which lay beside it was fumbled as if by a rat or a kitten. In our state of strained expectancy this sound was very startling indeed.

"What about that, Miller?" I asked, in a tone of exultation. "Who's doing that? Last time you suspected Howard, now here you must suspect the psychic. The movement of that pencil is of enormous significance. How can she possibly reach and handle that cone?"

"She can't, unless she has freed her hands," he admitted. "Let us touch hands." I gave him my left hand, and sitting thus, with all hands accounted for, we entered into communication with the "spirit" that was busy in the centre of the table.

"Are you present, 'Wilbur'?"

Tap, tap, tap.

"Are you moving the table?"

Tap, tap, tap.

Pg 106

"To get it out of reach of the psychic?"

Tap, tap, tap.

Suddenly, with a loud bang, something heavy fell upon the table. Releasing the hands of my fellow-investigators, I felt about for this object and found that a book had been brought and thrown upon the table. A shower of others followed, till twenty-four were piled about the cone. They came whizzing with power, yet with such precision that no head was touched and the cone remained undisturbed. It was as if some roguish poltergeist had suddenly developed in the room.

"Miller, I find this exciting!" said I, after silver fell upon the table. "Suppose we ask 'Wilbur' to fetch some small object whose position you know."

Mrs. Miller then said: "There is a box of candy on a shelf back of Mrs. Smiley. It is quite out of her reach. Can you bring that to me, 'Wilbur'?"

Tap, tap, tap! was the decided answer, and almost immediately the box was placed on the top of the table and shoved along toward Mrs. Miller.

"That's a good demonstration," I remarked, and 'Wilbur' drummed a sharp tattoo of satisfaction.

At my request he then wrote his name on a pad while Miller waited and listened, his mind too busy with surmise to permit of speech. He told me afterward that he was perfectly sure the psychic had wrenched free of her tacks and he was Pg 107 wondering how she would contrive to put herself back again.

Finally I asked: "Are you still with us, 'Wilbur'?"

The force tapped smartly on the tin.

"Now, just to show you that the psychic is not doing this, can't you hold up a book between me and the light? I want to see your hand."

Instantly, and to my profound amazement, a book rose in the air, and I could see *two hands* in silhouette plainly and vigorously thumbing the volume, which was held about three feet above the table, and to the psychic's left.

"Miller," I said, excitedly, "I see hands!"

"I do not," he answered; "but I hear a rustling."

Swift on the trail, I called out: "Now, show me your empty hand, 'Wilbur.' I want to see how big it is." A moment later I exclaimed, in profound excitement: "I can see a *large* hand against the window, and, strangest part of all, the spread fingers are pointing *toward* Mrs. Smiley, the wrist is nearest you and at least six feet from the psychic. It is a man's hand. You are not doing this, Miller?"

"Certainly not!" he answered, curtly.

"This is astonishing! It certainly is a hand and much larger than that of a woman, and *the wrist is toward you*. It is still at least four feet from the psychic. Oh, for a flash-light camera now! I Pg 108 was perfectly certain that this is not the psychic's hand, and yet to admit that it is not is to grant the whole theory of materialization."

At last the shadow disappeared. The book fell. With a ringing scrape the cone rose in the air and the voice of "Wilbur" came from it life-like—almost full-toned, and with a note of humorous exultation running through it. "*I told you I'd astonish you!*" he said. "*Don't get in a hurry; there's more coming.*"

For nearly two hours thereafter this "spirit voice" kept us all interested and busy. He was very much alive, and we alternately laughed at his quaint conceits or pondered the implications of his casual remarks. It was precisely as if a rollicking Western, or, rather, Southern, man were speaking to us over the 'phone. I asked: "Who are you? Is 'Wilbur' your surname?"

"*No; my middle name. My family name is Thompson.*"

His characterization was perfect. He responded to every question with readiness and perfect aplomb. At times he played jokes on us. He bumped Miller on the head, and touched him on the cheek farthest from the psychic. At my request he covered Mrs. Miller's ear with the large end of the horn, then reversed and nuzzled her temple with the small end. She said it felt like a caress, as if guided by a tender hand. She had Pg 109 become clairvoyant also, and saw many forms about the room. I could see nothing.

"Tell us more about yourself, 'Wilbur'?" I asked. "Who are you? What did you do on the earth?"

"*I was a soldier.*"

"In the Civil War?"

"*Yes.*"

"On which side?"

"*That's a leading question,*" he answered, with some hesitation.

"Oh, come now, the war is over!"

"*I was on the Southern side. I am Jeff. W. Thompson. I was a brigadier-general.*"

"Where were you killed?"

"*I was invalided home to Jefferson City, and passed out there.*"

"How do you happen to be 'guide' to this little woman?"

He hesitated again. "*I was attracted to her,*" he said, and gave no further explanation.

"Mitchell" then came and said: "*We are deeply interested in your experiments, Mr. Garland, and will afford you all the aid in our power. It is hard to meet your tests—hard, I mean, for our medium, but we will assist her to fill the requirements.*"

"Thank you. I don't see how any psychic could be more submissive."

Mrs. Miller, deeply impressed by all this, began to inquire concerning those of the invisible host Pg 110 whose names were familiar to her. It was evident that she, at least, was convinced of their reality.

Meanwhile, the movement of the cone interested Miller more than the messages. "How does she do it?" he exclaimed several times. "To touch Mrs. Miller means that the psychic must not only have free use of her hands: she must rise from her chair and pass behind me and the wall."

"The precision of the action is my amazement," I replied. "I've noticed this same thing many times. Apparently, darkness is no barrier to action on the part of these forces. That cone, you will observe, can touch you on the nose, eyelid, or ear, softly, without jar or jolt. It came to me just now like a sentient thing—like something human. Such unerring flight is uncanny. Could any trickster perform in the dark with such precision and gentleness? Of course this is not conclusive as argument, but at the same time it has weight. Whose is the eye that directs this instrument? Can you tell us, 'Wilbur'?"

A chuckle came through the cone. "*I'm doing it.*"

"How can you see?"

"*Day and night are all the same to me.*"

Miller held up his right hand. "Prove it; touch my knuckles!" he commanded.

After a moment's silent soaring the cone struck his left hand, which was farthest from the psychic, Pg 111 and a voice followed it with laughter, asking: "*What made you jump?*"

Before Miller had recovered from the surprise of this, the table seemed to be grasped and shaken as if by a man of giant strength—and yet the cone and the books did not shift position. Hands patted the pillows on a sofa at Miller's right, and one of these cushions was flung against his chair. The room seemed to swarm with tricksy Pucks. At last the cone took flight again, and moved about freely among the heap of books and over Miller's head, while a variety of voices came successively from it, some of them speaking to Mrs. Miller and some to me. Several of the names given were known to Mrs. Miller, and a few were recognizable by me. They all claimed to be spirits of the dead with messages of good cheer for friends on "the earth-plane," but they were all rather vague and stereotyped. Once I thought I could see the cone passing between me and the window, high above the table. It seemed to float horizontally as if in water. Some of the spirits were too weak to raise the cone—so "Wilbur" said; too weak, even, to whisper.

During all this time the psychic remained in trance—deathly still; but "between the acts" her troubled breathing and low moans could be heard. So far as hearing could define, she was still at the end of the table, where she had been placed at the beginning of the sitting. None of these Pg 112 movements occasioned the slightest rustling of the newspaper. When the cone was moving no sound was heard. The floor was of hard-wood, and, as one's hearing becomes very acute in the darkness, I am certain the psychic did not rise from her chair. She was, for the most part, silent as a dead woman.

The force expended on the table was very great, almost furious, and even if the psychic had been able to extend her foot or release a hand she could not have produced such movement, and if she had done so we could have detected it. Intelligent forces were plainly at work on the table, and writing was going on. So far as I was concerned, I was convinced that the psychic had externalized her power in some occult fashion, and that it was she who was speaking to us. It was as if she were able to *will* the cone to rise and then to project her voice into it, all of which seems impossible the moment it is stated.

At length "Wilbur" said: "Good-night." I rose, and Miller, eagerly, expectantly, turned the light slowly on. *Mrs. Smiley sat precisely as we had last seen her. Her eyes were closed, her head leaning against the back of her chair. Her hands were fastened exactly as we had left them, and, strangest thing of all, the table was pushed away from her so that the silk threads were tight.*

"Do you see that, Miller?" I exclaimed. "Will Pg 113 you tell me how that final movement was made? 'Wilbur' has given us an unexpected test. Even if she had freed her hands, she could not have tied the threads and returned to her bonds; and if she first returned to her bonds, how could she, then, have pushed the table away? The two things are mutually exclusive. Her feet are nailed to the floor, and the newspaper still on guard. Are we not forced to conclude that the table was moved by some supernormal expenditure of force? Her hands were here, the table there. Does it not seem to you a case of the 'psychic force,' such as Crookes and Richet describe?"

Miller was confounded, but concealed it. "She may have shoved the table with her feet."

"How? Your newspaper is unbroken. Not a tack is disturbed. But suppose she did! How about the books? Did she get the books with her feet? How about the broad hand which I saw? How about the candy-box which was moved from a point seven feet away? How could she slip from her bonds? See these threads, actually sunk into her wrists!" I continued. "No, my conviction is that she has not once moved."

"I cannot admit that."

"You mean you dare not!"

Mrs. Miller was indignant at our delay. "The poor thing! It is a shame! Unfasten her at once! You are torturing her!"

Pg 114

"Wait a few moments," said Miller, inexorably. "I want to make a few notes."

Meanwhile I took the psychic's pulse. It was very slow, faint, and irregular. It was, indeed, only a faint, sluggish throb at long intervals, and each throb was followed only by a feeble fluttering. Her skin was cold, her arms perfectly inert and numb, and she came very slowly back to consciousness. I had a conviction at the moment that she had been out of her body.

While I rubbed her hands and arms, Miller took notes and measurements. There were more than two dozen books on the table, and some of them had come from shelves three feet distant and a little above the psychic's shoulders. It was true she could have reached them with a free arm, but she had no free arm! The pad in the middle of the table was scrawled upon. "Wilbur" was written there, and short messages from "Mr. Mitchell" and other "ghosts." Therefore, it is of no value to say we were collectively hypnotized.

As she came to life, Mrs. Smiley complained of being numb. "My arms are like logs," she said, "and so are my feet. My 'guides' say that if you will put one palm to my forehead and the tips of your fingers at the base of my brain it will help me to liven up."

I did as she requested, and was at once conscious of great heat and turmoil in her head. It appeared Pg 115 to throb as if in receding excitement. I thought of Richet's observations that in cases of materialization the psychic seemed shrunk and weakened , and narrowly scanned the helpless woman. She seemed at the moment small and bloodless.

"Were you conscious of groaning and gasping?" I asked.

"No, I have no recollection of anything. I am told I do make a great fuss, but I don't know it. Did anything happen?"

"A very great deal happened," I answered.

She smiled in quiet satisfaction.

"I'm glad. Mr. Miller has been good and patient; it would have been a shame to disappoint him. If you will only keep from being too anxious you'll get anything you want."

"That's what 'Mitchell' said."

Mrs. Miller patted her hands. "You must be very tired, poor thing?"

"I do feel weak, but that will soon pass away. What time is it?"

Miller looked at his watch. "Great Scott! It's after one o'clock."

"Absorbing business, isn't it?" said I.

Mrs. Miller invited Mrs. Smiley to stay the remainder of the night and took her away to bed, leaving us to measure and weigh and surmise. It seemed absurd—like a dream; and yet there lay the visible, tangible proofs of the marvel.

Pg 116

"Everything took place within her reach, provided she could have freed her hands," Miller repeated, as he sat in her chair and studied the books on the table.

"Miller," said I, with conviction, "*that woman did not lift her wrists from that chair*!

"I don't see how she did it; but to say she did not, is to admit the preposterous. I wish she had permitted us to hold her hands."

"I don't know of another psychic in America who would have submitted to the test we put upon Mrs. Smiley to-night, but 'Mitchell' has assured me he will go further: he will let us hold her hands and turn on the light. I feel as if the great mystery were almost within our grasp. By the ghost of Euclid! I have the conviction at this moment that we are at the point of proving for ourselves the elongation of the psychic's limbs! Suppose Flammarion is right? Suppose that the psychic can extend her arms beyond their normal proportions? You should be ready to give a year, ten years, to demonstrating a single one of these physical effects. If I am any judge of character, this little woman is as honest and as wholesome as Mrs. Miller herself. It isn't this one performance alone which proves it. It is the implication of a dozen other sittings, almost as convincing as this, that gives me hope of proving something. Let us have our next sitting at Cameron's. It is only fair to Pg 117 readmit them, for we have proven that they had nothing to do with our performance that first night. Let us ask to be permitted to hold the hands and feet of the psychic, and also to take a flash-light picture of the floating cone. We may yet see these ghostly hands in the light of the lamp."

Miller was shaken. I could see that. He sat like one who has been dealt a stunning blow.

"I don't believe it—I can't believe it," he repeated.

"Crookes got some photos of 'Katie King,' and I fully believe that Mrs. Smiley may be developed further. Anyhow, let's test her. Now for a word of theory. This is the way it all appears to me at this time. She seems to enter successively three stages of hypnotic sleep. In the first stage the 'spirits' speak through her own throat—or she impersonates, as Mrs. Harris did. Her second and deeper sleep permits of the movement of the cone—'telekinesis,' 'independent slate-writing,' etc. But in this final deathly trance she has the power of projecting her astral hands, whatever that may mean, and the production of spirit voices. Perhaps she has an astral head—"

"I don't believe a word of it! It is all impossible, monstrous!"

"Well, how will you explain this performance? What about the tacks, the threads, the tapes that bound her? She brought books, shook the table, touched us—How?"

Pg 118

"I don't know; but there must be some perfectly natural way of explaining it. There is no place for the supernatural in my world. She seems a nice, simple little woman, and yet this very simplicity may be a means of throwing us off our guard. I will give a hundred dollars for permission to hold her hands while the cone is moving."

"If you do not believe in tacks, will you believe in the touch of your fingers?"

"If she permits me to hold her and the cone moves I will surrender."

"No, you won't. You think you will, but you won't. Don't deceive yourself. I've been all through it. You *can't* believe until some fundamental change takes place in your mind. You must struggle just as Richet did."

"Anyhow, let's turn the screws tighter. Let's devise some other plan to make ourselves doubly certain of her part in the performance."

With this understanding I said good-night, and took my lonely way to my apartment.

It was deliciously fresh and weirdly still in the street, and as I looked up at the glowing stars and down the long, empty street my mind revolted. "Can it be that the good old theory of the permanence of matter is a gross and childish thing? Do the dead tell tales, after all? I wish I could believe it. Perhaps old Tontonava was right. Perhaps if we were all to pray for the happy hunting-grounds Pg 119 at the same moment and in perfect faith, the lost paradise would return builded by the simple power of our thought."

Then Richet's moving confession came to me: "It took me twenty years of patient research to arrive at my present conviction. Nay to make one last confession , I am not yet absolutely and irremediably convinced. In spite of the astounding phenomena which I have witnessed, I have still a trace of doubt—doubt which is weak, indeed, to-day, but which may, perchance, be stronger to-morrow. Yet such doubts, if they come, will not be due so much to any defect in the actual experiment as to the inexorable strength of prepossession which holds me back from adopting a conclusion which contravenes the habitual and almost unanimous opinion of mankind."

Pg 120

V

At this point the sittings, which had begun so interestingly, suddenly began to fail of results. The power unaccountably weakened. Miller and several others of the circle believed these failures to be due to the increased rigidity of the restraint we had imposed upon the medium. The next "session" was held in Fowler's down-town office, against the hesitating protest of the psychic, who said: "The atmosphere of the place is not good." By which she meant that the associations of the office, with the hurry and worry of business, were in opposition to the mood necessary for the production of the phenomena.

"The real reason," declared Howard, "is this: we're now getting down to brass tacks in her business."

This was literally true. At Miller's suggestion a strong tape, perhaps half an inch wide, had been passed about the psychic's wrist and tied in a close, square knot, and finally a long brass tack was driven down through both strands of the tape into the chair-arm. This was in reality as secure Pg 121 as a handcuff. Nothing happened this night beyond the movement of the table and some rather weak raps, and we all rose from our seats worn and disappointed.

When we met the next night in the same place, and adjusted the ever-tightening bands upon the psychic, she sat helplessly for three hours. I began to lose confidence in her power to do anything beyond the ordinary. Howard, Mrs. Quigg, and Miss Brush dropped out before the sitting was over. Only Brierly and myself met the psychic at the Camerons' on the following Thursday. Again we sat patiently for long hours, with only the movement of the table and a drumming upon the top in response to our requests. Miller now said: "I would like to have one more sitting in my library, to see if we can duplicate the marvels of our previous séance."

We did not. The table alone moved, but it did this under absolutely test conditions. Over each of the psychic's arms a lady's stocking was drawn, and pinned to her dress at the shoulder. On each hand a luminous pasteboard star was fastened, and her wrists were tied and tacked, as before. Again we nailed her dress to the floor and covered her knees with a newspaper, and Miller and I held threads which were knotted to her wrists. Nevertheless, under these conditions the table moved while no one touched it, but always Pg 122 in a line away from the psychic. At the moment of the sliding of the table I closely watched the luminous stars, and asserted to the others that her hands did not stir. So that this movement, though slight, was genuinely telekinetic.

A very curious incident now cut short our sitting. Miller, who thought the left hand of the psychic was not in place, twitched the string which he held, and immediately Mrs. Smiley began to twist and sigh, and "Maud" complained that her mamma had been injured by the jerking of the thread by Professor Miller, and said that the sitting would have to stop. We lighted up and found the psychic apparently suffering keenly from a severe cramp all through her left side, and a good deal of rubbing was necessary to restore her to anything like a normal condition.

It really seemed like failure for my psychic, and I began to wonder whether the books really did fly from Miller's shelves. I could not suspect the gentle little lady of *conscious* deceit, but with a knowledge of the wonderful deceptions of somnambulists and hysterics, I began to doubt. I urged Miller to try one more sitting. He consented, and we met at Brierly's house. Nothing happened during the first two hours, and at ten o'clock, or thereabouts, Miller, Brierly, and Fowler withdrew, leaving me to untie and restore Mrs. Smiley, who was still apparently in deep sleep.

Pg 123

It was evident that the guides had not released the psychic, and "Maudie" soon spoke, asking me to put her mamma into a wooden chair, and to take the cone apart and put the smaller end upon the table. I did as she requested, and drew the psychic's chair and table together. "Wilbur" insisted that I tie the psychic as before, but I replied, rather dejectedly: "Oh no; let things go on as they are."

He insisted, and, with very little faith in the power of the psychic, I did as I was told. I tied her wrists separately and then together, and, drawing both ends of the tape into my left hand, I passed them under the tip of my forefinger in such wise that I could feel any slightest movement of the psychic's hands. The guides asked me to fasten her wrists to the chair, but I replied: "I am satisfied."

Again I was brought face to face with the mystery of mediumship. Sitting thus, with no one present but Mrs. Brierly, a woman to be trusted, the cone was drummed upon and carried about as if by a human hand. It touched my cheek at a distance of two feet from Mrs. Smiley's hands, and "Wilbur's" voice—strong, vital, humorous—came to me, conversing as readily, as sensibly, as any living flesh-and-blood person, *and all the time I held to my tapes, carefully noting that no movement, beyond a slight tremor*, took place in the psychic's arms. Just *before* each movement of the cone she Pg 124 shivered convulsively and sighed, but while the cone moved she was deathly still. Each time as the cone left the table it seemed to rock to and fro as though a hand were trying to grasp it, and a moment later it rose with a light spring. My impression was—my *belief* at the moment was—that Mrs. Smiley had nothing to do in any ordinary way with the movement of the horn. If there is any virtue in a taut tape and my sense of touch, her arms lay like marble during the precise time the voice was speaking to me. I could detect no connection between herself and the voice.

"Mitchell" assured me that he approved of every test we were putting upon "the instrument," and expressed confidence that she would triumph over Miller. "But the circles have been too often changed," he asserted, "and the places have not been well chosen. All must be unhurried and harmonious," he added, and I replied that I had been discouraged, but that this sitting had given me new interest. "I will be faithful to the end," I assured him.

"Wilbur" and "Mitchell" were perfectly distinct personalities, and appeared to confer and act together. I had a sense of nearness to the solution of the mystery that thrilled me. Here in the circle of my out-stretched arms the incredible was happening. I held Mrs. Brierly's hands, and controlled by means of my tightly stretched tape the Pg 125 movements of the psychic, and yet the megaphone was lifted, handled, used as a mouthpiece by "spirits." I felt that if at the moment I had been able to turn on a clear light I could have seen *my* ghostly visitors. This final hour's experience revived all my confidence in Mrs. Smiley, and not even another long series of absolute failures could destroy my faith in her honesty or my belief in her occult powers.

My patience was sorely tried by twelve almost perfectly useless sittings, during which everybody dropped away but Mr. and Mrs. Fowler, Dr. Towne, Brierly, and myself. They were not utterly barren sittings, but the phenomena were repetitious or slight and fugitive.

Mr. and Mrs. Fowler were friends of Brierly, and, like him, avowed spiritists, but they both lent their best efforts to make the tests complete and convincing. After trying sittings here and there, we finally settled upon a series of afternoon sessions in Fowler's own house. This was the twenty-sixth sitting of the series, and Cameron's Amateur Psychical Society was practically a memory. I was now going ahead pretty much on my own lines, but with an eye to catching Miller and the Camerons at a successful séance before concluding my search.

Mrs. Smiley was in great distress of mind over the failure of her powers. "I guess I'm no good any more," she said. "I never sit now without a feeling that perhaps my power is gone forever. Pg 126 This Eastern climate is so harsh for me, and I long for my own California. If you will not give up, I will keep trying as long as my guides advise it."

"You have done your part," I said, with intent to console her.

"Please don't give up," she pleaded.

"I am not giving up—on the contrary, I am only beginning to fight," I assured her, paraphrasing General Grant, or some other obstinate person. "I recognize the truth of what you complain about, but I am sure that at Fowler's, in a small, warm, well-aired room, you will feel at home and be secure of interruption."

Mrs. Fowler, a very sensitive, thoughtful, dark-eyed little lady, received us at the appointed hour with quiet cordiality, and suggested that her own room up-stairs would be a comfortable and retired place.

To this I agreed, and we set to work to prepare it for the sitting. Fowler and I assumed control of the psychic, though Brierly insisted that, as the house belonged to Fowler, it would be more convincing if he were not connected with the preparation of the room. "I don't think we need to consider hair-drawn objections," I retorted.

As before, we placed Mrs. Smiley in an arm-chair at one end of a small table; as before, we secured her ankles by looping a long tape about them and nailing the two ends to the floor behind her. Mrs. Pg 127 Fowler introduced an innovation by *sewing the tape to the sleeves of our psychic*. This made slipping out of the tape an impossibility, but, to push security still further, I drove a long brass tack down *through both tape and doubled sleeve*. Not content even with this, Fowler put a second tape about each wrist, to add further security and to take off the strain in case of any unconscious movement. Another tape was carried across Mrs. Smiley's dress about four inches below her knees, and pinned there. Next the ends were drawn tight and tied to the back rung of her chair. By this we intended to prevent any pushing action of the knees. As a final precaution, we nailed her dress to the floor in front with three tacks. The small end of the tin cone was then placed on the table at the request of the psychic and the large end deposited upright on the carpet near Fowler. Some sheets of paper and a pencil were laid upon the table. Everything movable was entirely out of the psychic's reach.

It was about three o'clock of the afternoon when, after darkening the windows, we took our seats in a little circle about the table. As usual, I guarded the psychic's right hand, while Fowler sat at her left. Brierly and Mrs. Fowler were opposite Mrs. Smiley. The room was lighter than at any other of our sittings—both on account of the infiltering light of day, and also because an open grate fire in Pg 128 the north wall sent forth an occasional flicker of red flame.

We sat for some time discussing Miller and Harris and their attitude toward the psychic. I remarked:

"To me our failures, some of them at least, have been very instructive, but the gradual falling away of our members makes evident to me how unlikely it is that any official commission will ever settle the claims of spiritualism. As Maxwell has said: 'It is a slow process, and he who cannot bring himself to plod patiently and to wait uncomplainingly for hours at a time will not go far.' I confess that the half-heartedness of our members has disappointed me. I told them at the outset not to expect entertainment, but they did. It *is* tiresome to sit night after night and get nothing for one's pains. It seems foolish and vain, but any real investigator accepts all these discomforts as part of the game. Failures are sure to come when the psychic is honest. Only the juggler can produce the same effects. A medium is not a Leyden-jar nor an Edison battery; materialization is not precisely a vaudeville 'stunt.'"

"I don't call the last sitting a failure," said Fowler. "The conditions were strictly test conditions, and yet matter was moved without contact. Of course, the mere movement of a table, or even of the trumpet, seems rather tame, as compared with the doings of 'Katie King'; but, after all, a single Pg 129 genuine case of telekinesis should be of the greatest value to the physicist; and, as for the psychologist, the fact of your friend, Mrs. Thomas, becoming entranced by 'Wilbur' was startling enough, in all conscience."

"I don't think Miller believed in her trance," said I.

"What happened?" asked Brierly, who had not been present at this particular sitting.

I answered: "Mrs. Thomas, a friend of mine, a very efficient, clear-brained person, whom, by-the-way, we had asked to come in order to fully preserve the proprieties, suddenly felt a twitching in her left hand, which was touching mine. This convulsive movement spread to her shoulder, until her whole arm began to thresh about like a flail in a most alarming way. The action became so violent at last that she called upon me for aid. I found it exceedingly difficult to subdue her agitation and silence her rebellious limb, but I did finally succeed. Nor was this all. A few moments later, while helping us in the singing, my friend suddenly stopped singing and began to laugh in a deep, guttural fashion, and presently a voice—the voice of a man, apparently—came from her throat: '*Haw! haw! I've got ye now! I've got ye now!*' It sounded like 'Wilbur.'"

This seemed to amuse Mrs. Smiley. "It was 'Wilbur,'" she said. "He loves to jump in and Pg 130 seize upon some one's vocal chords that way. It's a favorite joke with him."

"What horrible taste!" Mrs. Fowler shudderingly exclaimed.

"Oh, I don't know," remarked Brierly. "It is actually no worse than having your hand controlled."

"To have a spirit inside of one's throat is a little startling, even to me," I admitted, sympathetically. "But there was more of this business. Another member of the circle—a young man—became entranced, and proceeded to impersonate lost souls, 'earth-bound spirits,' in the manner of our friend Mrs. Harris, and wailed and wept and moaned in most grewsome fashion. However, I think Miller considered both of these performances merely cases of hysteria, induced by the darkness and the constraint of sitting about the table. And perhaps he was correct."

"Anything a doctor doesn't understand he calls hysteria," put in Brierly. "I consider these specialists nuisances."

"Well, anyhow, our 'Amateur Spook-spotter Association' seems to have come to an untimely end," said I, regretfully. "Of the original number, only Brierly remains. Wouldn't our deserters be chagrined if we should now proceed to enjoy a really startling session?"

"We will," Mrs. Smiley responded. "I feel the power all about me."

Pg 131

"Good!" cried Fowler. "That is the way you should feel. If you are at ease, the spirits will do the rest."

"Sit back and rest," I said. "We have plenty of time. You've been too anxious. Don't worry."

In the mean while, between the sitting at Miller's house and this present one, I had been reading much on the subject of the trance and of "the externalization of the fluidic double," of which the Continental philosophers have much to say. If not convinced, I was at least under conviction that the liberation of the astral self was possible if at all only in the deepest trance, and I now attempted to discover by interrogation of Mrs. Smiley precisely what her own conception of the process was.

"You told me once that you are conscious of leaving your body when in trance," I said. "Do you always have that sensation?"

"Yes, I almost always have a feeling of floating in the air," she answered. "It often seems as if I had risen a few feet above and a little to one side of my material self, to which I am somehow attached. I can see my body and what goes on around it, and yet, somehow, it all seems kind of dim, like a dream. It's hard to tell you just what I mean, but I seem to be in both places at once."

"Do you ever have any perception of a physical connection between yourself and the sitters?"

She seemed to me to answer this a bit reluctantly. Pg 132 "Yes, I sometimes feel as though little shining threads went out from me and those in the circle, and sometimes these threads meet and twine themselves around the cone or the pencil. This means that I draw power from all my sitters."

This was in accord with the accounts of a "cobwebby feeling" which both Maxwell and Flammarion had drawn from their mediums. Maxwell makes much of this curious physical sensation which accompanied certain of M. Meurice's phenomena. Here also seemed to be an unconscious corroboration of Albert de Rochas's experiments in the "externalization of motivity," as he calls it. The "cobwebby feeling" of the fingers might mean an actual raying-out of some subtle form of matter. Indeed, M. Meurice, Maxwell's medium, declared he could see "a sheath of filaments pass from his fingers to the objects of experimentation."

"Tell us about your journeys into the spirit land," I suggested. "You sometimes seem to go far away, do you not?"

Her voice became very wistful as she complied. "Yes, sometimes I seem to go to a far-off, bright world. I don't always want to come back, but there is a little shining white ribbon that unites my spirit with my body and holds me fast. Once when I had resolved never to return, that little band of light began to tug at me, and, although it broke my heart to leave my children, who were there with Pg 133 me, I yielded, and came back to life. It was very cheerful and lovely in that land, and I hated to come back to the cold and cruel earth-plane."

"Can't you tell us about it more particularly?"

"No; it is so different from this plane that I have no words in which to describe it. All I can say is that it seems glorious and happy and very light."

Something in her gentle accent excited Fowler's sympathy. "Mrs. Smiley, you have the blood of the martyrs in you. It takes courage to put one's self into the hands of a cold-blooded scientist like Miller. Even Garland, here, has no pity. He's like a hound on the trail of a fawn. It's all 'material' for him. Now, I am nothing but a mild-mannered editor. I have all the facts I require concerning the spirit world. I am busied with trying to make people happy here on this earth. But these scientific 'sharps' are avid for any fact which sustains the particular theory they happen to hold. Not one in a hundred will go where the facts lead. Their investigation is all a process of self-glorification, wherein each one thinks he must prove all the others liars or weak-minded in order to exalt himself."

To this I could only reply: "I'm not a scientist, though, I must say, I sympathize with the scientific method. And as for my treatment of Mrs. Smiley, I am following exactly the advice of her controls. They assure me that they will take care of her."

Pg 134

"And so they will," responded the devoted little psychic.

By the closest questioning I had never been able to change a single line of her simple faith. She was perfectly certain of the spirit world. She had daily messages from "Wilbur" and her spirit father, partly by voices, but mainly by intuition. Her children hovered over her while she slept. "Mitchell" healed her if she were ill. "Maudie" comforted her loneliest hours. These voices, these hands were an integral part of her world—as necessary and as dear to her as those of her friends in the flesh. As she talked on I experienced a keen pang of regret. "Why disturb her belief in the spirit world?" I asked myself. "Why attempt to reduce her manifestations to natural magic? To rob her of her conviction that 'Maudie' is able to come back to her would leave her poor indeed."

However, as the scientist cannot permit pity to hinder his purpose, I was determined to disassociate the *facts* of spiritualism from the *cult* of spiritualism. I was not concerned with faith or consolation. I returned to a study of the facts as a part of nature. I was now observing closely the three levels of sleep into which Mrs. Smiley seemed to lower herself at will, or upon the suggestion of those in the circle. I had adopted the theory that in the lighter trance she spoke unconsciously and wrote automatically. In the second, and deeper, Pg 135 trance she became the somnambulist possessed of diabolic cleverness, when, with the higher senses in abeyance, she was able to deceive and to elude all detection. In the third, or death-like, trance, I was ready to admit, for the sake of argument, that she was able, as De Rochas and Maxwell seem to have demonstrated, to exert an unknown form of force beyond the periphery of the body—that is to say, to move objects at a distance and to produce voices from the horn.

To prove that she actually left the body would do much to explain the phenomena, and I was very eager to push toward this demonstration. I had now been her chief inquisitor for nearly thirty sittings, and had developed apparently the power to throw her into trance almost instantly. A few moments of monotonous humming, intoned while my hand rested upon hers, generally sufficed to bring the first stage of her trance. As we had been sitting for half an hour, I now proceeded to chant my potent charm, with intent to liberate the "spirits" to their work.

In a few moments she responded to my suggestion. A nervous tremor, now expected and now familiar, developed in her hands. This was followed by a slight, convulsive, straining movement of her arms. Her fingers grew hot, and seemed to quiver with electric energy. Ten minutes later all movement ceased. Her temperature abruptly Pg 136 fell. Her breath grew tranquil, and at last appeared to fail altogether. This was the first stage of her trance. "Take your hand away, Fowler," I said. "We have nothing to do now but wait. The psychic is now in the hands of 'Mitchell.'"

Fowler remarked, with some humor: "I can tell by your tone that you're still unconvinced."

"I'm like the Scotchman—ready for convincement, but I'd like to see the man who could do it."

After a few minutes' silence Mrs. Fowler asked: "What is the most conclusive phenomenon you have ever witnessed, Mr. Garland?"

"That's a little difficult to answer," I replied, slowly, "but at the moment I think the playing of a closed piano, which I once heard, is the most inexplicable of all my experiments."

"What do you mean by 'the playing of a closed piano'?" queried Brierly.

"I'll tell you about it. It happened during the second sitting I ever had with Mrs. Smiley. I was lecturing in her home town at the time, and after the close of my address, and while we were talking together, some one who was aware of Mrs. Smiley's mediumship suggested: 'Let's go somewhere and have a sitting.' The plan pleased me, and, after some banter pro and con, we made up a party of six or eight people, and adjourned to the home of the chairman of the lecture committee, a certain Miss Halsey. I want to emphasize the high character Pg 137 of Miss Halsey, as well as the casual way in which we happened to go to her rooms, for it puts out of the way all question of collusion. There was no premeditation in the act, and Miss Halsey, who was the librarian of the city, and a pronounced disbeliever in spiritistic theories, had never met Mrs. Smiley before.

"The circle was made up about equally of men and women, all of them well-known residents of the town. So far as most of the phenomena resulting from this sitting are concerned, they have very little value, for they took place in the dark and the medium was not closely guarded. It was only toward the end of the sitting, which, by-the-way, took place in Miss Halsey's library and music-room, that the unexpected suddenly happened, the inexplicable came to pass.

"We were gathered about a long table, with Mrs. Smiley at one end sandwiched between the editor of the local paper and myself. Behind me, and just within reach of my hand, stood an upright piano, with its cover down, but not locked. We had heard drumming on the table for some time, and writing had apparently taken place on the pads in the middle of the table. But all this was inconclusive, for the reason that Mrs. Smiley was not fastened as she is now. I took it all with a pinch of salt. My mental reservations must have reached the minds of the 'guides,' for with startling suddenness they left the table and fell upon the top of Pg 138 the piano. After drumming for some time, the invisible fingers seemed to drop to the strings beneath, and a treble note was sounded as if plucked by a strong hand."

"You are sure the piano was closed?"

"I am coming to that. Highly delighted by this immediate response to my request, I said to the 'forces': 'Can't you demonstrate to us that these sounds are not accidental or caused by the jarring of cars in the street? Can't you pluck the bass strings?' Instantly, and with clangor, the lower strings replied. Thereupon I said: 'Can't you play a tune?' To this only a confused jangle made answer. I was unable to secure any orderly succession of notes. 'Can't you keep time while I whistle?' I insisted, with intent to show that intelligence guided these sounds. The 'spirits' twanged three times in the affirmative, and when I began to whistle 'Yankee Doodle' the invisible musician kept perfect time, playing according to my request—now on the treble, now on the bass. Leaning far back in my chair, I placed my hand upon the lid of the closed piano, and called out to the others in the circle: 'The lid of the piano is closed. My hand is upon it. So far as the sense of touch and hearing are concerned, we have here an action absolutely unaccounted for by any scientific law.

"This was at the moment absolutely convincing to me, as to the others, and I promptly reported the Pg 139 case to the American Psychical Society in Boston. Since then I may say I have had many experiments quite as convincing, but never a repetition of this peculiar phenomenon. It is useless to talk about secret wires, or a mouse running up and down the strings, or any other material explanation of this fact. It took place precisely as I relate it, and remains a mystery to this day."

Fowler remained very calm. "Crookes saw in a full light an accordion playing beneath the touch of invisible fingers."

"Yes," I retorted, in protest, "but this action of a closed piano happened in my presence, under my hand, and there is always so much more convincing quality in the miracle which happens in one's own house. But, seriously, that performance on the closed piano remains a profound mystification to me. If it had happened in the medium's house, or in the home of some one who knew her, I might have suspected fraud—but it did not! It happened in the study of one of the most respected women in the city, a student who did not believe in psychic phenomena. Furthermore, my own hand was on the lid of the piano. I was so convinced of Mrs. Smiley's possession of some occult force that I at once wrote to the society, telling them that a study of her phases would, in my judgment, be the most important work its directors could engage upon. This is one of my crack stories, and I wouldn't Pg 140 believe it as related by any one else. However, you may read my report, which I made at the time, if that will be of any satisfaction to you."

"Oh, I don't need it," responded Mr. Fowler. "I was merely trying to find out what your best experiments had been. Have they all been on the physical plane?"

"They are all on the physical plane—that is to say, on one plane for me. Any 'spirit manifestation,' so long as we are what we are, must be an agitation of what we call 'molecules of matter,' and is to that extent physical. I have no patience with those highfilutin teachers who speak of matter as though it were ignoble in some way. Matter to me is as mysterious as spirit."

At this moment a slight movement of the psychic arrested me, and as we listened the silvery sweet voice of "Maudie" issued from the darkness, saying: "*Mr. Mitchell wants Mr. Garland to change places with Mr. Fowler. Be very careful as you move about. Don't joggle mama. It's very dangerous to her.*"

As I rose to comply, "Maude" called out: "*Mr. Mitchell wishes the threads fastened to mama's wrists. He wants you and Mr. Fowler to hold them the way you did at Mr. Miller's house.*"

Turning up the lights, we tied a strong silk thread to each wrist, and passed the ends under each arm of the chair. Fowler took one of these ends while Pg 141 I retained the other. I then called the attention of Brierly to the fact that the table was seventeen inches from the feet of the psychic, and that the fastenings were unchanged. When his examination was completed, the lights were again turned off, and the circuit of hands restored.

"Maudie" then requested that the pieces of cone be put together and placed on the floor beside the table. Fowler did this, and drew a chalk mark about it, numbering it "Position No. 1." Immediately after his return to his seat the table was strongly pushed away from the psychic. It moved in impulses, an inch or two at a time, until it was certainly six or eight inches farther from the psychic.

It is impossible to conceive how this movement without contact takes place; but, then, what do we know about the action of the magnet on a pile of iron filings? How can a thought in the brain of man contract a set of muscles and lift a cannon-ball? At bottom we do not know how the will, as we call it, crosses the chasm between mind and matter—we don't even know there is a chasm.

"Do you feel any motion in your thread, Fowler?" I asked.

"Nothing but a faint quiver," he replied.

"Neither do I, and yet the table moved."

"The table is crowding against me!" called Mrs. Fowler, in some excitement.

The fact that the table moved toward us and Pg 142 directly away from the psychic was in itself suspicious; but, as a matter of fact, at other sittings we obtained sidewise movements of the table—generally to the left. The present experiment did not stand alone. You must remember also that the table was at this time more than two feet from Mrs. Smiley's toes, her dress was tacked to the floor, and her ankles controlled by a tape whose ends were nailed to the floor four feet behind her chair.

"So far as matter can testify, Mrs. Smiley is not concerned in this movement of the table," I said. "The question is now up to us. Which of us is doing this?"

"I am not," answered Brierly.

"Nor I," declared Fowler.

"Nor I," chimed in Mrs. Fowler.

At this moment the psychic began to stir again. "Look out!" I called, warningly. "Let every hand be accounted for. Some new demonstration is preparing. These periods of suffering are strangely like the pangs of childbirth. I wonder if, after all, Archdeacon Colley was not in the right when he asserted that he had seen the miraculous issue of phantoms. I confess that when I read it first I smiled with the rest, for his description of the process was not very poetic. He declared that he saw a white vapor steam from the side of the psychic, like vapor from a kettle, forming a little cloud, and from this nebulous mass various phantasms appeared, Pg 143 ranging from a little child to a full-grown man. It is curious how exactly similar all the reports of this process are. Crookes speaks of a milky-white vapor which condensed to a form, and Richet and Maxwell describe it as a sort of condensing process. I have seen it myself, but could not believe in the evidence of my own eyes. One can see all kinds of things in the dark."

Peace had again fallen upon our psychic—the peace of exhaustion; as if, her struggles being over, her flesh-free spirit were at large in the room. The silence was profound, yet somehow thrilling with potency.

In this hush the megaphone was lifted slightly and dropped, making us all start. It was as if a feeble hand had tried to manipulate it without success. "Let us keep test conditions," I urged. "Please do not make a movement now without warning me of your intentions. Keep the circuit closed." Here I addressed "Wilbur": "Let's see if you can handle the cone under strictly test conditions. Come now, lift it! Lift it!" I repeated the command with intent to concentrate all will-power of both psychic and sitters upon the thing desired, as Maxwell was accustomed to do in his experiments with Meurice.

Several times the forces strove to carry out my wishes, but could not. Twice the horn rose from the carpet, only to fall back helplessly. Fowler placed it in position each time, marking each new Pg 144 position, while I took note of the convulsive tremor which swept from time to time over the psychic. It was exactly as if she were a dynamo generating some unknown electrical energy, which, after accumulating for a time in her organism as in a jar , was discharged along the direction of our will, and yet I could not detect any marked synchronism of movement between these impulses and the movement of the horn.

After each fall of the cone she moaned and writhed, *but not till the hush of death came over her did the horn move.* So intense was the silence each time that we could hear the slightest breath, the minutest movement of the tin as it scraped along the rug.

"It is useless to talk of a confederate," I remarked; "it is of no value to refer this action to the hands of the psychic. We must look to subtler causes for this phenomenon. Perhaps Maxwell's theory that some magnetic power is liberated by the contraction of the larger muscles will account for it, but in no other way."

At last the megaphone soared into the air, passed over our heads, and dropped gently upon the table. It did not fall with a bang; on the contrary, it seemed to descend gently—*as if under perfect control of both hand and eye.* And yet I assert there was nothing to indicate that the psychic shared in these movements. She lay as still as a corpse. Nothing but a minute continuous tremor in the thread told that Pg 145 she was still alive. I was enormously impressed by the silence. The darkness seemed athrill with mystery—not the mystery of the discarnate soul, but the mystery of the X-ray. I felt that we were ourselves involved in a production of each and every one of these movements.

"There is no use attempting to deny this fact," I insisted to the other sitters. "Either the psychic is able to control that cone by the exercise of her will over some unknown invisible force, or she has left her body and is now at work, a sentient entity in the air about us. There is the same precision in all this which Lombroso observed. It really seems that the medium has the faculty of using her senses at a distance. To say that she is handling that cone with her ordinary physical limbs is absurd. This single inexplicable moving of a mass of matter from A to B makes the experiments of Crookes and Maxwell very much more vital to me. I shall reread their books with new interest."

This result should have awed me, but it did not. I felt a deep interest, of course, but no bewilderment. My mind was perfectly clear and my senses alert to every sound, every ray of light.

At this moment the psychic again began to twist and turn as if in pain, and at last the little voice of "Maudie" anxiously asked: "*Is Mr. Garland going to take a train at seven o'clock?*"

This query convinced me that deep in the Pg 146 subconscious mind of the psychic lay the knowledge that I had thought of catching this train, and that a sense of my plan was disturbing her and interfering with our experiment. To remove the uneasiness, I replied: "No, I am going to stay; for I think 'Mr. Mitchell' has something very special in store for me. Tell her not to think of it any more. I am in no hurry. I have no appointment elsewhere."

To this "Maudie" replied: "*Mr. Mitchell says, 'Thank you'; he will do the best he can for you. He says go down-stairs now and get your supper. Leave mama just where she is. He will take care of her.*"

As we had been sitting for nearly three hours in a dark close room we welcomed this suggestion from our thoughtful guide, although it tended to make the sitting less conclusive. As I followed my hostess down the stairs I shared her remorseful pity of poor Mrs. Smiley, bound and helpless in her inquisitorial seat. "Mitchell" did not ask that she be fed, only that she be covered with a shawl to keep her warm.

"If she is doing this for her own entertainment," I said, "she has singular tastes. If she is doing it to advance the cause of spiritualism, she is a noble creature—though a mistaken devotee, in the eyes of Miller."

Our hostess's uneasiness concerning the psychic made the meal a hurried one. None of us felt very much like eating, and I could see that Fowler was disposed to cut corners. "Well, Garland, what Pg 147 do you intend to do with the facts obtained this afternoon? You have plenty of authority behind which to shelter yourself. Why not admit the truth? So far as I am concerned, I am willing to swear that Mrs. Smiley had no actual hand in the movement of the cone."

To this I replied: "From one point of view, these phenomena are slight; but considered in the light of the manifestation of a totally new force, they are tremendous in their implication, and I must be absolutely sure of them before I assert their truth. The most impressive fact of all is that every phenomenon we obtain coheres with those obtained by Maxwell, Crookes, and Flammarion. It will not do to admit the spirit hypothesis, or grant the objectivity of phantasms, merely because we have proved the movements of a particle of matter from A to B without a known push or a pull, for such admission is far-reaching. If Maxwell is right, these phenomena—even the most complicated of them—are metapsychical, but perfectly normal. For example, he says: 'A movement without contact was forthcoming this afternoon. I placed a table upside down on a linen sheet. M. Meurice and I then put our hands on the sheet, some distance away from the table. The table turned completely over. The movement was performed slowly and gently. It was four o'clock in the afternoon, and the sunlight was streaming in through an open window.' Now Pg 148 here was a perfectly clear case of telekinesis, with no one present but Dr. Maxwell and his friend; but the turning over of the table does not imply the action of spirit hands."

"I don't see why not," responded Mrs. Fowler, "if Dr. Maxwell had mediumistic power."

"It was Meurice who had the power; but it was a physical power, which went out from his organism like heat. He was often ill after his experiments, and felt nausea and a disturbing weakness in the solar plexus, as though his bodily powers had been seriously drawn upon. I have felt this myself—or so it seemed; perhaps I imagined it."

Fowler struck in: "But what will you do with materializations such as Dr. Richet studied at the Villa Carmen in Algiers? What will you do with the photographs of the spectre of the helmeted soldier which he obtained under what he declares were test conditions?"

"But were they? That's the point."

"I am willing to trust a man of Richet's wide knowledge and known skill in experimentation. When he says he saw, touched, and heard the apparition of a man, I am ready to believe that he had taken quite as many precautions as his newspaper critics would have done. He saw a helmeted soldier leave the séance cabinet and walk about. He clasped his hand, he affirmed, and found it warm and jointed perfectly real , and he secured the Pg 149 breath of this phantom in a tube of baryta so unmistakably that the liquid was chemically changed in accordance with his test. There are thousands of other well-authenticated cases of materialization. I have seen scores of them myself. I am only quoting Richet because I know you believe in his methods."

"I do, indeed; but he may have been deceived, all the same. The failure of all his experiments in Algiers lay in the fact that he was never able to nail his psychic down, as we have done. He was the on-looker, after all—not the experimenter he should have been and wished to be. Really his photographs of the spirit 'B. B.' have not the weight as evidence of the physical manifestation, as the phenomena which we have this evening secured."

Fowler rose. "I have his report in my library. Let me get it."

He returned in a few minutes with a small blue book in his hand, from which he began to read with gusto: "'I saw, as it were, a white luminous ball floating over the floor; then rising straight upward, very rapidly, as though issuing from a trap-door, appeared B. B., born, so to speak, out of the flooring outside the curtain, which had not stirred. He tries, as it seems to me, to come among us, but he has a limping, hesitating gait. At one moment he reels as if about to fall, limping on one leg; then he goes toward the opening of the curtains of the cabinet. Pg 150 Then, without as I believe opening the curtains, he sinks down, disappears into the floor.'"

"What are you reading from?" I asked.

"I am reading from the report which Richet made to the Annals of Psychical Science. He goes on to say: 'It appears to me that this experiment is decisive, for the formation of a luminous spot on the ground, which then changes into a living and walking being, cannot seemingly be produced by any trick. On the day after this experiment I minutely examined the flagstones which made up the floor of the séance room , and also the coach-house and stable immediately under that part of the kiosque.' There was no trap-door, and the cobwebs on the roof of the stable were undisturbed. The photographs of the apparition were taken on five different plates simultaneously, and the figure is the same on each."

"Yes; but those experiments were afterward made of no value by the confession of a coachman, who admitted his complicity in the fraud."

"No; that story is not true. The experiments stand, and Richet still defends both himself and the circle against the charge of fraud."

"But read on," I insisted. "Does he not say that, in spite of all his proof, he will not even hazard an affirmation of the phenomena?"

"Yes, he does say that," admitted Fowler; "but he also says: 'I have thought it my duty to mention these facts in the same way as Sir William Crookes Pg 151 thought it his duty in more difficult times to report the history of "Katie King." I do not believe I have been deceived. I am convinced that I have been present at realities, not deceptions. Certainly I cannot say in what materialization consists. *I am only ready to maintain that there is something profoundly mysterious in it, which will change from top to bottom our ideas on nature and on life.*'"

"He apparently was profoundly affected by what he saw," I assented, "and I am perfectly willing to grant that the character of his friends in the circle add value to what he saw. But, after all, the fact of materialization is so tremendous in its implications that even to admit its possibility is to admit more than any man of our day, who has been trained in scientific ways, is willing to be answerable for. However, the most extraordinary story I have ever read is that of Archdeacon Colley, Rector of Stockton, Warwickshire, who declared in a public lecture—

and many times since, over his signature—that he saw the miraculous issue of phantoms born directly from the side of a psychic. He declares he saw a winsome little girl emerge—a laughing, golden-haired creature, as alive as any one. I confess that this is too much for me, and yet if a Spanish soldier can be born from a spot of light, anything at all that anybody may imagine can happen.—But let us return to our own psychics."

We found Mrs. Smiley sitting precisely as we left Pg 152 her, and, picking up our thread, Fowler and I located the table and the cone and reassumed our positions. The table, which was quite out of reach of Mrs. Smiley's hands, now stood with its end toward the three of us, sitting in a crescent shape opposite the psychic—a position which produced, so the guides said, one pole of a battery.

Hardly were we seated in our places when the psychic suddenly awoke and spoke in her natural voice, and I for one felt that the sitting was over. I was perfectly certain that nothing could happen out of the ordinary unless the medium were in either one or the other of her states of trance.

I was now both amazed and delighted to find that the cone could be drummed upon and voices delivered through it while Mrs. Smiley, mentally normal, took part in the conversation. My theories were upset. I was completely mystified, though I said nothing of this to Fowler.

Once or twice Mrs. Fowler declared she heard the sound of lips, and at last a voice came to her speaking the name of her father. His voice answered some of her questions correctly, but could not utter the pet name which her father used to call her. This breakdown of the individuality of the phantom voices is very characteristic. This ended the sitting. The voices had not been as strong as we had hoped for, but as we threw on the light we found a number of messages written upon the sheets of paper Pg 153 which Fowler had put in the middle of the table. These messages were lying with the writing wrong side up, so far as the psychic was concerned. Altogether we felt that the results were both significant and encouraging, and we agreed to meet three days later in the same room and under the same conditions.

"What I want to do now is to hold your arms while the horn is in the air, or while the writing is going on," I said to Mrs. Smiley.

And to this she replied: "You may make any test you please. I feel that in this house my powers will return."

"That is a real gain," I said, to encourage her.

Pg 154

VI

The next sitting was an almost exact duplication of the last so far as the binding and nailing of the psychic was concerned, except that we sewed *two* bands of tape to her sleeves and *four* tacks were used at each wrist. Her feet were tied separately in the middle of a long tape, and the ends brought together, carried back beneath her chair, and tacked to the floor. As before, we placed the large end of the cone on the floor, out of her reach, leaving the smaller end on the table, which we left just out of her utmost reach. On the table we placed some sheets of paper specially marked and dated, and took our seats as usual.

No one was present at this sitting but Mr. and Mrs. Fowler and myself. Even the faithful Brierly had been unable to share in this, the twenty-ninth experiment. I was delighted to have the circle narrow down, for Fowler was a good investigator and a man of vast experience in psychic matters. Outside interference was absolutely excluded. "Whatever happens to-night, Fowler," I said, "you and I or the spirits must be responsible for it."

Pg 155

We began, as usual, by putting Mrs. Smiley into hypnotic sleep. In a few moments the familiar shuddering action took place. Her palms grew moist. She said she found it difficult to submit to our touch. She asked us to put our fingers above hers, and soon after, in the midst of our singing, her voice ceased, her hands grew heavy as lead, and lay perfectly limp and dead in their bonds.

Again following the guidance of the raps, Fowler and I moved back and sat opposite her, with Mrs. Fowler between us. "Maudie" then spoke from the psychic's lips, asking us to move the table farther away. This I did, leaving it at least twelve inches from the utmost tips of her fingers. "Maudie" then asked us to take up the larger half of the cone and unite it with the smaller part, and lay the entire cone flat across the table.

We did so, marking its position by means of chalk. It was nearly three feet from the utmost extension of the psychic's hands, and yet, almost immediately, tapping came upon the cone keeping time to our singing. Later, sounds were produced like the beating of a kettle-drum. A hammering was then carried on as if within the cone, and "Maudie" spoke, telling us to go down and get supper, as before.

I regretted this necessity very much, for up to this moment all had been clear sailing; the tapping on the cone was inexplicable on the basis of any Pg 156 normal action of the psychic; but to leave her alone, even while so well accounted for, weakened the test.

I said as much to Fowler as we sat at the dinner-table. He admitted his own disappointment. "However," he added, philosophically, "we have to take these things as they offer. We can't construct them."

We discussed the implications of the sittings we had already held. "It isn't one thing only," he reminded me; "it is because of the larger fact that one phenomenon supports another that one comes to believe. Thus far to-night we have *proved* that Mrs. Smiley is not concerned with the drumming on the cone, haven't we?"

"Yes; but I want to hold her hands while the drumming takes place. I want to hear her voice at the same time with 'Mitchell's.'"

"We'll get it," he responded, confidently. And a little later we returned to the room where our psychic was sitting, still in deep trance.

After some moments of waiting, "Maudie" said: "Mr. Mitchell says take the table away and put the cone in its place."

We moved the table a short distance to the left, and I put the cone in the centre of the rug where the table had stood, and marked the position of the cone. The psychic then passed through a period of suffering, of effort, but nothing took place. Again "Maudie" spoke, asking us to restore the table Pg 157 and cone to their former positions. "Evidently the experiment designed by 'Mitchell' has failed," I said, "but these failures instruct us."

A convulsive restlessness again seized upon the psychic, and "Maudie" asked us to sing. I hummed softly, in order to hear anything that might take place. A minute clicking sound at once developed, as though some one were lightly beating the cone with a key. These clicks answered our questions. It was "Wilbur" once more. I asked him if he were going to be able to speak to us, and he tapped "*Yes*." Soon after this the cone was swung into the air and "Wilbur's" throaty whisper was heard. I asked him if the psychic could not be awake and speak while he was present, and he answered: "*Yes; we have planned that.*"

Even as he spoke Mrs. Smiley passed into what seemed like a struggle for breath and awoke!

"Are you with us, Mrs. Smiley?" asked Fowler.

"Yes. What time is it?"

"About half-past eight. How do you feel?"

"Very numb and cold," she answered, plaintively.

"I don't wonder at that," I remarked. "You've been sitting there for five hours."

"Is anybody present?" she asked, anxiously.

I knew what she meant, and answered: "Yes, 'Wilbur' is here—or was a few moments ago. Are you still with us, 'Wilbur'?"

Pg 158

A rapping on the cone made vigorous answer, and a few seconds later the cone took flight and "Wilbur's" voice resumed general conversation with us. It was noticeable to me all through this sitting, as at others, that neither "Wilbur" nor "Mitchell" nor "Maud" ever addressed the psychic;*they spoke of her, but never to her.*

I requested further tests. "'Wilbur,' I want the privilege of going to the psychic's side. I don't like this long-distance experiment. I want to get closer to these facts—if they are facts."

"*You shall have the privilege,*" was the reassuring answer.

"Shall I go now?"

There was no reply through the horn, but a tapping on the table gave a doubtful "*Yes,*" and I crept slowly forward and took a seat at Mrs. Smiley's right hand. "I am very close to the ultimate mystery, Mrs. Smiley," I said, as I placed my hand upon her wrist. "Proceed, 'Wilbur.' Let me hear your voice now."

With tense expectation, I put my ear close to the psychic's lips and listened breathlessly. The horn soared into the air and was drummed there, as if to show that it was out of the reach of the psychic, but no voice came from it! This was a disappointment to me, as well as to Fowler, and I banteringly said: "You know this failure is suspicious, Wilbur.' It seems to indicate that Mrs. Smiley is only Pg 159 a wonderful ventriloquist, after all. Can't you prove that she is independent of your voice? Can't you do something decisive at this moment?"

No reply came to this; but while my hand was firmly pressed upon her wrist both sleeves being nailed to the chair , the loose leaves of the paper in the centre of the table were whisked away to the left. I could follow their flight, and we all heard their deposition on a couch in a corner of the room.

"Fowler," I said, "are you controlling your wife's hands?"

"Yes; we had nothing to do with that noise."

This was another tense moment, for the movement of those papers was very ghostly indeed. We had demonstrated clearly that their movement was supernormal.

"May I come forward?" asked Fowler.

Tap—"*No,*" was the decided answer.

I then asked: "'Wilbur,' do you want me to change with Fowler and control Mrs. Fowler's hands?"

An emphatic "*Yes*" was rapped in reply.

"They seem as anxious for a conclusive test as we are," remarked Fowler. "Did you mean you didn't want Mrs. Fowler unaccounted for?"

A perfect fusillade of raps followed: "*Yes, yes, yes.*"

Fowler then came forward to Mrs. Smiley's left, Pg 160 while I returned to the table. Taking both of Mrs. Fowler's hands in mine, and setting the toes of my shoes upon hers, I awaited developments. At this moment, while Fowler was pressing the psychic's imprisoned wrists, the cone banged about most furiously, describing wide circles entirely out of Mrs. Smiley's reach. This action was another perfectly convincing test of the psychic's supernormal powers. As the same movement had taken place with *each* of us in control of the psychic, each was absolved from any complicity in the matter; but I did not forget my further test. "Mrs. Smiley," I said, "I want Mr. Fowler to return to his seat, and I want to place my hand over your lips—or to muffle you in some way. *I must* prove that you have nothing to do with the production of those voices. Will you permit this test?"

"Certainly," she answered, with patient sweetness. "You may gag me in any way you please. I am perfectly sure you can secure the proof you want." Upon this hint I acted. Taking a large kerchief from my pocket, I tied it tightly around her mouth, knotting it at the back, and then, in growing excitement, challenged the ghostly voice: "Now, 'Wilbur,' let's hear from you."

A moment later the voice came from the cone, but apparently very much muffled and blurred. "You are not articulating well," I rather sarcastically observed.

Pg 161

Instantly the voice came out clearly, more sharply than ever before. "*I was fooling you!*" jeered "Wilbur."

We all applauded. "There, that's better," I said. "Your voice improved wonderfully."

"Wilbur" chuckled with glee. "*I've taken a lozenge,*" he whimsically retorted, expressing a very human delight in our mystification.

Fowler then said: "Now let's consider this a moment, Garland. Suppose Mrs. Smiley has been able to loosen the gag. How does she handle the cone? We will suppose she is a marvellous ventriloquist. How does she write on the pads on the table, and how does she whisk them away? You see, it isn't the matter of one thing, but of all that has happened."

"Yes, I admit that everything points to an exercise of supernormal force. It really looks, so far as anything in the dark can look, like spirits, but I prefer to think Mrs. Smiley has the power to project her will in some way."

"I don't see how we are going to escape the spirit hypothesis," replied Fowler.

"'Mitchell,'" I said, addressing the phantom, "I want to examine that gag, and I want to hold both hands of the psychic. Will you permit that?"

There was no reply to this, and Fowler offered an explanation: "We had that test at a previous sitting."

Pg 162

I explained to the invisible ones: "'Wilbur,' it is absolutely essential that you should prove to me that your voice is not dependent upon the vocal chords of the psychic. You see the importance of this, do you not, Mrs. Smiley?"

"Indeed, I do," she earnestly answered, her voice sounding very faint and muffled through the kerchief. "I am anxious for the test."

"Very well, then. Now I want you to sing a song, and while you are singing I am going to insist on 'Wilbur's' speaking. Will you do that, 'Wilbur'?" The cone was drummed upon as if in vigorous promise of success.

Mrs. Smiley sang, or rather hummed; but there was no response on the part of the ghostly voices, and a moment later she called, faintly: "The kerchief is slipping down, Mr. Garland."

I rose and went to her side. As I untied the kerchief, she said, plaintively: "I am sorry we didn't get the voices. I am sure we can if we try again. Please try again." And a vigorous drumming on the cone seemed to second her plea.

However, it was getting very late, and I said: "I think we will postpone further experiment to-night. What are your sensations now?"

"I am almost paralyzed, and still deaf, too, but that often happens. My feet are as if they did not exist."

"But your mind is perfectly normal?"

Pg 163

"Yes, it seems to be."

Soon after this I returned to my seat; the cone was lifted high into the air silently, broken apart, and then, with the small end jangling inside the larger one, was carried over the table and back to the floor. It fell with a bang that seemed final and decisive. "That is 'good-bye,'" said Mrs. Smiley.

Upon lighting the gas we found our victim as before, sitting absolutely as we had left her. The table edge was twenty-four inches from her finger-tips. The place where the cone lay, which we had marked with chalk when it was first drummed upon, was thirty-six inches from one hand and forty inches from the other. But the most inexplicable of all—the tangible, permanent record—was the seven sheets of paper which were lying upon a couch six feet from Mrs. Smiley's left hand. *They were all written upon legibly, and pinned together with a black pin, which had been thrust through the writing.* "Wilbur" had scrawled his name, Mrs. Fowler's father's name was signed to a message, and there were other signatures unknown to any of us. The pencil was on the carpet, forty inches from Mrs. Smiley's hand. The leaves of paper, at the moment when they were grasped and lifted, were more than forty inches from her finger-tips. How this was done I do not know: but of this I am absolutely sure: the psychic did not remove them from the table by means of her ordinary, material limbs. Barring the failure Pg 164 to disassociate her voice from that of "Wilbur," she had met every demand upon her. Her powers were truly magical. I cannot say I *saw* the cone move, but I have proven that the psychic did not surreptitiously touch it or fraudulently write upon the papers during this sitting. I cannot swear that Fowler was controlling his wife's hands while the cone was floating and while I held the psychic's imprisoned hands , but I*believe* he was. In short, barring the one sense of sight—an all-important one, I admit—these happenings were convincing and fitted in with phenomena which I had secured with other psychics.

Nevertheless, I was not satisfied. I wanted Brierly, or some other fifth person, in the room, in order that *both* of the psychic's hands could be controlled at the same time that Mrs. Fowler's were secured. So long as a single hand was left free, the doubter would be warranted in questioning our results.

The next two or three sittings were partial failures—so much so that I made no record of them. Possibly, conditions were not strict enough. At any rate, the final and most conclusive sitting came three days later. It was held in Fowler's house. We followed the conditions of the previous sitting very closely—the same room, the same table, the same fastenings as before.

There was present a friend of Fowler's, a young Pg 165 man who was possessed of some psychic power. We will call him Frank. Fowler and I took entire charge of the psychic, and her bonds were even more carefully nailed than before. We began the séance, as before, by putting her to sleep.

Not long after "Maudie" spoke, saying: "*Mr. Mitchell wishes the thread fastened to mama's hands in the way Mr. Garland desires.*"

I fastened a strong thread to each wrist as I had done several times before, passing the ends under the chair-arm in such wise that any movement of the psychic would be plainly and instantly detected. We then returned to our seats, and, though conditions seemed favorable, no marked phenomena took place; the cone was lifted, it is true, but we were used to this now, and accepted it as quite commonplace.

At six o'clock the voice of "Maudie" came: "*Please go down to supper. Mr. Mitchell says he will be able to give you what you ask for after you return.*"

I did not ask to what he referred, but I had in mind the test to prove the voices independent of the psychic's vocal organs, and at the dinner we discussed methods by which this could be made clear.

"If they will let me put my hand over her mouth," I said to Fowler, "I will be satisfied."

"Do you mean that you will believe in spirits?" he smilingly challenged me.

Pg 166

"Oh, I won't go so far as to promise that, but I confess it would help to prove their existence."

"We may be about to get something more conclusive than that."

"Let us fix our minds on two things: first, to get the writing, or at least movement, with every hand controlled; and, second, the voices, while one of us covers Mrs. Smiley's mouth with a hand."

"Very well," acquiesced Fowler. "But the unexpected is what usually happens in these performances."

We were gone but twenty minutes, so eager were we for our demonstration. We found everything quite as when we left: the psychic was asleep, the fastenings undisturbed. Fowler and I regained our threads and resumed our places at the sides of the table, while Frank and Mrs. Fowler sat close together at the end opposite Mrs. Smiley. I ask the reader to recall that the psychic's ankles were encircled with tape which was nailed to the floor behind her chair. Two bands of tape, after being sewn to her cuffs, had been tacked solidly to the chair, three strong tacks were driven down through the hem of her dress, and, finally, Fowler and I were holding the threads which, after encircling the psychic's wrists, passed under the chair-arm.

And yet, in spite of all these bonds and precautions, the cone was almost immediately lifted, and "Mitchell" spoke through it. In a deep, clear, Pg 167 well-delivered, and decidedly masculine whisper, and with stately periods, he promised the complete co-operation of the spirit world in the great work to which I was devoting myself. He directed his exhortation to me, as usual; and for the benefit of those who think the spirits are always trivial or foolish, I wish to say that "Mitchell's" remarks were dignified and very suggestive. He produced in my mind the distinct impression of a serious man of seventy, ornate of rhetoric, but never vague or wandering in his thought, and he never went outside the circle of Mrs. Smiley's mind.

For fully a quarter of an hour he discussed with me the value of the investigation which we were pursuing. "*I and my band*," he assured me, "*are working as hard from our side as you are from yours, equally intent upon opening up channels of communication between the two worlds.*" He solemnly urged me to proceed in this "*grand work*," and at last said, "*Good-bye for the present*," and fell silent.

The cone was then deposited on the table, and "Maud" said: "*If Mr. Garland and Mr. Fowler will go quietly up to mama's side, holding all the time tightly to the threads, 'Mr. Mitchell' will do what Mr. Garland so much desires. Please be very careful not to touch mama until I tell you. Keep as far apart as you can as you go up to her. When you reach my mama's side, you may put one hand on her* Pg 168 *head and one on her wrist. 'Mr. Mitchell' says please have Frank take Mrs. Fowler's hands, so that every hand in the circle is accounted for.*"

I was now very eager and very alert. I felt that at last, after many, many requests and many trials, I was about to secure a clear, complete, and satisfying demonstration. Surely no trickster would permit such rigorous control as that toward which we were now invited. I was sorry that Miller was not present to share with me the satisfaction of the moment. My admiration went out toward this heroic little woman, who was enduring so much pain and suspicion for the sake of science. "She believes in herself," I thought. "If she succeeds, all honor to her."

Slowly we crept to her side, being careful to touch nothing until directed by the voice of "Maud." At last the childish voice said: "*Mr. Garland may put his right hand on top of mama's head and his left hand on her wrist. Mr. Fowler may place his left hand above Mr. Garland's and his right hand on mama's wrist. 'Mr. Mitchell' says he will then see if the voices will not come.*"

I then said aloud: "My right hand is on the psychic's head, my left is on her wrist."

Fowler repeated: "My left hand is above Garland's right, which is on the psychic's head, and my own right hand is on the right wrist of the psychic. Now, 'Wilbur,' go ahead."

Pg 169

Our challenge was almost instantly caught up. While thus double-safeguarding the psychic, the cone, which was resting on the table a full yard away, rose with a sharp, metallic, scraping sound, and remained in the air for fully half a minute, during which I called out, sharply: "We are absolutely controlling the psychic; her hands are motionless; Mrs. Fowler, be sure you are holding both of Frank's hands."

"I have both his hands in mine," she answered.

As the cone was gently returned to the carpet Fowler was moved to say: "Garland, that was a supreme test of the psychic. She was absolutely not concerned in any known way with that movement. Save for a curious throbbing, wave-like motion in her scalp, she did not move. If she lifted the horn, it was by the exercise of a force unrecognized by science."

To this I was forced to agree. I here definitely declare that the psychic was not concerned with the flight of the cone in any way known to biology. If she produced the voices, they too must have been examples of supernormal ventriloquism, for they came through the megaphone. Of that I am as certain as one can be of an auditory impression.

A few moments later we returned to our seats, while "Wilbur" and "Mitchell" and several other voices spoke to us. Fowler, now that I had admitted telekinesis, wanted me to go further. "Is Pg 170 the psychic speaking to us," he asked, "or are these voices independent of her?"

"An investigator is never satisfied," I answered. "I must have the voices *through* the cone while I am covering the psychic's mouth."

To this "Mitchell" replied: "*We are doing all we can, and we will yet be able to meet every demand you make upon us.*"

"I am anxious for conviction," I said. "I want to secure the voice of the psychic and your voice at the same time, 'Mr. Mitchell.' Can you do that for me?"

He seemed to hesitate, and at last said: "*We will try.*" I perceived in his tone a certain doubt and indecision. Again we were permitted to hold the psychic's wrists, and, as before, the cone was lifted and drummed upon as if to show its position high in the air; but no voices came. Hidden forces seemed to be struggling for escape beneath our hands; the woman's brain seemed a powerful dynamo. I could not rid myself of a sense that there was an actual externalization of the psychic's nerve force, and with this conviction I could well understand why the command had so often been given not to touch her unbidden. Suppose the poor naked "astral body" were abroad and a strong light were suddenly turned upon it!

Now came on a singularly engrossing game of "hide-and-seek." Convinced that Mrs. Smiley Pg 171 was innocent of any trick in the movement of the horn, I tried every expedient to satisfy myself that "Wilbur's" voice was independent of her own; but I did not succeed. Mrs. Smiley spoke*almost* at the same moment but never precisely synchronous with Wilbur's whisper. She answered all my questions perfectly unconcerned and unexcited, lending herself to my experiments. All in vain. At no time did I succeed in getting "Wilbur's" voice at *precisely* the same moment with her own, though the whisper, following swiftly on her speech, interjected remarks as if echoing her questions. There was always an approximate interval between her voice and the spirit whisper.

This was to me very significant, and strengthened me in my belief that the entire process, while inexplicable, was, after all, not the work of spirits.

When the gas was lighted we found the cone had been placed on the table, a distance of forty inches from the utmost reach of the psychic's hands. Her feet were twenty-three inches from the nearest leg of the table. We carefully examined the tapes which were sewed to her sleeves. They were tied, and the doubled ends tacked precisely as described so many times, and to remove the tacks we were forced to use a hammer. It is useless to talk of a possible release of her arms during the phenomena of the cone.

As I was about to leave the house that night, Pg 172 Mrs. Smiley said: "I do not feel able to sit any more for the present, Mr. Garland. I feel myself growing weaker, and 'Mitchell' tells me I would better stop for the present. I feel that my power belongs to the world, and I want to do all I can to convince you of the truth of spiritualism, but I feel the strain very greatly."

"I do not wonder at that," I responded, "and I cannot blame you for demanding a rest. No one could have endured more uncomplainingly. You have been a model subject, and we are deeply in your debt. I am sorry Miller was not with us to-night; he would have been convinced of your supernormal power at least. Have no fear of my report; for while I am not convinced of the spirit hypothesis, I have found you honest and patient and very brave. I thank you very sincerely for what you have done."

And in this spirit we parted. 1

FOOTNOTE:

1 Since these words were written I have *seen* the cone move. In the presence of another medium, with no one in the room but myself, I held the psychic's hands what time the horn circled over my head. It shone like a golden rod as it moved. I could see the gleam of light along its entire side. At last it came softly down and laid itself across my shoulder. In order to satisfy myself of its presence, I bent and touched it with my forehead. The touch seemed to disturb conditions, to break the current, for it dropped instantly to the floor. Twice it answered to my request in this manner until my doubts were satisfied. It seemed to move with the swiftness of a dragonfly as silent and horizontal it hung in the air about my head.

Pg 173

VII

Cameron's Amateur Psychic Club, which had so nearly disintegrated by reason of the long series of barren sittings, was drawn together again by the news of my startling success at Fowler's house. Cameron at once decided that the members should hear my report, and I was notified to be ready to relate my experiences in full. We met, as before, at Cameron's table, and even before the soup-plates were removed the interrogation began, and by the time the company was in full possession of the facts the coffee and cigars had appeared.

"Why didn't these wonders take place in our presence?" asked Mrs. Quigg, who had returned to something like her original truculence of doubt. "Why should you and Brierly be so favored?"

"In this business everything comes to him who waits," I replied, a tinge of malice in my voice. "You obtained a few results, Miller a few more; but Fowler and I, for our pains, reaped the rich reward. By remaining long on the watch-tower we saw the armies pass. Harmony and patience are Pg 174 essentials in the production of these marvels. With people yawning or shuffling about uneasily, results are necessarily unimportant."

Miller continued firm in his agnosticism. "Although puzzling, I cannot grant so much as even one of the phenomena. Belief in the smallest of those manifestations at my house would be uprooting to all established theories of matter—not to mention time and space."

"Were not the notions of Galileo and Darwin also subverting?" asked Fowler. "Is there anything sacred in error? If we are wrong in our theories about the universe, let's correct them. You do not stand out against wireless telegraphy or the Röntgen ray?"

Miller fired at this. "I'm not going to take instruction from a tipping table or a flying hair-brush!" he fiercely retorted.

"I'll take illumination from any source whatsoever," responded Fowler.

Here I interposed: "The only question that concerns me at this stage is: Does the table tip and the brush really fly? No physical fact is trivial, for it stands related to mountains and the clouds."

Fowler's eyes gleamed with contempt. "That's the way of you so-called scientists: you narrow the mighty fund of occult phenomena down to a floating feather. As a matter of fact, there is a sea of evidence accumulated by the investigations of men quite Pg 175 as scientific as Miller, testimony that is neither petty nor ignoble. It is because you and your associates are so trifling in methods that the tables and the chair play leading parts in your drama."

"Good for you!" cheered Brierly. "You're quite right. When these materialistic investigators get done with trying to prove that independent slate-writing exists, they'll begin to give some attention to the fundamental truths of the messages which the slates set forth. Going after small things, they get small things. If Miller and his like went forth seeking the essentials of the faith, they would find them instead of being amazed with foolish tricks of hand."

"Essentials such as what?" interrupted Harris, with snappy suddenness.

"Such as—as—direct spirit communication, a knowledge of the astral, the reincarnation of souls, and—and—faith in the upward progression of the self," stammered Brierly, much disturbed.

Here again I interposed a quieting word: "I confess that it begins to look as though the theosophist's theory of the astral at which some of us have smiled were in a fair way to be scientifically demonstrated. Since our last meeting I have been studying the bound volumes of *The Annals of Psychic Science,* and I have found them full of comfort. They sustain Mrs. Smiley at every point. To my mind, the most important event in the history of spiritism is the entrance of Eusapia Paladino into the clinical Pg 176 laboratory of Cesare Lombroso. Nothing since Crookes's experiments has had such value for the scientist."

"We have heard of Lombroso, but who is Paladino?" asked Mrs. Quigg. "Is she a psychic?"

"She is the most renowned now living. Though only an illiterate peasant woman, she has been able for more than twenty years to baffle every scientist who has studied her. Her organism remains the most potent mystery on this earth."

"Tell us about her! Who is she? Where does she live?"

"She was born at Minerva-murge, a mountain village near Bari, in Italy. According to Lombroso's daughter, who has written a sketch of her, she is about fifty-three years of age. Her parents were peasants. She is quite uneducated, but is intelligent and rather good-looking. Her hands are pretty and her feet small—facts which are of value when studying her manifestations, as you will see later on. Her mother died while Eusapia was a babe, and her father 'passed over' when she was twelve, leaving her at large in the world 'like a wild animal,' as she herself says. A native family of her village took her to Naples, and her own story is that she was adopted soon after by some foreigners 'who wished to make me an educated and learned girl. They wanted me to take a bath every day and comb my hair every day,' she explains, with some humor.

Pg 177

"She didn't like the life nor the people, and she soon ran away back to her friends, the Apulians, and it was while she was in their house and at the precise moment when they were planning to put her in a convent that her occult powers were discovered. Some friends came in to spend the evening, and, in default of anything better to do, formed a circle to make a table tip. No sooner were they all seated, as she herself relates, than 'the table began to rise, the chairs to dance, the curtains to swell, and the glasses and bottles to walk about, till everybody was scared.' After testing every other person present, the host came to the conclusion that the medium was his little ward, Eusapia. This put an end to her going into a convent. She was proclaimed a medium, much to her disgust, and made to sit whole evenings at the table. 'I only did it,' she says, 'because it was a way of recompensing my hosts, whose desire to keep me with them prevented their placing me in a convent. Finally I took up laundress work, thinking I might render myself independent and live as I liked without troubling about spiritualistic séances.'"

"It is remarkable how many of these women psychics begin their career when they are ten or twelve years old," said Miller. "Mrs. Smiley was about that age, wasn't she?"

"Yes, and so was Mrs. Hartley, another psychic of my acquaintance. Mrs. Smiley complained of the Pg 178 tedium of sitting. She tells me that her father kept her at it steadily, just as Eusapia was not permitted to escape her fate. One day an Englishwoman, wife of a certain Mr. Damiani, came to a séance, and was so impressed by what took place that she interested her husband in Eusapia's performances. Damiani then took up the young medium's development along the good old well-worn lines of American spiritualism, and she acquired all the tricks and all the 'patter.' Among other notions, she picked up the idea of an English 'control' known as 'John King,' who declared himself a brother of 'Kate King,' of Crookes fame, and from that day Eusapia has been a professional 'mejum.'"

"What does she do?" asked Cameron. "What is her 'phase,' as you call it?"

"It must be confessed that most of her phases are of the poltergeist variety, but they are astounding. She produces the movement of mandolins, chairs, sofas, and small tables without contact at least, such is the consensus of opinion of nearly a score of the best-known scientists of France and Italy , and also materializes hands and arms. There is vastly more than the poltergeist in her, that is evident; for she has conquered every critic with her miracles. Take, for instance, Lombroso's conversion, a fairly typical case. He was not only sceptical of spirit phenomena, but up to 1888 was openly Pg 179 contemptuous of those who believed in them. However, in an article called 'The Influence of Civilization upon Genius,' published in 1888, he made this admission: '*Twenty or thirty years are enough to make the whole world admire a discovery which was treated as madness at the moment when it was made.... Who knows whether my friends and I who laugh at spiritualism are not in error, just like hypnotized persons, or like lunatics; being in the dark as regards the truth, we laugh at those who are not in the same condition.*'"

"True enough," said Fowler. "The man who has made no study of these phenomena is like one color-blind: he has never seen a landscape."

"It was this candid statement by Lombroso that moved Professor Chiaia, a friend of Eusapia's, to write the great alienist a letter which was in effect a challenge. After recounting a score or two of the wonderful doings of Paladino, whom he had studied carefully, he ended in this amusing fashion: 'Now you see my challenge. If you have not written the paragraph cited above simply for the fun of writing it, if you have the true love for science, if you are without prejudices—you, the first alienist of Italy—please take the field. When you can afford a week's vacation, indicate a place where we can meet. Four gentlemen will be our seconds: you will choose two, and I will bring the other two.... If the experiment does not succeed, you will consider me but as a man suffering from hallucination, who longs to be cured Pg 180 of his extravagances.... If success crowns our efforts, your loyalty ... will attest the reality of these mysterious phenomena and promise to investigate their causes.'"

"I hope Lombroso was man enough to accept the challenge," said Cameron. "Nothing could be fairer than the spook-man's offer."

"He did not at once take up the gage. It was not, in fact, till February, 1891, that he was able to go to Naples to meet Eusapia, who had begun to interest some of his trusted scientific friends. He found the great psychic quite normal in appearance and rather attractive in manner. She was of medium size, with a broad and rather serious face lit with brilliant dark eyes. The most notable thing about her physical self was a depression in her skull caused by a fall in her infancy. This scar figures largely in nearly all the reports of her."

"Why?" asked Harris.

"Because they all agree that a singular sort of current of force, like a cool breeze, seems to come and go through this spot."

Harris groaned, and Howard said: "Oh, rubbish!"

"Rubbish or not, they all speak of this scar and its singular effects. At the time when Lombroso saw her first, Eusapia was just beginning to be known to scientists, but no one of special note had up to this time 1891 reported upon her. She was known as the wife of a small shop-keeper in Naples, and Pg 181 seemed a decent, matronly person, quite untouched by mysticism. Although not eager to sit for Lombroso and his party of scientists, she finally consented. Among those who took part in these celebrated experiments were Professor Tamburini, an eminent scientist; Dr. Bianchi, the superintendent of the Insane Asylum of

Sales; and Dr. Penta, a young nephew of Lombroso, a resident of Naples. Lombroso had charge of the sittings, which were held in a room of his own choice and with the medium entirely under his control. He was astonished at the prompt response obtained. At the first sitting, while he and Professor Tamburini held the psychic's hands, a bell was carried tinkling through the air and a small table moved as if it were alive. Many other mysterious movements took place. Lombroso was very much disturbed by these inexplicable phenomena, and could not rest till he sat again. At the second séance spectral hands developed, profoundly mystifying every sitter, and Lombroso went away, promising to carry forward a study of spiritism. In a letter written the following June he manfully said: '*I am filled with confusion, and regret that I combated with so much persistence the possibilities of the facts called spiritualistic. I say facts, for I am opposed to the theory.*'"

"Did Lombroso say that?" asked Harris.

"He wrote it, which is still more to the point, and it was his acceptance of the main *facts* of Paladino's Pg 182 mediumship that led other groups of scientists to take up her case. Professor Schiaparelli, Director of the Observatory at Milan; Gerosa, Professor of Physics; Ermacora, Doctor of Natural Philosophy; Aksakof, Councilor of State to the Emperor of Russia; and Charles du Prel, Doctor of Philosophy in Munich, were in the next group, which met at Milan with intent to settle the claims of this bold charlatan.

"The sittings took place in the apartment of Monsieur Finzi at Milan, and were more rigid and searching than any Paladino had ever passed through, but she was again triumphant. She bewildered them all. Lombroso himself was present during some of the sittings. The results of the series of experiments were very notable and very far-reaching. For the first time, so far as I know, a table was photographed while floating in the air—"

"No!" shouted Howard.

"Yes; and certain other telekinetic happenings were proved, to the stupefaction of most of those in the group. One special experiment, the success of which confounded the shrewdest, was the attempt to secure on a smoke-blackened paper the print of one of the spectral hands."

"Did it succeed?"

"Yes. The impression was made while Paladino's hands were imprisoned beyond all question, and, what was most singular of all, the hand *that made the print smudged the wrists of one of the Pg 183 experimenters, and yet not a particle of black appeared on the fingers of the psychic*."

"That ought to have convinced them of her honesty," remarked Fowler, with a note of amusement in his voice, "but it didn't; these scientific folk are so difficult."

"No," I replied, "it didn't convince them, but it jarred them not a little. In their report they admitted this much. They said, 'We do not believe we have the right to explain these things by the aid of insulting assumptions.' By this they meant to acquit the psychic of fraud. 'We think, on the contrary, that *these experiments have to do with phenomena of an unknown nature*, and we confess that we do not know what the conditions are that are required to produce them.'"

"That seems to me like a very mild statement, but I suppose they considered it epoch-making," remarked Fowler.

"From this time forward learned men in Russia, France, and Italy successively sought Paladino out and tried to expose her to the world. Professor Wagner, of the Department of Zoölogy at the University of St. Petersburg, made a study of her in 1893, and found her powers real. A year later M. Siemeradski, correspondent of the Institute, experimented with her in Rome, obtaining, among other miracles, the plucking of the strings of a closed piano under strictly test conditions."

Pg 184

"You had that experience, did you not?" asked Mrs. Cameron.

"Yes, I've had that."

"How do you account for a thing of that sort?"

"I don't account for it—or if I did give my theory, you would laugh at me. Wait till I tell you what these Italians are doing. Among the most eminent and persuasive of all Eusapia's investigators was Professor Charles Richet, the French physiologist and author. Eusapia came to revere and trust him, and gave him many sittings. He, too, was bowled over. He tells the story of his conversion very charmingly. 'In my servile respect for classic tradition,' he writes, 'I laughed at Crookes and his experiments; but it must be remembered in my excuse that as a professional physiologist I moved habitually along a road quite other than mystical.' His attention, he goes on to say, was first drawn to spiritist phenomena by the word of a friend who had discovered a power that caused a table to move intelligently. He was trying to explain this and one or two other little things like telepathy and prophetic vision by the word 'somnambulism,' when his friend Aksakof, a great psychical expert, reproached him for not interesting himself more keenly in experiments with mediums. 'Well,' said Richet, 'if I were sure that a single true medium existed, I would willingly go to the ends of the world to meet him.'"

Pg 185

"That's the spirit!" exclaimed Fowler. "That is the way the scientist should feel. What then? Aksakof told him all he needed to do was to go round the corner, didn't he?"

"Not exactly. Two years later Aksakof wrote to him: 'You needn't come to the end of the world; Milan will do.' So Richet went to Milan, and took part in those very celebrated séances with Eusapia. 'When I left Milan,' Richet says, 'I was convinced that all was true; but no sooner was I back in my accustomed channels of work than my doubts returned. I persuaded myself that all had been fraud or illusion.'"

Here Harris interrupted: "Miller can testify to this inability to retain a conviction. He, too, has slumped into doubt. How about it, Miller?"

"I never professed to believe," declared Miller.

"You were pretty well convinced that night in your study, weren't you?" I asked.

"I was puzzled," he replied, guardedly.

There was a general smile of amusement at his manifest evasion, and I resumed: "Richet went to Rome, and together with Schrenk-Nötzing, the philosophic expert, and Siemeradski, the correspondent of the French Institute, made other and still more convincing experiments, and yet doubt persisted! 'I was not yet satisfied,' he says, further. *'I invited Eusapia to my house for three months. Alone with her and Ochorowicz, a man of penetrating* Pg 186 *perspicuity, I renewed my experiments in the best possible conditions of solitude and quiet reflection. We thus acquired a positive proof of the reality of the facts announced at Milan.'"*

"By George, that's going it strong!" said young Howard. "You've got to believe that a man like Richet has seen something after three months' experiment in his own house."

Miller faced them all stubbornly: "And yet even Richet may have been deceived."

"Are *you* the only one competent to study these facts?" asked Brierly, hotly. "The egotism of you professional physicists is a kind of insanity. The moment a man like Richet or Lombroso admits a knowledge of one of these occult facts, you who have no experience in the same phenomena jump on him like so many wolves. Such bigotry is unworthy a scientist."

"Would you have us accept the word of any one man when that word contradicts the experience of all mankind?" asked Miller.

"Listen to what Richet says in confession of *his* perplexity," I called out, soothingly. "He writes: 'It took me twenty years to arrive at my present conviction—nay! to make one last confession. *I am not yet absolutely and irremediably convinced.* In spite of the astounding phenomena which I have witnessed during my sixty experiments with Eusapia, I have still a trace of doubt. Pg 187 *Certainty does not follow on demonstration; it follows on habit.*' So don't blame Miller or myself for inability to believe in these theories, for our minds are the kind that accept the mystical with sore struggle."

"Go on with Eusapia's career," said Harris. "I am interested in her. I want the story of the investigations."

"Her story broadens," I resumed. "Her fame spread throughout Europe, and squad after squad of militant scientists grappled with her, each one perfectly sure that he was the one to unmask her to the world. She was called before kings and emperors, and everywhere she triumphed— save in Cambridge, where she made a partial failure; but she redeemed herself later with both Lodge and Myers, so that it remains true to say that she has gone surely from one success to another and greater triumph."

"But there have been other such careers—Slade's and Home's, for instance—which ended in disaster."

"True, but nothing like her courage has ever been known. The crowning wonder of her career came when she consented to enter the special laboratories of the universities of Genoa and Naples. It is in the writings of Morselli, Professor of Psychology at Genoa, and in the reports of Bottazzi, head of the Department of Physics at Naples, that scepticism, such as my own, is met and conquered. I defy Pg 188 Miller or any man of open mind to read the detailed story of these marvellous experiments and deny the existence of the basic phenomena produced by Eusapia Paladino."

"You speak with warmth," said Harris.

"I do. I am at this moment fresh from a reading of the reports of Bottazzi's up-to-date experiments, and I am compelled to grant that he has not only sustained Crookes at every point, but has gone beyond him in his ingenuity of test and thoroughness of control. He adds the touch of certainty that we all needed to complete our own experience. He has given me courage to say what I believe Mrs. Smiley did for us."

"Won't you tell us all about it?" pleaded Mrs. Cameron. "Please do."

"It is too long and complicated. You must read it for yourself. It is too incredible to be told."

"Never mind, Garland; we'll take it as part of your fiction. Go ahead."

As I looked about me, I could detect in the faces of some of my friends an expression of apprehension. The coffee had grown cold. Our ice-cream had melted with neglect. Every eye was fixed upon me. It was plain that Harris and Miller considered me "on the high-road to spiritualism." Quite willing to gratify their wish to be startled, I proceeded:

"You will find the latest word on all these matters in a small but valuable review, published Pg 189 simultaneously in London and in Paris, called *The Annals of Psychic Science*. It is edited by César de Vesme in France, and by Laura I. Finch in England, and is a mine of reliable psychic science. Its directors are Dr. Dariex and Professor Charles Richet. Its 'committee' is made up of Sir William Crookes, Camille Flammarion, Professor Lombroso, Marcel Mangin, Dr. Joseph Maxwell, Professor Enrico Morselli, of Genoa; Dr. Julien Ochorowicz, head of the General Psychologic Institute of Paris; Professor Porro, the astronomer; Colonel Albert de Rochas, author of *The Externalization of Motivity*, and others of like character."

"We don't want the review, we want your account," said Harris. "Don't spare us. Give us detail—lots of it."

"Thank you; you shall have it hot-shot, but I'll have to generalize the story for you. The most decisive of all the tests have been made during the last eighteen months, and the final and most convincing of all within the year, under the direction of Lombroso, Morselli, and Bottazzi. It is safe to say that with these experiments and the reports which accompany them a new era has dawned in biology. The facts of mediumship are in process of being scientifically observed by a score of the best-qualified men in Europe, and at last we are about to study mediumship apart from any question of religious tenets."

Pg 190

Fowler took issue with me here: "It is absurd to say that no one but these physicists has ever properly studied spiritualistic phenomena; spiritists themselves have put the screws on quite as effectively as ever Crookes or Richet has done. Some of the best investigators ever known have been spiritists."

"Even if that were true, their testimony would lack the convincing power that flames from Morselli's book or Bottazzi's report. The essential weakness of the spiritist's testimony lies in the fact that for the most part he assumes that the facts of mediumship are somehow, and necessarily, in opposition to somebody's religion. He finds it sustained or opposed by the Bible, or he fancies it mixed with deviltry or the black art. He trembles for fear it will affect the scheme of redemption or assist some theosophical system. Whereas, a man like Bottazzi is engaged merely with the facts; he lets the inferences fall where they may. He is not concerned with whether Eusapia's manifestations oppose Christian theology or not; he wants the phenomena. He is alert to note their effect on biologic science, but he does not shrink from any report of them. So far as I am concerned, my lot is cast with these men who put the clamps on the fact and wait for larger knowledge before constructing a system of religion on the half-discovered."

Pg 191

"I'm with you there," said Miller. "And if our university officials took the same view, we Americans would hold higher rank in the world's thought."

"Bottazzi himself says, with reference to his experiments: 'In spite of all the hundreds of those who have observed Eusapia, it still remained true to say that hitherto she had been free to throw things about as she pleased.' But all this took a sharp turn when she came into Bottazzi's laboratory."

"Just who is Bottazzi?" Harris asked.

"He's the head of the Physiological Institute of the University of Naples; of his age and general character I am not precisely informed, but he writes delightfully of his experiments. Morselli, who preceded him in his study of Eusapia, is the Professor of Psychology in the University of Genoa. Foà and Herlitzka are of the same university. Within the last two years Eusapia has also been rigorously studied in Lombroso's clinical laboratory at Turin. All honor to her for breaking away from the traditions of mediumship!"

Mrs. Quigg caught me up on this: "What do you mean by 'traditions of mediumship'?"

"I mean that for the most part investigators have nearly always been kept at arm's-length by the fiction that the 'guide' should control everything, that the séance is a religious rite, that the medium must not be touched nor exposed to the light, and so on, till _{Pg 192} the scientist was reduced to the feeble rank of an on-looker in the dark, so that no real test was possible. These Italians did not grant any of these traditions. They were scientists, not devotees at a new shrine."

"However, I am ready to grant that some of the good old rules were justified. As you have seen in my own experiments, I have proceeded cautiously, for if you suppose mediumship to be a psycho-dynamic adjustment of the organisms in the circle—a subtle physical relationship—there is all the more reason to be careful. I did not find it necessary to mistreat Mrs. Smiley in order to test her powers. But *Eusapia has set a new pace for mediums*. She has gone into the lion's den alone and unarmed—not once, but a hundred times. She entered Lombroso's study, a room previously unexplored by her, and there placed herself before a cabinet that she was not permitted to examine—a cabinet filled with machines for dividing the true from the false. In Morselli's presence she submitted to tests the like of which not even Crookes was permitted to apply, and all sacred rules and regulations, all ideas of religion or questions of morality, vanished when she entered the cold, clear air of Bottazzi's physiological laboratory."

"This begins to sound like the grapple of a cuttlefish and a mermaid. Was the woman crushed?"

"No; she more than sustained her great _{Pg 193} reputation. She conquered the remorseless scientist and performed the impossible."

I had the strained attention of my audience now. Time was forgotten, and cries of "Tell us!" "Tell us all!" arose.

"It is an exciting story, an incredible story—"

"So much the better!" exclaimed Miss Brush.

"I am full of enthusiasm for Bottazzi," I resumed. "His was the kind of investigation I should like to put through myself. It appeals to me as no spiritualistic performance has ever done. In a sense the facts he has demonstrated make all material tests inoperative. Matter is all we have to cling to when it comes to physical tests. A nail driven down through the sleeve of the medium's dress *seems* to increase our control of her, and a metronome or a Morse telegraphic sounder does add value to our testimony, and yet Zöllner seems nearer right than Miller: matter seems only a condition of force, and subject to change at the will of the psychic.

"Up to the beginning of last year Bottazzi confesses that he had read little or nothing on the subject, and, like our friend Miller here, considered it beneath the dignity of a scientist to be present at spiritualist circles. It is highly instructive to note that Paladino, the most renowned medium of her time, was in Naples at his very door; but that doesn't matter—a scientist is blind to what he does not wish to see. In this case Bottazzi's eyes were opened by Pg 194 a young friend, Professor Charles Foà, of Turin, who sent him an account of what he and Dr. Herlitzka had witnessed in Eusapia's presence."

"They really seem to be taking the phenomena seriously over there," said Harris.

"These particular sittings at Turin made a great sensation in Italy. They were under the direction of Drs. Herlitzka, Foà, and Aggazzotti, assistants to Professor Mosso, of the University of Turin. Dr. Pio Foà, Professor of Pathologic Anatomy, was also present during one séance. The conditions were all of the experimenters' own contriving. They were young men and had been companion workers in science for many years, and were accustomed to laboratory work. They all came to this experiment perfectly sure that no mediumistic phenomena could endure the light of science. At the end of their three sittings they manfully said: '*Now that we are persuaded of the authenticity of the phenomena*, we feel it our duty to state the fact publicly in our turn, and to proclaim that the few pioneers in this branch of biology destined to become one of the most important generally saw and observed correctly.... We hope that our words may serve to stimulate some of these colleagues to study personally and attentively this group of interesting and obscure phenomena.' You will note they relate their tests, not to theology, but to unexplored biology."

Pg 195

"I like the ring of that declaration of theirs," said Harris. "Go on! Come to Hecuba!"

"Bottazzi was enormously impressed by this account, which detailed coldly, critically, the most amazing experiments. With ingenuity that would have seemed satanic to Paladino had she known of it , Foà and Aggazzotti had laid their pipes and provided for every trick. They were confident that nothing genuine could occur, but, as a matter of record, weird performances began at once. Bells were rung, tables shifted, columns of mercury lifted, mandolins played, and small objects were transported quite in the same fashion as the books were handled during our own sittings at your house, Miller—in fact, the doings were much the same in character. A small stand was broken to pieces under the very eyes of the learned doctors, *and hands hit and teeth bit those whom the medium did not like*. Each of the machines for registering movement, though utterly out of reach of Paladino, was operated, and some of these movements were systematically recorded.

"It was this care, these scrupulous and cold-blooded tests, that so profoundly affected Bottazzi. These men were his friends. He knew their level-headed and remorseless accuracy. The fact that they considered the whole investigation biologic in character, and that the results of their experiments strengthened their theory of the physiological Pg 196 determinism of the phenomena, added to his eagerness to try for himself."

"Wait a moment," said Cameron. "What do you mean by 'physiological determinism'?"

"He means that the phenomena began and ended in the psychic's organism."

"Do you intend to convey that they considered the medium dishonest?"

"Oh no. Merely that they did not relate the phenomena to the intervention of the spirits of the dead."

"Oh!" gasped Mrs. Cameron.

"Merely!" exclaimed Harris. "'Merely' is good in that case."

"'After reading these articles with avidity,' Bottazzi's report begins: 'Professor Galeotti, my associate, and I looked at each other astounded, and the same thoughts in the same words came simultaneously to our lips: "We, too, must see, must touch with our hands—and at once—here in this laboratory where experiments of the phenomena of life are daily carried on, with the impartiality of men whose object is the discovery of scientific truth, here in this quiet place where sealed doors will be superfluous. Everything must be registered. Will the medium be able to impress a photographic plate? Will she be able to illuminate a screen treated with platino-cyanide of barium? Will she be able to discharge a gold-leaf electroscope without touching Pg 197 it?" And so we travelled on the wings of imagination, always having before us the plummet of the strictest scientific methods.'"

"Now you're getting into my horizon," said Miller. "That is the way I wished to proceed in Mrs. Smiley's case. Did Bottazzi get these things done?"

"You're as impatient as Miss Brush," I replied, highly amused at his eagerness. "First you must catch your medium. Bottazzi succeeded at last in getting Paladino's consent, but only through the good offices of Professor Richet, whom she deeply loves and reverences. Submissively she entered into this most crucial series of tests. She was no longer afraid of any scientist, but it was not precisely a joy to her. Bottazzi invited his friend Galeotti, Professor of General Pathology in the University of Naples; Dr. de Amicis, Professor of Dermatology; Dr. Oscar Scarpa, Professor of Electro-chemistry at the Polytechnic High School of Naples; Luigi Lombardi, Professor of Electro-technology at the same school; and Dr. Pansini, Professor Extraordinary of Medical Semiotics; and these gentlemen certainly made up a formidable platoon of investigation. The room in which the experiments took place was an isolated one, connected with the laboratory of experimental physiology, and belonged to that part of the university set aside for Bottazzi's exclusive use. Nothing could have been Pg 198 further from the ordinary stuffy back parlor of the 'materializing medium.' No women were present, and no outsider; as you see, conditions were as nearly perfect as the ingenuity of Bottazzi and his assistants could make them."

The members present nestled into their chairs with looks of satisfaction, and Mrs. Cameron said: "Don't leave anything out. Tell it all."

"It is hardly necessary to say that every precaution was taken. Photographs of the cabinet were made before the sittings and afterward, in order that all displacements might be recorded. Provision was made for registering the action of 'John King's' spectral hands. Some of these devices were concealed in an adjoining room and watched by other attendants. One little touch early in Bottazzi's account impressed me deeply. A little electric motor was used to furnish power for the lamps and other apparatus, and Bottazzi, in speaking of it, says: 'At the moment when the phenomena to be registered began to manifest, the circuit was closed, *and suddenly in the complete silence of the night the feeble murmur of the motor was heard.*' I thrill to the action of that faithful little material watch-dog. Ghosts and hobgoblins could not silence or affright it. After all, matter is both persistent and bold."

"But not sovereign," defiantly called out Brierly; "the psychic dominates it."

"We shall see. Bottazzi declares in italics that Paladino neither put her hand into the cabinet nor knew the contents of it. 'Rarely has she been surrounded by such an assembly of unprejudiced minds, by such strict and attentive intellects,' he declares. And when you consider the absence of women, the mystery of the machinery, together with the stern character of the sitters, the medium's courage becomes marvellous. Perfect honesty alone can sustain a medium in such an ordeal. I am ready to agree that a new era began for spiritism when Eusapia entered that room, April 17, 1907."

"Poor Paladino!" sighed Mrs. Cameron. "I tremble for her."

"Bottazzi grimly says: 'We began by restraining her inexhaustible mediumistic activity. We obliged her to do things she had never done before. We limited the field of her manifestations.... I was convinced that it was much easier for her to drag out of the cabinet a heavy table than to press an electric knob or displace the rod of a metronome.' And this theory he set himself to prove. It was beautiful to see the way he went about it."

Howard was also impressed. "I see Eusapia's finish. She won't do a thing. The influences will criss-cross. Bottazzi's cabinet is her Waterloo."

"Observe that Bottazzi was not perverse. He met the psychic half-way by forming the usual chain about the table, placing Eusapia before the curtains Pg 200 of the little cabinet, which was a recess in the wall. Bottazzi himself and his assistants had constructed this cabinet and placed everything in position before Eusapia entered the room at all, and throughout the sitting she was controlled by at least two of the investigators so that she could not so much as put a hand inside the curtains. She was very uneasy, as though finding the conditions hard. Nevertheless, *even at this first sitting, everything movable in the cabinet was thrown about.* The table was violently shaken and the metronome set going. Bottazzi ends his first report by saying: 'The séance yielded very small results, but this is always the case at first séances. Nevertheless, how many "*knowing* people and *savans*" have formed a judgment on phenomena after séances such as this one?'"

"That's a slant at you, Miller," remarked Harris.

"Yes," I agreed, "it's a slant at all commissions and committees who think they can jump in and settle this spiritistic controversy in the course of half an hour. Bottazzi, like Lombroso and Richet, was aware that he had entered upon a long road. He knew that a tired or worried medium was helpless. He called the same circle together for the 20th, willing to try patiently for developments. All came but Lombardi, whose place was taken by M. Jona, an engineer. The second sitting was a wonder. Warned by his first experience, Bottazzi nailed or screwed every movable thing fast to the Pg 201 walls of the cabinet. He was resolute to force 'John,' the supposed 'guide,' to touch the electric button and press the ball of India-rubber that connected with a mercury manometer. He intended to teach the spirit hand to register its actions on a revolving cylinder of smoked tin. He wanted graven records, so that no wiseacre like Harris, here, could say: 'Oh, the thing never moved. You were all hypnotized!' In effect, he said: 'They tell us that a cold wind blows from the cabinet. I will put a self-registering thermometer in the cabinet and see. They say tables weighing forty pounds have been lifted. All I ask is that the bulb of a self-registering manometer be pressed. They say a Morse telegraphic key has been sounded by spirit hands. Very well; I will arrange a connection so that every pressure of the key will be registered on a sheet of smoked paper, so that the fact of the sound of the key shall be recorded by an infallible instrument.'"

"Did he get the records?" asked Harris.

"Wait and see!" commanded Cameron.

"These indicate the methods which Bottazzi and his assistants brought to bear on the medium. No more worship here, no awe, no hesitation, no superstition. Among other things, he put into the cabinet a small table weighing about fifteen pounds, and on top of it arranged a hairbrush, a hen's feather, a bottle full of water, and a very thick glass. Pg 202 These articles and the table were the only objects that could be moved. His aim was to limit the spirit hands to a few movables—to see whether they could not be taught to do what was required of them. Well, *that little table came out of the cabinet of its own accord in a light that made it perfectly visible*, at the precise time when three of the inexorable professors were rigidly clasping the psychic. But that is not the most remarkable thing. The psychic's feet were held by the engineer, and he observed that at *the exact moment when Paladino pushed against his knee the table moved*. 'Each advance of the table corresponded,' says Bottazzi, 'with the most perfect synchronism, to the push of Eusapia's legs against Jona's knees'; in other words, she really executed movements identical with those that she would have made had she been pushing the table out of the cabinet with her *visible* limbs."

As I paused for effect, Fowler said: "You say that as if you considered it very significant."

"I do. In my judgment, it is the most valuable fact developed by these most searching experiments. Flammarion noted this same significant relation between the movements of the psychic and the spirit hands, and so did Maxwell. Maxwell proved it by experiments on his own person, and now Bottazzi is proving it in a larger way. 'A few moments later,' he says, 'a glass was flung from the cabinet by these invisible agencies, and this fling coincided exactly Pg 203 with a kick which Paladino gave to Jona, as if the same will governed both movements.'"

Miller was thinking very hard. "That certainly is very strange," he said, "but I observed nothing of it in Mrs. Smiley's case; on the contrary, it seemed to me that our strongest manifestations came when she was perfectly still."

"Hasten!" urged Fowler. "Come to the phantoms. I perceive his theory, but it will all be upset later by the materialized forms."

"On the contrary, Bottazzi declares the phantoms also conformed to this same law. He was determined upon educating 'John King,' and kept insisting that the invisible hands press the rubber ball, or lower the registry balance, or set the metronome going, and Eusapia repeatedly moaned: '*I can't find,*' '*I can't see,*' or '*I don't know how.*' Once she complained that the objects were *too far off—that she could not reach them!*—all of which sustained Bottazzi in his belief that these activities were absolutely under her psychic control, just as the synchronism of movements convinced him that she was 'the physiologic factor in the case.' All of this is very exciting to me, for I have had the same feeling with regard to the several mediums whose activities I have closely studied. Bottazzi says, with regard to the results of the first two sittings: 'These first séances show that Eusapia needed to learn how to make these movements with which her invisible hands Pg 204 were unfamiliar, just as she would have had to learn to make them with her visible hands. You will all observe that he did not permit awe or superstitious reverence for the medium or her phantoms to balk his experiments.' A convinced spiritist who attended one of the séances was scandalized by the tone and character of the tests. These professors were continually bobbing up to see what was going on, disturbing conditions, stirring things up as with a spoon to see how it was all going on. They broke the chain of hands whenever they wanted to see what 'the spirits' were doing. In other words, these scientists were students, not devotees. They were experimenting, not communing with the dead."

"Others have tried that," said Fowler. "But they succeeded in preventing any manifestations whatsoever."

"It didn't work out so in this instance. Bottazzi says that during the first séance Professor Scarpa irritated Eusapia greatly by his impertinent curiosity, but Bottazzi himself quieted her by saying: 'You see, dear Eusapia, we are not here only to admire the marvellous phenomena you are able to produce, but also, and chiefly, to observe and verify and criticise. We do not doubt you or suspect any fraud, but we want to see clearly, and to follow the development of the phenomena. That is why M. Scarpa surveys the cabinet between the Pg 205 curtains, illuminating it occasionally with an electric pocket-lamp. Which do you prefer, passive admiration, of which you must have had more than enough already, or the calm affirmation of physicists who are accustomed to extort from Nature secrets which she hides from physical eyes? 'In this way,' adds the master, 'Eusapia's irritation was softened; she rebelled no further, but yielded with docility to the sharp, attentive scrutiny of the observer, who finally declared himself beaten, not having been able to discover at any point a shadow of fraud.'"

"Hurrah for Eusapia!" shouted Howard. "She must be a wonder!"

"A spiritist would say that her guides were insisting on the most rigid test. The account goes on to say that the psychic, when entranced, was not satisfied with the grasp of two of the spies; she frequently asked, in a faint voice, for a third or even a fourth hand in order that there could be no question of her freedom from connection with the phenomena. As in the case of our own psychic, Mrs. Smiley co-operated to the utmost with us. She never refused to permit any test."

Miller here remarked: "I can't but think that our control of Mrs. Smiley was complete, and yet I could not under the conditions assert that she was not the author of the acts we witnessed in my library. I cannot bring myself to entertain, even Pg 206 for an instant, the spirit hypothesis, but in Bottazzi's theory I glimpse an alternative."

"Yes, Bottazzi plainly hints at his conclusions by saying: '*The invisible limbs* of the psychic explored the cabinet.' He repeats, 'I am convinced that these *"mediumistic limbs" are capable of being taught unfamiliar duties*, like pressing an electric button of squeezing a rubber ball,' and this he proceeded patiently to exemplify. At the third sitting Madame Bottazzi was present Lombardi and Jona being absent , and the 'force' was much greater and more active than before, probably because of the psychic's growing confidence. A small table floated in the air '*while we watched it in amazement*,' he says. One levitation lasted long enough to count fifty. 'We all had time to observe that the piece of furniture was quite isolated,' he adds. Furthermore, a big black hand came from the curtain and touched Madame Bottazzi on the cheek, and frightened her from her place beside the medium."

"I can understand that," said Mrs. Cameron. "Think of being touched by even one's own dead!"

"Professor de Amicis was not only touched on the arm but forcibly pulled, as if by an invisible hand. The curtain of the cabinet then enveloped him as if to embrace him, and he felt the contact of another face against his, and a mouth kissing him—"

Pg 207

The women cried out at the thought, but I hurried on to make Bottazzi's point: "*'At the same time Eusapia's lips moved as if to kiss, and she made the sound of kissing, which we all distinctly heard.'* Here again, you see, is that astounding synchronism which Maxwell and Morselli observed between the movement of objects and the contraction of the muscles in the medium's arms and legs. Bottazzi pauses to generalize: 'Whatever may be the mediumistic phenomena produced, there is almost always at the same time movement of one or several parts of the medium's body.'"

"What does he mean? Does he mean that Eusapia performed all these movements with her 'astral hands'?" asked Mrs. Quigg.

"That is precisely his inference. 'Mysterious hands,' Bottazzi calls them."

"But how will he account for the difference in size between Eusapia's hands and the *large black hand* that she saw and felt?" asked Fowler.

"Bottazzi himself remarks upon this discrepancy. 'To whom does this hand belong?' he asked—'this hand, a half a yard away from the medium's head, seen while her visible hands are rigorously controlled by her two neighbors? Is it the hand of a monstrous long arm which liberates itself from the medium's body, then dissolves, to afterward "materialize" afresh? Is it something analogous to the pteropod of an amœba, which projects itself from Pg 208 the body, then retreats into it only to reappear in another place? Mystery!' But this is not the most grewsome sight; one of the professors, stealing a glance behind the medium, saw remnants of legs and arms lying about the cabinet."

"Horrible!" exclaimed Mrs. Cameron. "I'd rather believe in spirits. What does he mean to infer?"

"Apparently he would have us believe that materialization is a process due to the medium— or at least dependent on her will—and that these partially completed forms represent fragmentary impulses. But I'm not so much concerned just now with that as with the course of schooling through which he drove Eusapia. He stuck to his plan. He put into his cabinet each time certain sounders, markers, and lamps, which could be moved, ticked, or lighted only by hands in the cabinet, and he kept the same rigid control of his medium *outside* the cabinet. For the most part she was in the light. By means of a series of lamps the séance-room could be lighted dimly or brightly at a touch, and, while many of the phenomena in the cabinet were being performed by 'John,' Eusapia's hands could be plainly seen in the grasp of her inquisitors. After seeing a mandolin move and play of itself, after having the metronome set in motion, stopped, and set going again, after having the registrations he most desired, Bottazzi concludes his third sitting by Pg 209 saying: 'An invisible hand or foot *must* therefore have forced down the disk,*must* have leaned on the membrane of the receiving-drum of my apparatus, because I assured myself next day that to obtain the highest lines registered the disk had to be pressed to the extreme point. This was no ordinary case of pushing or pulling. The mysterious hand had to push the disk, and push it in a certain way. *In short, the "spirit hand" was becoming educated to its task.*'"

Miller asked: "Did these performances take place, as in the case of Mrs. Smiley, within the reach of her ordinary limbs?"

"Yes, many of them took place within a yard of her head; but some of them, and the most marvellous of them, not merely took place out of her reach, but under conditions of unexampled rigor. 'Eusapia's mediumistic limbs penetrated into the cabinet,' says Bottazzi. 'I begged my friends not to distract the medium's attention by requests for touches, apparitions, etc., but to concentrate their desires and their wills on the things I asked for....' What he wanted her to do was very simple, but conclusive. He wished 'the spirit hand' to press an electric button and light a red lamp within the cabinet. The coil and the switch had been dragged out of the cabinet and thrown on the table. Bottazzi begged them all not to touch it. No one but Scarpa, Galeotti, and Bottazzi knew what it was for. 'At Pg 210 a certain moment Eusapia took hold of the first finger of my right hand and squeezed it with her fingers. A ray of light from the interior of the cabinet lit up the room'—she had pressed the contact-breaker with her invisible fingers at the precise time when she had squeezed with her visible hand the forefinger of Bottazzi. She repeatedly did this. 'If one of us, be it observed, had lit the lamp, she would have screamed with pain and indignation.'"

"Was this the climax of his series? Is this *all* he is willing to affirm?" queried Harris, with ironic inflection.

"Oh no, indeed. The greatest is yet to come. At the fourth sitting a new person, Professor Cardarelli, was introduced, and this new sitter disturbed conditions. Nevertheless, the inexplicable took place. Small twirling violet flames were seen to drift across the cabinet curtains, and hands and closed fists appeared over Paladino's head. These have been photographed, by-the-way. Some of them were of ordinary size, and others at least three times larger than the psychic's hand and fist. These flames interest me very much, for I have seen them on several occasions, but could not believe in them, even though Crookes spoke of handling them. I must admit their objective reality now. It is absurd to suppose they were fraudulently produced in this laboratory.

"A stethoscope was taken from Cardarelli's Pg 211 pocket and put together—a movement requiring the action of two hands. The noise of fingers running over the keys of a typewriter in the cabinet was plainly heard, although no writing came. At the fifth sitting the mandolin again moved as if alive no one touching it , in a light that made all its movements observable; and as it did so *Eusapia's hand* tightly controlled by Bottazzi *made little movements as if to help the instrument to move.Each movement, though it ended in the air, seemed to affect the mandolin.* Bottazzi says: 'It would be necessary to have Paladino's fingers in the palm of one's hand, as I had that evening, in order to be convinced that the evolutions, twangings of the strings, etc., all synchronized with the very delicate movements of her fingers.... I cannot describe the sensation one experiences when seeing an inanimate object moved, not for a moment merely, but for many minutes in succession, by a mysterious force.'"

"We observed no such synchronism," repeated Fowler. "We not only controlled Mrs. Smiley's hands, but nailed her to her chair. In a way, our test was more rigid than those you are describing. Our results were not so dramatic, but they were produced under test conditions, and their significance is as great as that of Bottazzi's lamp-lighting."

"But we did not have as much light on the medium, and, by-the-way, Miller, the spectral hands Pg 212 that I saw in your study, each larger than Mrs. Smiley's hands, were as real to me as those Scarpa studied, and the books deposited on your table form as good a record, in their way, as the marks on his smoked-glass cylinder."

"Furthermore, we had writing," added Fowler. "All of which Bottazzi would explain by his theory of an 'astral arm.'"

"Yes, but he secured something still more marvellous. He obtained the print of human hands in clay and also on smoked glass. He demonstrated that the invisible limbs of the psychic cannot only move objects at a distance, *but that they can feel at a distance.* 'Eusapia's attitude was that of a blindfolded person exploring space with her hands to find a lost object!' he exclaims, at one point. 'Eusapia opened my right hand, stretched out my three middle fingers, and, bending them on the table, tips downward, said, in a whisper: "How hard it is! What is it?" I did not understand,' says Bottazzi. 'She continued: "There, on the chair." "It is the clay," I said, quickly; "will you make the impression of a face?" "No," she replied, "it is too hard; take it away."' Some one broke the chain to carry out her desire. He looked at the desk and saw the imprint of three fingers."

"What I would like to know at this point," Harris quickly interposed, "is this: were the fingermarks lined like Bottazzi's or like the medium's?"

Pg 213

"He does not say in this case, but, as I recall it, they found in other instances that the lines on the impressions made by Eusapia's invisible fingers were precisely like those of her material fingers, and yet no mark of flour or lamp-black remained attaching to her hands. In one case a perfumed clay was used, and, although the impressions secured 'resembled Eusapia's face grown old,' no scent of the wax could be detected on her cheeks. Bottazzi gives much space to these 'mediumistic explorations of the cabinet.' He could follow these blind, mysterious gropings of the invisible Eusapia by closely controlling the real Eusapia. 'Presently she asked: "What is that round object? I feel something round."' This was, in fact, the rubber ball which connected with a tube—the tube, in its turn, passing through the wall into another room where it operated a manometer. She pressed this ball with her invisible limbs, and the column rose and registered the pressure. This was entirely satisfactory to Bottazzi, who then says: 'I desire again to affirm that with her invisible limbs Eusapia feels the forms of objects and their consistency, feels heat and cold, hardness and softness, dampness and dryness neither more nor less than if she were touching and feeling with the hands imprisoned in ours. She feels with other hands, but perceives with the same brain with which she uses to talk with us.'

Pg 214

"The most astonishing physical phenomena came when the contact-breaker was thrown on the table, and Eusapia called out: 'See how it moves!' *We all directed our gaze toward the small object,*' says Bottazzi, '*and we saw that it oscillated and vibrated at an elevation of an inch or two above the surface of the table, as if seized with internal shivering—Eusapia's hands, held by M. Galeotti and myself, being more than a foot from the contact-breaker.*'"

My auditors were now in the thrall of Bottazzi's story, and the silence was eloquent. At last Cameron said: "It certainly seems like a clear case of 'astral.' I begin to believe in our first sitting with Mrs. Smiley. What do you want us to do—announce ourselves converted?"

"Certainly not," I replied. "We must not relax our vigilance, even though Bottazzi, Morselli, and their fellows seem to have proved the genuineness of the phenomena. At the same time, I admit it is a source of satisfaction to me to know that these Italian scientists, with conditions all their own, are willing to affirm that Eusapia '*feels with her invisible limbs,*' and explores a cabinet while sitting under rigid control more than a yard away from the objects moved. My experiences point to this. How else could the cone be handled with such precision as was shown at your house, Miller? Lombroso observed that chairs and vases Pg 215 moved as if guided by hands and eyes, and that the psychic could see as well behind her as in front. Mrs. Smiley has always been able to direct me *exactly* to the point where the cone or pencil had been flung. How can letters within closed slates be formed so beautifully and so precisely without some form of seeing?"

Fowler was ready with an answer: "At the final analysis all perception is due to some form of vibration. To be clairaudient is simply to be able to lay hold upon a different set of pulsations in the ether, and to be clairvoyant is to perceive directly without the aid of the eye, which is only a little camera, after all."

"All this is merely a kind of prelude," I resumed, "for Bottazzi apparently proved that the invisible hand of Eusapia's invisible arm could not penetrate a cage of wire mesh that covered the telegraphic key in the cabinet. 'How, then, can we consider it to be a spirit hand—an immaterial hand—when a wire-netting can stop it?' he very pertinently inquires."

"That's what troubles me," said Miller. "If a phantom hand can bring a real book and thumb its leaves, or drum with a real pencil or write, why isn't it, for all practicable purposes, a real hand?"

"What *is* a real hand?" retorted Fowler. "Isn't the latest word of science to the effect that matter like the human body is only a temporary condition of force?"

Pg 216

"Precisely so; and every advance along the line of these experiments goes to prove the power of mind to transform matter. It almost seems to me at times as though these psychic minds were able to reduce matter to its primal atom and reshape it. In Bottazzi's seventh sitting, under the same rigorous restraint of Eusapia, a vase of flowers was transported, a rose was set in a lady's hair, a small drum was seized and beaten rhythmically, an enormous black fist came out from behind the curtain, and an open hand seized Bottazzi gently by the neck. Now listen to his own words: 'Letting go my hold of Professor Poso's hand,' he says, 'I felt for this ghostly hand and clasped it. *It was a left hand, neither hot nor cold, with rough, bony fingers which dissolved under pressure. It did not retire by producing a sensation of withdrawal—it dissolved, "dematerialized," melted.*'"

I paused to say: "Remember, this is not the tale of a perfervid spiritist. On the contrary, it is the scientific account of a laboratory experiment by a physiologist of high rank. The incident is not a part of a séance in the home of a medium in a dark parlor full of side-doors and trick windows. It is a registered phenomenon in the physiological department of a great university, occurring under scientific test conditions. I confess it gives verity to many a doubtful thing I have myself seen."

Pg 217

"It certainly staggers me," said Cameron. "How does the scientific gentleman explain it?"

"He goes on to say: 'Another time, later on, the same hand was placed on my right forearm—I saw a human hand, of natural color, and I felt with mine the back of a lukewarm hand, rough and nervous. *The hand dissolved I saw it with my own eyes and retreated as if into Madame Paladino's body, describing a curve.* If all the observed phenomena of these seven séances were to disappear from my memory, this one I could never forget.'"

Fowler was smiling with calm disdain. "Let him go on with his psycho-dynamic theories. He will be confounded yet. These are only the first stages of the game."

"But all this happened while the hands of the psychic were merely held," protested Miller. "He says he controlled her hands rigorously. Why didn't he handcuff her, or nail her down? The facts he claims to have established are too subversive to accept on his word alone."

This amused me. "There you go again! Not satisfied with wonders, you want miracles. Happily, you may be satisfied. In the eighth sitting, which took place in the same room of the physiological laboratory, with Bottazzi, Madame Bottazzi, Professor Galeotti, Doctors Jappelli and d'Errico present, Eusapia submitted to the most rigorous Pg 218 restraint of her life. Two iron rings were fastened to the floor, and by means of strong cords, which were sealed with lead seals like those used in fastening a railway car, her wrists were rigidly confined. She was, in fact, bound like a criminal; and yet the spectral hands and fists came and went, jugs of water floated about, and as a final stupendous climax, while Galeotti was controlling Eusapia's right arm, which was also manacled, he *saw* the duplications of her left arm. 'LOOK!' he exclaimed, 'I SEE TWO LEFT ARMS IDENTICAL IN APPEARANCE. ONE IS ON THE LITTLE TABLE. THE OTHER SEEMS TO COME OUT OF THE MEDIUM'S SHOULDER, TOUCH MADAME BOTTAZZI, AND THEN RETURN TO EUSAPIA'S BODY AGAIN. THIS IS NOT AN HALLUCINATION. I AM CONSCIOUS OF TWO SIMULTANEOUS VISUAL SENSATIONS WHEN MADAME BOTTAZZI SAYS SHE HAS BEEN TOUCHED.'"

For a moment the entire company sat in silence, as though stunned by the force of my blow. Then all turned to Miller as though to ask: "What do you think of that?"

He slowly replied: "To grant the possible putting forth of a supernumerary arm and hand would make physiological science foolish. It is easier to imagine these gentlemen suffering a collective hallucination."

"Ah! Bottazzi provided against all that. He called in the aid of self-registering contrivances. Pg 219 It won't do, Miller—he proved the objective reality of 'spirit phenomena.' He lifted the whole performance to the plane of the test-tube, the electric light, and the barometer. His experiments, his deductions, came as a splendid sequence to an almost equally searching series by Crookes, Zöllner, Wallace, Thury, Flammarion, Maxwell, Lombroso, Richet, Foà, and Morselli. His laboratory was the crucible wherein came the final touch of heat which fuses all the discordant facts into a solid ingot of truth."

"But, to me, he is misreading the facts," objected Fowler. "I maintain that he is as prejudiced in his way as the spiritist. He says: 'The mediumistic limbs explored the cabinet.' A spiritist would say: '*John King* explored the cabinet.' The synchronism he speaks of might exist, and only be a proof of what the spiritist admits—that the presence and activity of the materializing spirit are closely circumscribed by the medium."

"Bottazzi proved the relationship to be something more intimate than that. He demonstrated that the movement of the hands in the cabinet and of those outside had a common origin— namely, the will and brain of Eusapia. He proved that these invisible hands were, after all, material, and limited in their powers. He proved that the 'spirits' shared all Eusapia's likes and dislikes, and knew no more of chloride of iron or ferro-cyanide Pg 220 of potassium than she herself possessed—in short, while admitting the mystery of the process, he reduces all these phenomena to human, terrestrial level, and relates them wholly and simply to the brain and will of the psychic. Perhaps his state of mind is best expressed at the close of his statement concerning the registration of the movements of 'the spirit hand.' He says, in effect: 'These tracings demonstrate irrefutably that the keys were repeatedly pressed with perfect synchronism, the outside key with Eusapia's left hand, the one inside the cabinet by another, which a convinced spiritist would call that of a "materialized spirit," and which I believe to be neither the one nor the other, although I am not able to explain what it was.'"

"Oh, lame and impotent conclusion!" exclaimed Brierly. "After that superb test, why didn't he frankly say the discarnate had been proved?"

"Because his proof, his knowledge, was not yet sufficient. Besides, it requires heroic courage to admit our ignorance. 'I don't know,' he says, and that is the attitude of Morselli. Dr. Foà believes the phenomena to come within the domain of natural law, and to result from a transmutation of energy accumulated in the medium. He calls this 'vital energy' or 'psychic energy,' and adds: 'If these phenomena appear strange by virtue of their comparative rarity, they are not really more Pg 221 marvellous than the biological phenomena which we witness every day.'"

"According to this theory, then," said Miller, "Mrs. Smiley has remained, as you believe, motionless in her chair, but has been able to 'energize' at a distance."

"More than that. She has been able to emit supernumerary etheric limbs, perhaps a complete material double of herself, which is able to move with lightning speed and perfect precision. It is this actual externalization of both matter and sense that makes darkness so essential to the medium. Vivid light forces this effluvia, this mysterious double, back into its originating body with disrupting haste. Witness the several times when Mrs. Smiley was convulsed merely by being touched at the wrong moment."

"There is a different interpretation to be put upon the psychic's hatred of light," remarked Howard.

"By-the-way, yet bearing on this very subject, I read in the *Annals of Psychic Science* the account of a singular experiment in the matter of independent writing. A certain Dr. Encausse, in giving a lecture before the Society for Psychical Research at Nancy, said that in 1889, having heard that a professional magnetizer named Robert was able to put a subject into such a state of hypnosis that he could project lines of writing on paper without use of pen or pencil, he was curious to see the Pg 222 performance. Together with a colleague, Dr. Gibier, Encausse hastened to witness this marvel. One of the subjects was a girl of seventeen. The magnetizer put her to sleep, 'and during this séance,' says Dr. Encausse, 'we were able to obtain in full light on a sheet of paper signed by twenty witnesses, the precipitation of a whole page of written verses signed "Corneille." I examined under the microscope the substance that formed the writing, and I was led to the conclusion that it consisted of globules of human blood, some scattered as if calcined, others quite distinct. I thus verified the theory of the occultists of 1850 that the nervous energy as well as the physical force of a medium, the material of which he is constituted, such as his blood, could exteriorize itself and reconstruct itself at a distance.'"

"What a stunning experiment!" exclaimed Cameron.

"Important, if true," sneered Harris.

"What do you know about this learned doctor?" asked Miller.

"Nothing; but you will see that these later experiments of the Italian scientists are sustaining De Rochas and Aksakof in their claim that the medium is in a sense dematerialized to build up the phantasms. Dr. Encausse goes on to say: '*Moreover, the medium who had produced this phenomenon was preparing for the stage and had been studying* Pg 223 *Corneille during the whole of the preceding day.* I was thus able to discover the origin of the substance of the materialization of the writing, and also its psychic origin.' In other words, he claims that the message was not from the shade of the great dramatist, but was a precipitation of the blood of the psychic and an exercise of her subconscious mind, all of which accords with Bottazzi's theory.

"Now, then," said I, in the tone of one about to conclude, "in the light of these experiments, my own sitting at Miller's, and especially those that I held at Fowler's house, take on the greatest significance. Miller, Mrs. Smiley's *visible limbs* did not handle the books—of that I am positive—and yet I am equally certain that she governed every movement."

"But what about the voices?" asked Fowler. "Does this theory cover the whispering personalities we heard? What about 'Wilbur' and 'Maudie'?"

"That's easy," retorted Howard. "Once you explain the manipulation of the cone, the rest is merely clever ventriloquism."

"There is nothing 'easy' about any of these phenomena," I answered. "As Richet says, they are absurd, but they are observed facts. It would not be fair to the spiritists to end the account of these sittings without frankly stating that there Pg 224 were many other phenomena very difficult to explain by Bottazzi's theory. There came a time, as he admits, when 'a mysterious entity behind the curtain, among us, almost in contact with us, was felt all the time.' This entity was supposed to be 'John King,' the psychic's control. This being, invisible for the most part, gave roses to those he liked, conversed freely, and in one case threw a bunch of flowers in the face of one of the sitters to whom Eusapia had taken a dislike. A little later 'John' presented a small drum from behind the curtain, and, when Galeotti tried to take it, 'John' pulled it out of his hands. Again he offered it, and Galeotti seized it, and the two fought for its possession with such violence that the drum was nearly torn to pieces."

"Where was Paladino meanwhile?" asked Miller.

"Seated quietly in the grasp of Bottazzi and Madame Bottazzi. Galeotti then raised the drum in his hand, high above his head and against the curtain, and requested 'John' to beat it. 'John' pushed a hand against the drum and beat a muffled tattoo. All this was utterly out of the psychic's reach. The strife over the drum would seem to argue a complete and powerful figure behind the curtain."

"In other words, a spirit," said Brierly.

"Not so fast," put in Miller. "I am content to plod with these Italian scientists. Let us establish Pg 225 one supernormal fact and then reach for another. You fellows with your 'reincarnations,' and the spiritist with his foolish messages from Cleopatra, Raphael, and Shakespeare, have confused the situation. We must begin all over again. If all that Garland is detailing is true—I have not read these reports he speaks of—then it is our duty to take up the scrutiny of these facts as a part of biologic science."

Fowler clapped his hands. "Bravo! that is all we ask of you. To study frogs and mosquitoes, to peer close into the constitution of the blood or the brain of man, is useful; but, to my mind, the questions raised by these Continental experimentalists are the most vital now clamoring for answer."

"Bottazzi says, with regard to his eighth and final sitting: 'The results of this séance were very favorable, because they eliminated the slightest trace of suspicion or uncertainty relative to the genuineness of the phenomena. We obtained the same kind of assurance as that which we have concerning physical, chemical, or physiological phenomena. Henceforth sceptics can only deny the facts by accusing us of fraud and charlatanism. I should be very much surprised if any one were bold enough to bring the charge against us, but it would not disturb our minds in the least. From this time forward the medium who wishes to prove the truth of her phenomena will be obliged to Pg 226 permit the same kind of experimentation which Eusapia so adequately sustained.'"

"Well, now," said Cameron, "the practical question is this: are we to go on with our investigation?"

"I am ready," said Miller, promptly. "Garland, will you purvey another psychic and conduct the pursuit?"

"Yes, provided you all come in with spirits attuned, ready to wait patiently and observe silently. The law of these materializations seems to be this: the forces of the psychic are proportional to the harmoniousness of the circle and in inverse proportion to the light. Accepting this law as proved by our illustrious fellow-experimenters abroad, are you ready to try again along the lines they have marked out?"

As with one voice, all agreed.

"Very well," said I; "I will see what I can do for you in the way of a new psychic and new phenomena. We will now experiment with design to prove the identity of the reappearing dead. Of this I am fully persuaded. Men will be discovering new laws of nature ten thousand years from now, just as they are to-day. It is inconceivable that the secrets of the universe should ever be entirely made plain. The world of mystery retires before the dawn. Nothing is really explained—what we call familiar facts are at bottom inexplicable mysteries, and must ever remain so."

Pg 227

"Then why go on? Why not stop now and save ourselves the trouble of investigation?"

"Because there is joy in the pursuit—because it is in the nature of man to pursue this quest. Who knows but the conclusions of Venzano and Morselli, of Bottazzi and Foà, have opened new vistas in human nature? These 'supernormal powers' may chance to be of immense value to the race, quite aside from their bearing upon the problem of death. Furthermore, these reports come at a time when a hard-and-fast literalism of interpretation is the fashion among scientists like Miller. Perhaps they and the art of the day will alike be offered new inspiration by these mystifying enlargements of human faculty. I for one feel profoundly indebted to these brave and clear-brained Italian scientists. I should like to see the physicists of our own universities busying themselves with this most absorbing and vital problem."

"But they don't," retorted Fowler. "They will not even read Bottazzi's reports."

And I fear he is justified in his belief.

As I am reading proof on this page a fat letter from a friend in Naples comes to my desk, filled with the several corroborative accounts of a special sitting with Paladino which Professor Bottazzi kindly arranged for them. My correspondent is a New York editor, and in his party of six was the associate professor of chemistry in a big Eastern college. After detailing the many marvellous phenomena which took place in his presence, Professor M—— says: "In view of the phenomena with which I am habitually concerned, I did Pg 228 not *want* to believe in Paladino's supernormal powers, but I had to accept what I saw." These reports bring Bottazzi's experiments closer to the dead. I hope they will bring them a little nearer to my readers. "Bottazzi has no slightest doubt of the phenomena," is the concluding line of my friend's letter.

VIII

Cameron's society never came together again in formal session, and I was not able to carry out my plan for developing a psychic along the line of proving the identity of the spirits manifesting. However, between the final sitting of the club and my next meeting with Fowler and Miller, I passed through a series of very interesting experiences more or less corroborative of the phenomena which the members had witnessed either individually or as a body. These additional experiments I proceeded at once to lay before my friends as we met at the club one quiet afternoon a couple of weeks later.

"We haven't heard of any new psychic," Miller began at once, as we settled into easy-chairs in a retired corner.

"No," I replied. "I've been unable to get the consent of any other psychic to undergo just the inquisition I know you'd like to give, but I've had some extremely suggestive sittings recently with a young professional man who does a little mediumistic 'work' on the side."

"A male psychic? That's amusing. I thought they were all female."

"No. There are men psychics," replied Fowler, "but they're scarce. One of the most wonderful I have ever known is a big, burly fellow of most aggressive manner. The reason why there are so few men in the business I take to be this: men are less subjective, less passive, than women, and the psychic's rôle seems to be a negative one. Men are aggressive and impatient, engaged in some kind of struggle with material things, or they are intolerant of the process of developing their psychic gifts. If Garland has found a male psychic, he is in luck."

"So I thought. The young fellow, whom we will call Peters, is only about twenty-four, a boyish professional man of refined habits. He comes of good family, and, being ambitious in his profession, is careful not to permit a knowledge of his psychical powers to reach the ears of his employers. I heard of him through a friend who is deeply interested in these matters, and who procured for me an invitation to be present at a sitting in the home of a certain Dr. Towne, on the East Side.

"We met at dinner, and during the meal Dr. Towne told us all he knew of Mr. Peters, which was little, and, turning to me, said: 'We expect you to take charge of the circle, Mr. Garland; it's all new to us.'

"'The first thing to do,' I answered, 'is to put Pg 231 the young fellow at his ease. It is a mighty good sign when a medium is willing to come into a strange house to perform for a circle as critical and as unfriendly as this.' 'Oh, not unfriendly,' said Dr. Towne. 'Well,' I said, 'I wouldn't call three practising physicians, who have never seen a psychic at close range, a friendly group.'"

"Were there three doctors present?" asked Fowler.

"Yes, and my friend was a notably keen-eyed man himself. I really had no faith that the young fellow could do anything remarkable for us, but I didn't say so.

"We were still at the table when our young psychic was announced, and, with a knowledge of how necessary it was that he should be in a comfortable frame of mind, I went out to the library to meet him and make his acquaintance. I wished to put him at his ease—so far as I was concerned, at least.

"I found him to be but a pale stripling, with slender limbs and brilliant eyes. He was plainly nervous and a little dogmatic in manner. He told me that he was twenty-four years of age, but he did not look to be nineteen. He said he had been aware of his power about four years, and that his grandfather and a man named 'Evans' were those who most frequently spoke. 'I have no "guides,"' he said, rather contemptuously.

Pg 232

"The place for the sitting was not especially favorable. It was a reception-room midway between the doctor's office and the dining-room, and was rather large and difficult to close off from the rest of the house. After the windows had been darkened in the usual manner, Peters arranged the chairs so that his seat came between Dr. Towne and Mrs. Towne. Dr. Merriam came next to Towne. This brought me two places away from Peters and next to a stout German woman whose name, as I understood it, was Mrs. Steinert. On Mrs. Towne's right sat Dr. Paul and Professor Franks, my friend. Within the circle Towne had set a small table, on which were placed pencils and paper. The chain was formed by locking our little fingers tightly. If we may depend on the word of those present, this chain of hands remained unbroken for two hours. The room at first was perfectly dark.

"For half an hour we sat at ease, talking a little now and then, but leaving the direction of the whole affair to Peters. He hinted to us—and this I wish to particularly emphasize—that he went out of his body. He said: 'When I think toward any one or toward a thing, I am there. I am all around it. If I think toward a person, I am there—all around him—inside of him.' In pursuit of this idea, I then asked: 'Are you conscious of your body which you have left behind? Are you conscious of being Pg 233 in the upper part of the room, for instance, and do you see your body below you?'

"'No,' said he; 'I am conscious of being in a certain place, but I am not conscious of being in two places at the same time.' He told us of his development, which came about through attendance on a circle with another psychic. He said he had been experimenting for about four years. I asked him if it had affected his health in any way, and he replied: 'No, it does not weary me any more than prolonged study might do. I am very fond of playing chess, and I find that I do not play so well after a sitting—that's all.' He said the only sign of the special condition which produced these phenomena was a nervous tremor in his limbs.

"The first evidence of 'the force' came in steady tappings upon Mrs. Towne's chair. The young man said: 'This is my friend "Evans,"' and thereupon I began to direct the sitting through 'Evans.' In answer to my questions, he said that he would do what he could do for us. I asked him if he would write, and he answered by tapping that he would try.

"Shortly after this promise, sounds as of hands were heard about the table. Sheets of paper were plainly being written upon and torn off the pad. One of these was flourished in my face, while the linked fingers of the psychic were firmly held by Dr. Towne and his wife. All of those in the circle Pg 234 excepting Mrs. Steinert and myself were new to this business, and much impressed.

"At the precise moment when these hands were at work writing, and a little later while they patted Mrs. Towne's cheek and tapped on the doctor's shirt-front, I asked: 'Are you controlling his hands?'

"'Yes,' responded the doctor, who, by-the-way, is a vigorous young scientist and had never before experimented with these forces. His reply was echoed by Mrs. Towne, who remained perfectly calm and clear-headed throughout the entire sitting.

"Thus far the phenomena were precisely similar to those we have had with Mrs. Smiley, but we were soon to have proofs of greater power. While the chain of hands continued unbroken, mysterious fingers clutched Dr. Towne's arm and drummed upon his shirt-front. At length the same mystic fingers began to take off his tie, and, while I warningly called out, 'Be sure of your psychic's hands,' the doctor's collar was taken away and put around his wife's neck. His tie was then added to the collar. Mrs. Towne announced that, while holding firmly to the psychic, she felt the touch of *two* hands about her face, and a few moments thereafter Dr. Merriam, seated next to Dr. Towne, said he felt a strong pressure upon his arm, as if some one were leaning upon it.

"A little later these hands began to unbutton Dr. Towne's shirt-front, and several pencils were Pg 235 stuffed inside. Hands patted and touched those who sat within a radius of about a yard of the psychic; apparently the forces could not reach to where I sat. I complained of this, and almost immediately the psychic said there was some one for me, and in answer to my question, 'Is there some one present for me?' the pencil rapped three times upon the table in the affirmative. At my request this 'spirit' wrote his name upon a piece of paper, tore it off, and threw it in my lap. A moment later something hard and crackling came over the table. 'My cuffs have been removed,' the psychic called out.

"Having in mind one of the extraordinary experiments of Zöllner, I then asked 'Evans' to remove Dr. Towne's vest. I said: 'If we can get that, it will be in effect a confirmation of Zöllner's theory of the fourth dimension.'

"For a few moments hands touched and patted Dr. Towne as if with intent to make this experiment but gave it up, and Peters announced that they were at work around him. It could not have been more than a minute later when I felt something soft thrown in my lap. I did not know what this was, and did not care to break the circle at the moment to find out, and the information was volunteered by the psychic that the 'spirits' had removed his vest, and this we afterward found to be the case, for at the close of the sitting his vest was lying at my feet."

Pg 236

"Oh, come now," said Miller, "you don't intend to convey—"

"I am telling exactly what took place," I replied.

"Peters then said to Dr. Towne: 'Think of some signature, not your own, that you know very well, and I will reproduce it.' After a little silence the sound of writing could be heard, and the tap of a pencil announced that its task was done. The sheet of paper was then ripped from the pad, a very definite action, as you may believe, and the sound of the sheet being folded was plainly heard."

"That would require a thumb and finger and afterward two hands," remarked Miller.

"Precisely; and they were there, notwithstanding the hands of the psychic could be felt so Dr. Towne and Mrs. Towne both said with no movement but a convulsive quivering.

"I then asked 'Evans' if he could not lift the table for us, and he replied by tapping that he would try; and a few moments later the psychic, whose hands and feet began to pass through a period of tremor, warningly called out: 'Now please be very quiet, and don't break the circle.' I could hear him take a deep breath, and a moment later the table rose and passed over Mrs. Towne's head so closely that she was obliged to lean to the right to avoid it, and we all heard it gently deposited not far from the psychic's right hand. While this was done, both Dr. Towne and Mrs. Towne affirmed Pg 237 that their fingers were locked with those of the psychic.

"Here, again, was a phenomenon, inconclusive in itself, from the fact that we could not see the table move, and yet which coheres with an immense body of inexplicable similar movements in the reports of Flammarion and Lombroso. It was impossible for the medium to lift this weight over Mrs. Towne's head, even if his right arm had been completely free, for the stand, though small, was heavy. I regarded this, at the moment, as an authentic case of telekinesis, and my further experience with this psychic has not weakened that conviction.

"Shortly after this the psychic broke up the circle, saying that, as conditions were favorable, he would try to produce materialized forms.

"Taking the chair which was occupied by Mrs. Steinert, he withdrew into the passage-way leading to the dining-room, requesting that the circle resolve itself into a half-circle facing the cabinet. You will remember that we were in a private house, and that all question of collusion is barred out. Shortly after he took his seat in this little recess, two or three brilliant lights, like the twisting flame of a small candle—a curious, glowing, yet not radiant violet flame—developed, high up on the outside of the portières which formed the cabinet, and drifted across and up toward the ceiling, where they silently vanished. I think there must have Pg 238 been three of these, which were followed by a broad, glowing mass of what looked like white-hot metal—a singular light, unlike anything I had ever seen. It made me think of the substance described by Sir William Crookes and other experimenters abroad. At the moment this appeared—or possibly a little before it—a wild whoop was heard—very startling indeed, as if a door had suddenly been opened by a roguish boy and closed again. This practically ended the séance.

"As we lighted up I had first interest for the object which had been thrown across to me. It proved to be a vest, which the psychic said was his. It was a soft gray vest, and matched his suit, and was without any trick seams—so far as I could see—being whole and uninjured. In the inside pocket a folded leaf of the paper from the pad was stuffed, and on this was the signature 'Alfred Towne,' which Dr. Towne said was an exact reproduction of his brother's autograph. On the sheet of paper which had been thrown to me was the simple word 'Taft.' This was taken by the circle to be a prophecy on the election, but, as my wife's family name is Taft, I put a different interpretation upon it. On the whole, the sitting made a profound impression upon me. It was not so much one thing as many things, all cohering with what I already knew of telekinetic phenomena. It was not a test sitting, as Peters acknowledged, but it was by no Pg 239 means easy to deceive under the control we exercised.

"There were many things of interest aside from the physical happenings. The young man did not go into a trance, but remained perfectly normal. He took part in the conversation, answered all questions, and lent himself perfectly to the experiment. He said that if we would sit with him again he was sure we could have more light. 'I don't care to be known as a medium,' he declared. 'I like the study of law, and I want to be a lawyer—not a sensitive. In the first place, the law pays better, and, in the second place, it isn't considered a nice thing to be a medium. However, I will sit again for you, if you want me to, and I am sure you will get many other things in the light.' And he added to me later: 'We can get all these phenomena with no one present but ourselves. Come down to my home some evening and we will try again.'"

"Did you accept his invitation?" asked Miller.

"Yes; but before I did so we had another sitting at Dr. Towne's house, which gave me a closer view of all that went on, for I was permitted to sit at his left and grip his little finger. The circle was slightly changed the next time, and on his right sat a young lady whom we will call Miss Brown. She was a wide-awake and very unexcitable person, and I believe kept close hold on the psychic's right hand. Pg 240 In addition to our linked fingers, the psychic's hands were tied to ours with dental floss.

"There was considerable light in the room this time, and as the nervous tremor developed in the psychic's hands and legs I imagined I could see a grayish vapor form just between and a little above our clasped hands. Suddenly I saw a shadowy arm dart forth from the cloud, and I felt the clasp of a firm hand on my wrist. It was a right hand. 'Are you controlling the psychic's hand?' I demanded of Miss Brown. 'Yes,' she replied, alertly. Even as I spoke I saw the mysterious limb dart out and seize upon a pencil which lay upon the table. Again and again I saw this 'apparition' emerge from that vaporous cloud and handle the pad in the middle of the table. I could see three fingers on the under-side of the pad as it was held before the psychic's face, and these facts I announced to the other members of the circle, who could not see as plainly as I could. Sometimes the arm seemed white, sometimes black, and always it appeared to be a right hand."

"That is to say, *your* control was more vigorous than that of Miss Brown," remarked Miller.

"A doubter might say so, and yet the thread which bound us had some value. One of the most extraordinary performances was the lifting of a glass of water which set in the centre of the table. I could see the glass plainly as it rose to the Pg 241 psychic's lips. It seemed to be sustained by a broad beam of vapor, or it may have been a slim arm clothed in white."

"Probably the psychic's."

"Possibly; but I don't see how it could have been. However, I do not place very much value upon it as standing alone, but considered in connection with the performances of Eusapia, it becomes a little more nearly credible."

"But all this is very far from being an evidence of anything like intelligence," protested Fowler. "It seems very trivial to me."

"It does not seem trivial to me," I answered; "but I will admit that is has nothing like the value of a series of sittings I held last spring with a psychic in a mid-Western city."

IX

The reader will have observed that up to the present moment I have not emphasized in any way the question of the identity of the "intelligences" that have manifested themselves. The reason for this lies in the fact that I was still seeking evidence concerning the processes of mediumship. However, being convinced by reason of my own experiments, supported by those of Lombroso, Morselli, and Bottazzi that the facts of mediumship exist, it is my purpose to take up definitely the question of identity, which is the final and most elusive part of the problem—it may turn out to be the insoluble part of the problem.

If you ask why it should be insoluble, I reply, because it concerns the mystery of death, and it may be that it is not well for us to penetrate the ultimate shadow. Among all the men of the highest rank who admit the reality of apparitions and voices, there are but few as yet who are willing to assert that the dead manifest themselves. By this I mean that though some of them, like Crookes, for example, believe in "the intervention of discarnate Pg 243 intelligences," they are not ready to grant that these intelligences are their grandfathers returning to the scene of their earthly labors.

I said something like this to Miller and Fowler, when we met at the club one afternoon not long after the final meeting of Cameron's Amateur Psychical Society, and I added: "I must confess that most of the spirits I have met seem to me merely parasitic or secondary personalities to use Maxwell's term , drawn from the psychic or from myself. Nearly every one of the mediums I have studied has had at least one guide, whose voice and habit of thought were perilously similar to her own. This, in some cases, has been laughable, as when 'Rolling Thunder,' a Sioux chief Indians are all chiefs in the spirit world , appears and says: 'Goot efening, friends; id iss a nice night alretty.' And yet I have seen a whole roomful of people receive communications from a spirit of this kind with solemn awe. I burn with shame for the sitters and psychic when this kind of thing is going on."

"You visit the wrong mediums," said Fowler. "Such psychics are on a low plane. I never go to those who associate with Indians."

"But mediums are all alike in this respect. I don't suppose Mrs. Smiley realizes that 'Maudie' would be called by a doubter a falsetto disguise of her own voice, and 'Wilbur' a shrewd and humorous personification of her subconscious self; or, if Pg 244 she does, she probably ascribes it to the process of materialization which 'takes from' the medium. Never but once have I had the sensation of being in the presence of a real spirit personality, and that happened to me only a few days ago."

"It must have been an extraordinary experience to have made so deep an impression upon you," said Fowler.

"Yes, it was extraordinary. It had the personal element in it to a much greater degree than any case I had hitherto studied, and seemed a direct attempt at identification on the part of a powerful and original individuality but recently 'passed out.' It came about in this way:

"I met, not long ago, at the home of a friend in a Western city, a woman who was said to be able to produce whispers independent of her own organs of speech. I was assured by those in whom I had confidence that these voices could be heard in the broad light of day, in the open air, anywhere the psychic happened to be, and that her 'work' was of an exceptionally high character. I was keenly interested, as you may imagine, and asked for a sitting. Mrs. Hartley, as we will call her, fixed a day and hour in her own house for the trial, and I went to the sitting a few days later with high expectations of her 'phase.' I found her living in a small frame house on a pleasant street, with nothing to Pg 245 indicate that it was a meeting-place of mortals and their 'spirit guides.'

"Mrs. Hartley was quite evidently a woman of power and native intelligence. After a few minutes of general conversation she took me up to her study on the second floor, a sunny little den on the east side of the house, which was not in the least suggestive of hocus-pocus. A broad mission table, two bookcases, a few flowers, and a curious battered old black walnut table completed the furnishing of the room, which indicated something rather studious and thoughtful in the owner.

"Mrs. Hartley asked me to be seated, and added, 'Please write on a sheet of paper the names of such friends as you would like to communicate with.' She then left the room on some household errand, and while she was gone I wrote the name of her guide, 'Dr. Cooke' out of compliment , and added that of a musical friend whom I will call 'Ernest Alexander.' I also wrote the names 'Jessie' and 'David,' folded the sheet once, and retained it under my hand. Upon her return the psychic seated herself at the battered oval table, and, taking up a pair of hinged school slates, began to clean them with a cloth. I am not going to detail my precautions. You must take my detective work for granted. Moreover, in this case I was awaiting the voices; the slate-writing was gratuitous. She took the slates between which I had dropped my slip Pg 246 of paper , and, putting them beneath the table, asked me to hold one corner."

"I *wish* they wouldn't do that," protested Fowler. "It isn't necessary. I've had messages on slates held in my own hands six feet from the psychic."

"As we sat thus she told me that she had never been in a trance, and that she never permitted the dark. 'I force my guides to work in the light,' she said. She declared that the whispers which I was presently to hear came to her under all conditions, and that her spirit friends talked to her familiarly as she went about her household duties. She assured me that 'they' were a great help and comfort to her. 'Dr. Cooke' was her ever-present guide and counsellor, and her father and brother were always near.

"It was plain that she did not stand in awe of them, for after half an hour's wait she grew impatient and called out in an imperious tone: 'Come, dear, I want you. Come, anybody.' Two or three times she spoke loudly, clearly, as if calling to some one through a thick wall. This interested me exceedingly. Generally psychics are very humble and patient with their 'guides.' A few moments later the slates began to slam about so violently beneath the table that her arm was bruised, and she protested sharply: 'Don't do that. You will break the slates and the table both!' Thereupon the 'forces' quieted down till only a peculiar quiver Pg 247 remained in them. I could hear writing going on steadily.

"At last a tap came to announce that the messages were written. The psychic withdrew the slates and handed them across the table to me. I opened them and took out my paper. On one slate was a message from 'Dr. Cooke,' the guide; on the other were these words, written in slate-pencil: '*I would that you could see me as I am now, still occupied, and happy to be busy.*' This was followed by four lines and three little marks, evidently intended to symbolize a bar of music, and the whole was signed, 'E. Alexander.' The writing was firm and manly, but I did not recognize it as that of my friend.

"The second trial resulted in this vague communication: '*My dear friend, don't overdo. Earth is but one life. Many I recall. I tried to give expression to my one talent.*' This was signed 'Ernest Alexander.' Both these replies, as you see, were very general in phraseology, but the third message came closer to the individual: '*I was so tired and not myself. I am well and in the world of progress. Ernest Alexander.*' The bar of music again appeared, this time much more 'developed.'"

Miller stopped me here. "All this is quite simple. Mrs. Hartley opened and read your note and, following up the clew, simply did some neat trick-writing beneath the table."

"It is not so simple as all that," I answered. "She was interrupted about this time by the doorbell, and while she was gone I wrote on another piece of paper: 'Ernest, give me a test of your identity. Write a bar from the "—— Sonata."' This note I folded close and put in an inside pocket.

"In answer to this request, when the medium returned I got these pertinent words: '*I was not a disappointment to myself, but I was at a point where nerve force failed me.*' This was signed 'Ernest,' and was accompanied by another sketchy bar of music. It all looked like a real attempt to give me what I had asked for, and yet it was the kind of reply that might have been made by the medium had she known the history of my musical friend, or had she been able to take it out of my mind."

"Even that is a violent assumption to me," remarked Miller.

"So it is to me," I answered. "I can't really believe in thought transmission, and yet— I then asked for the signature of the staff, and a small '*c*' was written in the bar above, and another bar was added. Now on the slates there came with every evidence of eager haste intimate questions concerning Alexander's family: '*Is my wife cared for?*' and the like. To these I replied orally. I must tell you that all along the whisper spoke of Alexander's wife as 'Mary,' which was wrong, although it was close to the actual name. Also, after I began Pg 249 to speak of him as 'E. A.' the messages were all signed in that manner, all of which would seem to argue a little confusion in the psychic's mind.

"A little later, *while I held the slate myself*, the mysterious 'force' wrote, '*I thank you for what you have done. I have been told my mind is clear,*' which was particularly full of meaning to me, for the reason that my friend's mind was clouded toward the close of his life."

"All of which proves nothing," insisted Miller. "Your friend, if I conjecture rightly, was a well-known man, and the psychic could have read, and probably did read, all about his illness in the public press."

"It may be so. About this time I began to hear a faint whisper, which*seemed* to come from a point a little to the right of and a foot or two above the psychic's lips. This, she informed me, was the voice of 'Dr. Cooke,' her guide. I could catch only a few of the whispered words, and Mrs. Hartley was forced to repeat them. 'Dr. Cooke,' thus interpreted, said: '*Your friend Alexander is present, and overjoyed to talk with you.*' The conversation went on with both 'Dr. Cooke' and the psychic standing between the alleged spirit and myself; but even then I must admit that 'Alexander's' queries and answers were to the point.

"Under what seemed like test conditions I got two more bars of music, both much more definitive Pg 250 in form than the others; and these, the whisper declared, were from the third movement of the '—— Sonata.' This message was accompanied by a curious little device like the letter*C* with a line drawn through it, and I said to myself: 'If this should prove to be a mark which "Ernest" used in signing his manuscript, something like Whistler's butterfly, I shall have a fine test of thought transmission.'

"I now secured under excellent tests the writing of a singular word, which was plainly spelled but meant nothing to me. It looked like '*Isinghere.*' In answer to oral questioning, the whisper said that these bars of music were part of an unpublished manuscript, a fragment, which the composer had meant to call 'Isinghere.'"

"What about the process?" asked Miller. "Did the writing appear to be supernormal?"

"Yes, and so did the whispering. I could detect no connection between the lips of the psychic and the voice. In one way or another I varied the conditions, so that I was at last quite convinced of the psychic's supernormal power; but that was not my quest. I was seeking proof of the identity of my friend 'E. A.'

"Seeing that the chief means of identification might be in the music, I persuaded my friend Blake, who is a fairly competent musician, to sit with me and decipher the score which 'E. A.' persisted in Pg 251 setting down. I was now eager to secure a complete phrase of the music. I saw myself establishing, at the least, the most beautiful case of mind-tapping on record. 'If we can secure the score of an unpublished manuscript of Alexander's composition we shall have worked a miracle,' I said to Blake.

"Our first sitting, which took place in the home of a common friend, was mixed as to results; but the second, which we held in Mrs. Hartley's study one bright morning, was very fruitful. The 'powers' started in at once as if to confound us both. Blake received a message written on a slate under his foot, and I got the name '*Jessie,*' with the word '*sister*' written beneath it; and then suddenly the whispers changed in character. The words became swift, impetuous, imperious. '*Line off all the leaves of a slate,*' the voice commanded. I understood at once, for in the previous sitting 'E. A.' had seemingly found it difficult to draw a long line.

"We had brought some silicon slates of the book variety, and Blake now proceeded to rule one of them with the lines of a musical staff, and on these slates, held as before beneath the table, we began to get bars of music of a character quite outside the knowledge of the psychic and myself; and, more remarkable still, the whispers, so the psychic informed us, were no longer from 'Dr. Cooke'; Pg 252 'E. A.,' she declared, was there in person and directing the work.

"Furthermore, the requests that we now received were entirely different in character from 'Cooke's' impersonal remarks. The whispers were quick and masterful, wonderfully like 'Alexander' in content. 'He' was humorous; 'he' acknowledged mistakes in the score, calling them '*slips of the pen.*' 'He' became highly technical in his conversation with Blake, talking of musical matters that were Greek to me and, I venture to say, Coptic to the psychic. 'He' corrected the notations himself, sometimes when Blake held the slate, sometimes when I held it. Part of the time 'he' indicated the corrections orally. 'He' asked Blake to try the air.

"At last 'he' broke off, and imperiously said: '*Take the table to the piano.*' This seemed to surprise the psychic, but she acquiesced, and we moved the small stand and our slates down to the little parlor; and there, with Blake now holding the slate beneath the table and now playing the notes upon the piano, the score grew into a weird little melody with bass accompaniment, which seemed to me at the moment exactly like a message from my friend Alexander. The first bar went through me like the sound of his voice."

"Now you are getting into the upper air of spiritualism," exulted Fowler. "You are now receiving a message that has dignity and meaning."

Pg 253

"So it seemed at the moment, both to Blake and to myself. The music was manifestly not the kind of thing that Mrs. Hartley could conceive. It was absolutely *not* commonplace. It was elliptical, touched with technical subtlety, although simple in appearance. At last a complete phrase was written out and partly harmonized. This, 'E. A.' said, was the beginning of a little piece that he had intended to call 'Unghere' or 'Hungarie.' Nothing in all my long experience with psychics ever moved me like the first phrase of that sweet, sad melody. It seemed like the touch of identification I had been seeking."

"But your friend Blake was a musician," interrupted Miller. "And how about your own subconscious self? You are musical, and your mind is filled with your friend Alexander's music."

"That is true, and I had that reservation all along. 'E. A.' may have been made up of our combined subconscious selves; I admit all that. But no matter; it was still very marvellous, even on its material side, for some of this music was written in while the slates were in Blake's entire control. At times he not merely inserted them himself but withdrew them—the psychic merely clutched one corner of them. Furthermore, throughout all this composition 'Ernest' was master of the situation. 'Dr. Cooke' was superseded. There was neither feebleness nor hesitation in the voice. I could now distinguish most Pg 254 of the words, and the dialogue went forward exactly as if a master musician were dictating to an intelligent amanuensis a new and subtle sketch."

"Did the medium look at the music?" asked Miller.

"Yes, now and then. However, most of the corrections were put in upside down, as regards her position, and during the last sitting she appeared to be no more than a mere on-looker. Once as we sat holding the slate 'Ernest' whispered to me: '*Blake is a fine fellow. I met him twice.*'"

"'Can you tell me where?' asked Blake.

"'*It was in New York City,*' was the reply; then, after a moment's hesitation: '*It was at dinner—both times!*' 'You are right,' said Blake, much impressed. 'Can you tell me the places?' '*Once was on Fifth Avenue. The other was—I can't tell the location exactly; but it was where we went down a short flight of steps.*' 'That is correct also,' said Blake. 'How many persons were there?' '*Five.*' 'Quite right. Can you tell me who they were?' '*Well, Mary was there, and you, of course; but I can't be sure of the others.*'

"Blake looked at me in astonishment, and our minds flashed along the same line. Suppose the whisper were only a bit of clever ventriloquism, how did the psychic secure the information conveyed in this dialogue? It was given as I write it, with only a bit of hesitation once or twice; and yet, it may have been merely thought transference."

Pg 255

"*Merely* thought transference!" exclaimed Miller. "I consider thought transference quite as absurd as slate-writing."

Fowler interposed. "I consider this a simple case of spirit communication. You should be grateful for such a beautiful response."

"This significant fact is not to be overlooked," I resumed: "the psychic secured almost nothing else that concerned either Blake's affairs or my own. Mainly the whispers had to do with 'E. A.,' which, of course, bears out Miller's notion that the psychic could deal only with what was public property, and yet this little colloquy about the dinners in New York is very convincing so far as mind-reading goes.

"During the third sitting, Blake again being present, 'E. A.' took control, as before, from the start, and carried forward the recording of the musical fragment. '*I want you to fill in the treble, Blake,*' he said. '*It's nothing but the bare melody now.*' Blake protested: 'I'm not up to this.' And the whisper came swiftly, '*You're too modest, Blake*'; and a moment later it said: '*I hope you're not bored, Garland.*' If all this was a little play of the psychic's devising it was very clever, for after a few minutes of close attention to Blake, 'E. A.' turned toward me and asked, with anxious haste: '*Where's Garland?*' 'I am here,' I answered. '*Don't go away,*' he entreated. It was as if for the Pg 256 moment he had lost sight of me by reason of fixing his attention upon Blake."

"That is singular!" exclaimed Fowler. "Their field of vision is evidently much more restricted than we thought."

"It must be very small indeed, for Blake and I sat touching elbows. Two or three times the whispering voice called, '*Is Garland here?*' and once it asked: '*What is Garland doing? I see his hand moving.*' I explained that I was making notes. '*Don't do it!*' was the agitated request."

"A very neat little touch," remarked Miller.

"We worked for a long time over this music, directed by the voice, both in the notation and in the execution of it. The lines were drawn for both bass and treble lengthwise of the slate, and Blake found the little piece difficult to play, partly because the staves were on different leaves of the slate and partly because the notes, especially some of those put in at the beginning by the composer, were becoming blurred. It was marvellous to see how exactly these dim notes were touched up by the mysterious pencil beneath the table. But our progress was slow. 'E. A.' was very patient, though now and then he plumply opposed his will to Blake's. Once, especially, Blake exclaimed: 'That can't be right!'"

"'*Yes, it is right!*' insisted 'E. A.'"

"'But it is very unusual to construct a measure Pg 257 in that way.' For there was a seeming confusion of three-four time with six-eight time."

"'*It is a liberty I permit myself,*' was the swift reply."

"In the last bar, which did not appear to be filled satisfactorily, the composer directed the insertion of a figure 2. This meant, as became clear through a subsequent reference to his printed scores, the playing of two quarter-notes in the time of three eighth notes, but was not understood at the moment by Blake."

"'*Never mind,*' said 'E. A.,' pleasantly, '*I will write it differently.*' The figure '2' was cancelled, and the measure was completed by a rest. This is only one of many astonishing passages in this dialogue."

"In all this work 'E. A.' carried himself like the creative master. He held to a plane apparently far above the psychic's musical knowledge, and often above that of his amanuensis. He was highly technical throughout in both the composition and the playing, and Blake followed his will, for the most part, as if the whispers came from Alexander himself. And yet I repeat the music and all may have come from a union of Blake's mind with that of the psychic, with now and then a mixture of my own subconscious self."

"What was the psychic doing all this time?" asked Miller.

"She was listening to the voice and repeating the words which Blake could not hear. She seemed merely the somewhat bored interpreter of words which she did not fully understand. It was precisely as if she were catching by wireless telephone the whispered instructions of my friend 'E. A.' I can't believe she consciously deceived us, but it is possible that these ventriloquistic voices have become a subconscious habit.

"One other very curious event I must note. Once, when Blake was asking for a correction, the whisper exclaimed: '*I can't see it, Blake!*'

"'*Cover it with your hand,*' interjected the 'control.' Blake did so, and 'E. A.' spoke, gratefully: '*I see it now.*"

"Seeing cannot mean the same with them that it does with us," exclaimed Fowler. "You remember Crookes put his finger on the print of a newspaper behind his back, and the 'spirit' spoke the word that was under his finger-tip. They apprehend by means of some form of etheric vibration not known to us."

I resumed: "Let me stop here for a moment to emphasize a very curious contradiction. Between my first séance with Mrs. Hartley and this, our third attempt to secure the music, I had held two sittings in the home of a friend. Mrs. Hartley had come to the house about ten o'clock in the morning, bringing nothing with her except a few tips of soft Pg 259 slate-pencil. During the sitting I had secured in the middle of a manila pad a pad which the psychic had never seen and which I had taken from my friend's desk these words: '*Have Schumann.—E. A.*' This writing I had taken to mean that 'Ernest' wanted to hear some of Schumann's music, and in that understanding I had called Blake in to play. This had seemed at the moment perfectly conclusive and entirely satisfactory; yet now, in this final sitting, 'E. A.' suddenly reverted to this message, and whispered: '*Garland, there is a certain étude which I took to Schumann. I want you to regain it and take it to Smart. Mary will know about it. I meant to take it away, but did I? I was so badly off mentally that I don't know whether I did or not.*' Whereupon Blake said: 'Do you mean Schumann the publisher?' '*Yes,*' 'E. A.' replied; and I said: 'And you want the manuscript recalled from Schumann and given to Smart?' '*Yes,*' was his very definite answer.

"'Very well, I will attend to it,' I replied. 'What do you want done with this fragment, "Isinghere"?' I pursued. 'Shall I publish it?' '*That is what it is for,*' he answered, curtly.

"'How many bars are in it?' asked Blake. 'Forty?' '*More,*' returned the whisper.

"Blake made the mistake of again suggesting an answer. 'As many as sixty?'

"'*Yes, sixty or seventy,*' was the answer, like an Pg 260 echo. Here Blake's thought governed, but it was evident that the psychic had no clear conception of what this reference to Schumann meant in the first instance, for 'E. A.' was unable to complete his sentence, which should have read: '*Have Schumann return a certain étude which I took.—E. A.*' Furthermore, the psychic evidently believed in the truth of the message or she would not have gone into it with such particularity; she would have been lacking in caution to have given me such definite and detailed information, knowing that it was all false.

"So far as my own mind is concerned, I had no knowledge of such a music publisher as Schumann. Smart I had met. Blake, however, knew of both firms. The entire message and the method of its communication were deeply exciting at the time, and completed what seemed like a highly intellectual test of identity, and we both left the house of the psychic with a feeling of having been very near to our dead friend.

"'To identify one of these bars of music would be a good test,' said Blake, 'but to find that *étude* at Schumann's would be a triumph.'

"'To find the manuscript fragment would be still more convincing,' was my answer.

"Imagine my disappointment when, in answer to my inquiry, Schumann replied that no such *étude* had ever been in his hands, and Alexander's family Pg 261 reported that no fragment called 'Unghere' could be found among the composer's manuscripts."

Fowler shared my regret. "What about the other messages? Were they all disappointing?"

"No; some of them were not. The most intimate were true; and a signature which came on the slate under test conditions, and which I valued very little at the moment, turned out to be almost the exact duplicate of Alexander's signature as he used to write it when a youth twenty years ago. As a matter of fact, it closely resembled the signature appended to a framed letter which used to hang upon the wall of his study. But, even so, its reproduction under these conditions is sufficiently puzzling."

"What was Blake's conclusion? Did he put the same value upon it all that you did?"

"Yes, I think he was quite as deeply impressed as I. He said the music seemed like Alexander's music, somehow distorted by the medium through which it came. 'It was like seeing Alexander through a pane of crinkly glass,' he put it. And he added: 'I had the sense of being in long-distance contact with the composer himself.' He had no doubt of the supernormal means through which our writing came, but he remains doubtful of the value of the music as evidence of 'Ernest's' return from the world of shadows."

"Have you tried to secure more of the music?" Fowler asked.

Pg 262

"No, not specifically; but I've had one further inconclusive sitting since then with Mrs. Hartley. Almost immediately 'Ernest' whispered a greeting and said: '*I want to go on with that music, Garland. I want to put B and D and A into the first bar—it's only a bare sketch as it stands.*'

"To this I replied: 'I can't do it, 'Ernest.' It's beyond me. Wait till I can get Blake again.'

"This ended his attempt, although he was 'terribly anxious,' so the psychic said. I am going to try for the completion of this score through another psychic. If I can get that eighth bar taken up and carried on by 'Ernest' through another psychic the case will become complicated.

"I have gone into detail in my account of this experiment, for the reason that it illustrates very aptly the inextricable tangle of truth and error which most 'spirit communications' present. It typifies in little the elusive problem of spirit identification which many a veteran investigator is still at work upon, after years of study. Maxwell gives a case of long-continued unintentional and unconscious deception of the general kind which went far to prevent his acceptance of the spirit hypothesis."

"I don't think the failure to find the musical fragment invalidates this beautiful communication," declared Fowler. "You admit that many of the messages were to the point, and that some of them were very intimate and personal."

Pg 263

"Yes, speaking generally, I would say that 'E. A.' might have uttered all the words and dictated all the messages except those that related to the publishing matter; but there is the final test. Schumann declares that no such manuscript has ever been in his hands."

"He may be mistaken, or 'E. A.' may have misspoken himself—for, as William James infers, the spirits find themselves tremendously hampered in their attempts to manifest themselves. Furthermore, you say you could not hear all that 'E. A.' spoke—you or the psychic may have misunderstood him. In any case, it all seems to me a fine attempt at identification."

"I wish I could put the same value on it now that I did when Blake played the first bar of that thrilling little melody; but I can't. As it recedes it loses its power over me."

"What did Alexander's family think of the music?"

"They thought it more like a Cheyenne or Omaha love-song than like a melody of 'Ernest's' own composition."

"But that only adds to the mystery of the mental process," objected Miller. "That supposes it to have come out of your mind."

"I can't believe that I had any hand in the musical part of it, and I can't persuade myself that my dead friend was present."

Pg 264

"Suppose you had been able to find that musical fragment, would it have converted you?" This was Miller's challenge.

"No, for even then some living person might have known of it—must have known of it; and if a knowledge of it lay in some other mind, no matter where and no matter how deeply buried in the subconscious, that knowledge, according to Myers and Hudson, would have been accessible to the supernormal perception of the psychic."

Fowler interrogated me: "But suppose a phantom form resembling 'E. A.' had *spoken* these things to you face to face—what then?"

"I would not have believed, even then."

"Why?"

"Well, for one reason, belief is not a matter of the will; it is not even dependent upon evidence."

Miller interrupted me. "I am interested in the writing. How do you account for the writing? As I understand it, the psychic did not, in some instances, touch the slate while the writing was going on. Are you sure of Blake?"

"Blake is as much to be trusted as I am. No, I am forced to a practical acceptance of the theory of the fluidic arm, and yet this is a most astounding admission. We must suppose that the psychic was able to read our minds and write down our mingled and confused musical conceptions by means of a supernumerary hand. It happens that I have Pg 265 since seen these etheric hands in action, which makes it easier for me to conceive of such a process. I have seen them dart forth from another medium precisely as described by Scarpa. I have seen them lift a glass of water, and I have had them touch my knees beneath a table while slate-writing was going on—so that, given the power to read my mind, there is nothing impossible having regard to Bottazzi's definite experiments in the idea of the etheric hand's setting down the music and reproducing the signature of 'E. A.' In fact, at a recent sitting in a private house with a young male psychic, we had this precise feat performed. Said the psychic to our host, Dr. Towne, 'Think hard of a signature that is very familiar to you,' and Dr. Towne fixed his mind upon the signature of his brother, and immediately, while the young man's material hands were controlled, his etheric hand seized a pencil in the middle of the table and reproduced the signature."

"Could you see this hand?" Miller asked.

"Not in this case; but at a sitting which followed this, during such time as I sat beside the psychic and controlled one hand, I plainly saw the supernumerary arm and hand dart forth and seize a pencil. I saw a hand very plainly cross my knee and grasp me by the forearm. All of this has its bearing upon this very curious phenomenon of the reproduction of 'E. A's.' youthful signature, which remained very puzzling to us all."

Pg 266

"But did you not say that 'E. A.' at times represented an opposing will?" questioned Fowler— "that he disputed certain passages with Blake, and that he finally carried his point in opposition to every mind in the circle?"

"Yes, that happened several times, and was all very convincing at the time. And yet this opposition may have been more apparent than real. It may have concerned our conscious wills only; our subconscious selves may have been in accord, working together as one."

Fowler was a bit irritated. "If you are disposed to make the subconscious will all-powerful and omniscient, nothing can be proved. It seems to me an evasion. However, let me ask how you would explain away a spirit form carrying the voice, the features, and the musical genius of 'E. A.'?"

"Well, there is the teleplastic theory of Albert de Rochas. He claims to have been able not merely to cause a hypnotized subject to exteriorize her astral self, but to mould this vapory substance as a sculptor models wax. So I can imagine that a momentary radiant apparition might have been created in the image of my sister or 'David' or 'E. A.'"

"To my thinking, that is more complicated and incredible than the spirit hypothesis," objected Fowler.

"Nothing can be more incredible to me than the spirit hypothesis," I replied. "But, then, Pg 267 everything is incredible in the last analysis. I am the more disposed to believe in the teleplastic theory, for the reason that I have recently had an opportunity to witness a particularly incredible thing: the materialization of a complete human form outside the cabinet and beside the psychic—a phenomenon which has a special bearing upon the matter of identity which we are discussing. The sitting took place in a small private house here in the city. The psychic in the case was a young business man who is careful not to advertise his power. For four years he has been holding secret developing circles whereto a few of his friends only are invited. I was present last Sunday, and shared in the marvels. The place of the séance was the parlor of his apartment, his young wife and little daughter being present. There was, in addition, an elderly lady, mother-in-law of the psychic, and a Polish student whom I will call Jacob. I am quite sure that no one else entered or left the room during the evening. Mrs. Pratt, the mother-in-law, occupied a seat between me and Jacob. The little girl sat at the window, and was under my eye all the time. The wife spent most of the evening at the piano on my right. The room was fairly dark, though the light of a far-away street lamp shone in at the window.

"The psychic retired into a little alcove bedroom, which served as cabinet, and the curtain had hardly fallen between him and our group when the spirit Pg 268 voices began. The first one to speak was 'Evan,' the 'guide,' and I remarked that his voice was precisely like a falsetto disguise of the psychic's own.

"Soon 'Evan' and other spirits appeared at the opening of the curtain. The wife called them each by name, but I could see only certain curious fluctuating, cloud-like forms, like puffs of fire-lit steam. The effect was not that of illuminated gauze, but more like illuminated vapor. At length came one that spoke in a deep voice, using a foreign language. Jacob, the young Pole, sprang up in joyous excitement, saying that he had sat many times in this little circle, but that this was the first time a spirit had spoken to him in his own tongue. As they conversed together, I detected a close similarity of accent and of tone in their speech. It certainly sounded like the Polish language, but I could not rid myself of the impression that the Pole was talking to himself."

"What do you mean by that?"

"I mean that the accent, inflection, and quality of the ghost's voice were identical with that of the living man, and this became still more striking when, a little later, Jacob returned to his seat, and the 'Count,' his visitor, called for the Polish national hymn. Jacob then sang, and the phantom sang with him. Now this seemed like a clear case of identification, and was perfectly satisfactory to Jacob, but I had observed this fact: the Pole was Pg 269 an indifferent singer—having hard work to keep the key—and the 'Count' was troubled in the same way. His deep, almost toneless, singing struck me as a dead, flat, wooden echo of Jacob's voice. In short, it was as if the psychic had built up a personality partly out of himself, but mainly out of his Polish sitter, and as if this etheric duplication were singing in unison with its progenitor."

"What nonsense!" exclaimed Fowler.

"Did he manufacture a double out of you?" queried Miller.

"No one spoke to me from the shadow, except the 'guide,' although I was hoping for some new word from 'Ernest,' and kept him uppermost in my mind. A form came out into the centre of the room, which the wife said was 'Evan,' and requested me to shake his hand. This I did. The hand felt as if it were covered with some gauzy veiling. My belief is that it was the psychic himself who stood before me, probably in trance. I could see nothing, however. I do not remember that I could detect any shadow even; but the hand was real, and the voice and manner of speech were precisely those of the psychic himself."

"I repeat that this does not necessarily imply fraud, for the mind and vocal organs of the psychic are often used in that way," Fowler argued.

"I grant that. Up to this point I had been able to see nothing but dim outlines. But toward the Pg 270 end of the evening the psychic advanced from the cabinet and in a dazed way ordered the lamp to be lit. This was done. He then asked that it be turned low. This was also done. Thereupon, directing his gaze toward the curtain, he called twice in a tone of command, 'Come out!'

"I could place every one in the room at the moment. I could see the psychic distinctly. I could discern the color of his coat and the expression of his face. He stood at least six feet from the opening in the curtain. At his second cry, in which I detected a note of entreaty, I saw a luminous form, taller than himself, suddenly appear before the curtain and stand bowing in silence. I could perceive neither face, eyes, nor feet, but I could make out the arms under the shining robe, the shape of the head and the shoulders, and as he bowed I could see the bending of his neck. It certainly was not a clothes-horse. The covering was not so much a robe as a swathing, and we had time to discuss it briefly.

"However, my eyes were mainly busy with the psychic, whose actions impressed me deeply. He had the air of an anxious man undergoing a dangerous ordeal. His right hand was stretched stiffly toward the phantom, his left was held near his heart; his knees seemed to tremble, and his body appeared to be irresistibly drawn toward the cabinet. Slowly, watchfully, fearfully, he approached the Pg 271 phantom. The figure turned toward him, and a moment later they met—they clung together, they appeared to coalesce, and the psychic fell through the curtain to the floor of the cabinet, like a man smitten with death."

"What do you wish to imply?" asked Miller. "Do you mean that the man and the ghost were united in some way?"

"Precisely so. The 'spirit' seemed drawn by some magnetic force toward the psychic, and the psychic seemed under an immense strain to keep the apparition exterior to himself. When they met the spectre vanished, and the psychic's fall seemed inevitable—a collapse from utter exhaustion. I was at the moment convinced that I had seen a vaporous entity born of the medium. It seemed a clear case of projection of the astral body. In the pause which followed the psychic's fall the young wife turned to me and said: 'Sometimes, if my husband does not reach the spirit form in time, he falls *outside* the curtain.' She did not seem especially alarmed.

"The young psychic himself, however, told me afterward that he was undergoing a tremendous strain as he stood there commanding the spirit to appear. 'I had a fierce pain in the centre of my forehead,' he said. 'I couldn't get my breath. I felt as if all my substance, my strength, was being drawn out of me. My legs seemed about to give Pg 272 way. It is always hard to produce a form so far away from me when I am on the outside of the cabinet in the light. The greater the distance, the greater the strain.' I asked him what happened when he and the form rushed together, and he answered: 'As soon as I touched it, it re-entered my body.'" 2

"I wonder why the spirits are always clothed in that luminous gauze?" queried Miller.

"They are not," replied Fowler. "More often they come in the clothing which was their habitual wear."

"I asked this young psychic if drapery were used out of respect to us mortals, and he replied: 'No; the forms are swathed not from sense of propriety so much as to protect the body, which is often incomplete at the extremities.' The wife and Jacob told me that at one of their meetings a naked Hercules suddenly appeared before the curtain. The Pole declared: 'He was of giant size and strength. I felt of his muscles he was clothed only in a Pg 273 loincloth , and I closely studied his tremendous arms and shoulders. The medium, as you know, is a small, thin man. We called this figure "the man from Mars." He was at least six feet high, and strong as a lion. He rushed back into the cabinet, and came out holding the medium above his head on his upraised palms. It was very wonderful.'"

"You didn't see anything like that, did you?" asked Miller.

"No," I replied; "but I did see the development of a figure apparently from the floor between me and the curtain of the cabinet. My attention was called to something wavering, shimmering, and fluctuating about a foot above the carpet. It was neither steam nor flame. It seemed compounded of both luminous vapor and puffing clouds of drapery. It rose and fell in quivering impulses, expanding and contracting, but continuing to grow until at last it towered to the height of a tall man, and I could dimly discern, through dark draperies edged with light, a man's figure.

"'This,' the young wife said, 'is Judge White, the grandfather of the psychic,' and she conversed with him, but only for a few moments. He soon dwindled and faded and melted away in the same fashion as he had come, recalling to my mind Richet's description of the birth and disappearance of 'B. B.,' in Algiers. I know this sounds like the veriest dreaming, but you must remember that Pg 274 materializations much more wonderful have been seen and analyzed in the clinical laboratories of Turin and Naples. Morselli, Bottazzi, Lombroso, Porro, and Foà have been confronted by similar apparitions. They saw 'sinister' faces, and were repelled by 'Satanic hands agile and prompt' in cabinets of their own construction, surrounded by their own registering machinery, and Richet photographed just such figures as this I have described.

"The question with me is not, Do these forms exist? but, What produces them? I am describing this sitting to explain what I mean by the ideoplastic or teleplastic theory. If, for example, this psychic had known me well enough to have had a very definite picture of 'E. A.,' he might have been able to model from the mind-stuff that he or the circle had thrown off, a luminous image of my friend, and, aided by my subconscious self, might have united the presence and the musical thought of Ernest Alexander."

"It won't do!" exclaimed Miller. "It's all too destructive, too preposterous!"

"I insist that the spirit hypothesis is simpler," repeated Fowler.

"It isn't a question of simplicity," I retorted. "It's a question of fact. If the observations of scientific experimentalists are of any value, the teleplastic theory is on the point of winning acceptance."

Pg 275

"I will not admit that," rejoined Fowler. "For, even if you throw out all the enormous mass of evidence accumulated by spiritistic investigators, you still have the conversion of Wallace, Lodge, and Lombroso, not to speak of De Vesme, Venzano, and other well-known men of science, to account for. Even Crookes himself admits that nothing but some form of spirit hypothesis is capable of explaining *all* the phenomena; and in a recent issue of the *Annals of Psychic Science*Lombroso writes a paper making several very strong points against the biologic theory. One of these is the simultaneous occurrence of phenomena. 'Can the subconscious self act in several places at once?' he asks. A second objection lies in the fact that movements occur in opposition to the will of the psychic—as, for example, when Eusapia was transported in her chair. 'Can a man lift himself by his boot-straps?' is the question. 'The centre of gravity of a body cannot be altered in space unless acted upon by an external force. Therefore, the phenomena of levitation cannot be considered to be produced by energy emanating from the medium.'"

"I don't think that follows," I argued. "Force may be exerted unconsciously and invisibly. Because the psychic does not *consciously*will to do a certain thing is no proof that the action does not originate in the deeps of her personality. We know very little of this obscure region of our minds."

Pg 276

Fowler was ready with his answer: "But let us take the case that Lombroso cites of the beautiful woman spirit whose hand twice dashed the photographic plates from the grasp of those who wished to secure her picture. Here was plainly an opposing will, for the psychic was lending herself to the experiment, and the spectators were eager for its success. Notwithstanding which co-operation this phantom bitterly opposed the wishes of every one present, and it was *afterward* learned that there was a special reason why she did not wish to leave positive proofs of her identity. 'It is evident, therefore,' concludes Lombroso, 'that a third will can intervene in spiritistic phenomena.'

"Furthermore, Dr. Venzano, as well as De Vesme, have taken up the same body of facts upon which Foà and Morselli base their theory, and arrive at a totally different conclusion. They call attention to a dozen events that can be explained only on the theory of discarnate intelligences. Venzano observed that the forms occurred in several places at once, that they appeared in many shapes and many guises. Some were like children, some had curly hair, some had beards. In one case identification was made by introducing the finger of one of the sitters within the phantom mouth to prove the loss of a molar tooth. Sometimes the hair of these heads was plaited like that of a girl. Some of the hands were large and black, others fair and pink Pg 277 —like a child's. In short, he argues that the medium could not have determined the size, shape, or color of the phantoms."

"All that does not really militate against the ideoplastic theory," I retorted. "It is as easy to produce a phantom with hair plaited as it is to produce one with hair in curls. If it is a case of the modelling of the etheric vapor by the mind of the psychic, these differences would be produced naturally enough. The forcible handling of the medium by the invisible ones is a much more difficult thing for me to explain, for to imagine the psychic emitting a form of force which afterward proceeds to raise the psychic herself against her will—as Mrs. Smiley testifies happened again and again in her youth—is to do violence to all that we know of natural law. And yet it may be that the etheric double is able to take on part of the forces resident in the circle of sitters, and so become immensely more potent than the psychic himself, as in the case of the 'Man from Mars'—the Hercules I have just been telling you about. Then, as to the content of these messages, they may be impulses, hints, fragments of sentences caught from the air as one wireless operator intercepts communications meant for other stations than his own. So that my interview with 'E. A.' may have been a compounding of the psychic, Blake, and myself, and fugitive natures afloat in the ether. In fact, I am not as near a Pg 278 belief in the return of the dead as I was when I began this last series of experiments. These Italian scientific observers, I confess, have profoundly affected my thought."

"Your idea is, then," said Miller, "that these apparitions are emanations of the medium's physical substance, moulded by his will and colored by the minds of his sitters?"

"That is the up-to-date theory, and everything that I have experienced seems capable of a biologic interpretation against it."

Fowler hastened to weaken the force of this statement. "Spiritists all admit that the forms of spirits are made up—partly, at least—of the psychic's material self, but that does not prove that the mind of the ghost is not a separate entity from that of the psychic. I grant that the only difference between the psycho-dynamic theory and the spiritualistic theory lies in the question of the origin of the intelligences that direct the manifestation. Foà would say they spring from the subconscious self of the psychic. We say they come from the spirit world, and there we stand."

Miller's words were keen and without emotion. "Until all phenomena are explained there will be obscure happenings and things to be explained by some one who can, but it is no final explanation to say 'a man did it' or 'an intelligence did it.' I have often been told that things cannot move in certain Pg 279 ways or certain things cannot be done except by intelligent action or guidance, but it may be remembered that Kepler thought guiding spirits were needful for making the planets move in their elliptical orbits."

"Your scientists are feeding millions of people stones," exclaimed Fowler. "They ask for bread, and you give them slices of granite."

"Better granite than slime," said Miller. "I am with the biologists in this campaign. Let us have the truth, no matter how unpalatable it may be. If these phenomena exist, they are in the domain of natural law and can be weighed and measured. If they are imaginary, they should be swept away, like other dreams of superstition and ignorance."

Fowler was not to be silenced. "I predict that you and your like will yet be forced, like Lombroso, to take your place with Aksakof, Lodge, Wallace, Du Prel, and Crookes, who have come to admit the intervention of discarnate intelligences. Lombroso says, 'We find, as I already foresaw some years ago, that these materialized bodies belong to the radiant state of matter, which has now a sure foothold in science. This is the only hypothesis that can reconcile the ancient and universal belief in the persistence of some manifestation of life after death with the results of science.' He adds: 'These beings, or remnants of beings, would not be able to obtain Pg 280 complete consistency to incarnate themselves, if they did not temporarily borrow a part of the medium. *But to borrow force from the medium is not the same thing as to be identical with the medium.*'"

"Well," said I, "of this I am certain: we cannot afford to ignore such experiments as those of Morselli and Bottazzi. I am aware that many investigators discountenance such experiments, but I believe with Venzano that the physical phenomena of mediumship cannot be, and ought not to be, considered trivial. It was the spasmodic movement of a decapitated frog that resulted in the discovery of the Voltaic Pile. Furthermore, I intend to try every other conceivable hypothesis before accepting that of the spiritists."

"What is your reason for that?" asked Fowler.

"Because I am a scientist in my sympathies. I believe in the methods of the chemist and the electrician. I prefer the experimenter to the theorist. I like the calm, clear, concise statements of these European savans, who approach the subject, not as bereaved persons, but as biologists. I am ready to go wherever science leads, and I should be very glad to *know* that our life here is but a link in the chain of existence. Others may have more convincing knowledge than I, but at this present moment the weight of evidence seems to me to be on the side of the theory that mediumship is, after all, a question of unexplored human biology."

Pg 281

"I don't see it that way," rejoined Fowler, calmly. "Suppose your biologists prove that the psychic can put forth a supernumerary arm, or maintain, for a short time, a complete double of herself. Would that necessarily make the spiritist theory untenable? Is it not fair to conclude that if the soul or 'astral' or 'etheric double' can act outside the living body, it can live and think and manifest after the dissolution of its material shell? Does not the experimental work of Bottazzi, Morselli, and De Rochas all make for a spiritual interpretation of life rather than for the position of the materialist? I consider that they have strengthened rather than weakened the mystic side of the universe. They are bringing the wonder of the world back to the positivist. Let them go on. They will yet demonstrate, in spite of themselves, the immortality of the soul."

"I hope they will," I replied. "It would be glorious at this time, when tradition begins to fail of power, to have a demonstration of immortality come through the methods of experimental science. Certainly I would welcome a physical proof that my mother still thinks and lives, and that Ernest and other of my dearest friends are at work on other planes and surrounded by other conditions, no matter how different from the conventional idea of paradise these environments might be; but the proof must be ample and very definite."

Pg 282

Miller put in a last word of warning: "Because a phenomenon has not been explained, and no one knows how to explain it, is no reason for supposing there is anything extraphysical about it. No one has explained the first cause of the development of an embryo. No one knows what goes on in an active nerve, or why atoms are selective in their associates. Ignorance is not a proper basis for speculation, and if one must have a theory, let it be one having some obvious continuity with our best physical knowledge."

And at that point our argument rested. We separated, and each went his way, to be met by questions of business and politics, and to be once more blended to the all-enveloping mystery of life.

FOOTNOTE:

2 Since this conversation I have had a letter from another well-authenticated psychic, a man making his living by honest labor as a carpenter, who gives very definitely his experience on emitting an etheric double. He says: "One evening, while sitting at the table, I began to feel as if I were swelling up. My thumb felt as big as my arm, and my arm as big as my leg. While I was perfectly aware that I was at the dinner-table, I also felt myself in the hall trying to enter the dining-room. I found the knob, I opened the door. The others saw me traverse the room toward myself. My dual body came close beside me and vanished with a snap."

Pg 283

ADDENDUM

A CORROBORATIVE AND TECHNICAL ACCOUNT OF PSYCHICAL PHENOMENA, INVOLVING THE PRODUCTION OF A MUSICAL SCORE ON A SLATE, SECURED BY "BLAKE." 3

This record was secured during three sittings, which took place on the forenoon and afternoon of Friday, March 13th, and on the forenoon of Saturday, March 14, 1908. These sittings were held in a dwelling-house on a quiet street of ordinary character. They began in a second-story front room, and were transferred to a parlor just below, where there was a piano. The room, in either case, was fairly light; now and then the window-shades were lowered, but reading and writing were easy at all times. Three persons were present: the psychic, a robust, alert, intelligent woman of thirty-five; Hamlin Garland; and the writer, who combined the functions of amanuensis and editor.

Pg 284

The psychic was not in a trance, and stated that she had never gone into one. She conversed throughout in ordinary voice and manner, save when, with a certain emphasis, she undertook to hasten the pace of her lagging "controls." The three sittings were attended by little noise, pounding, or violence; there was no breaking or crumpling up of slates, as had been the case during an earlier sitting on Thursday.

The psychic's principal "control"—to be known here as "Dr. Cooke"—spoke in whispers, and his words were repeated aloud by the psychic herself. These whisperings were only occasionally audible to the writer, but they were plainly heard by Mr. Garland. It may be added that on at least two occasions, however, the writer heard and understood replies which the psychic declared had not been audible to her. During the latter portion of these sittings, especially that of Saturday, the "control" seemed to withdraw altogether, and for two or three hours the circle was in apparent communication—direct, rapid, uninterrupted—with an intelligence that may conveniently be termed the "Composer."

The paraphernalia for these sittings comprised the following:

1. A small, light, walnut centre-table, which Mr. Garland himself had assisted in repairing before the proceedings began.

Pg 285

2. A silicon book-slate, eight inches by five inches. There were six pages—the insides of the covers and a double leaf. These leaves lay close and flat, like those of a book.

3. A few bits of slate-pencil, from one-quarter of an inch to three-eighths of an inch in length; also a longer slate-pencil used by the writer.

4. A small writing-pad and lead-pencil, for general memoranda and notations.

5. Certain fruits and flowers, such as roses, sweet-peas, pineapples, and grape-fruit. These met the psychic's needs or fancies, and were brought into close relation with pad or slate when the "forces" seemed inclined to weaken.

6. The piano.

Shortly after the opening of the Friday-morning sitting the Composer requested that the whole slate be ruled with staves for writing music. Throughout the preceding Wednesday and Thursday attempts at the writing of music had been of constant occurrence; they had come on slates, on writing-pads, and on the leaves of closed books. These bits of musical notation had been very fragmentary and obscure; often they had consisted of less than half a dozen notes placed upon staves consisting of but three or four lines, instead of five. The most successful of these earlier efforts had been produced on a double school-slate, with a wooden, list-bound frame: two measures on a treble staff Pg 286 had been sprinkled with vague indications of musical script. No attempts had yet been made to bring even the best of these various writings to order and intelligibility. We were soon to learn that a scrap of music set down within three or four minutes was to require as many hours for revision, emendation, elucidation—for editing, in brief. It is but fair, however, to state that some of this time was taken up by the registering of irrelevant messages from other quarters and by digressions toward the Composer's own private concerns.

The staff drawn on the wooden-framed slate had been ruled crosswise. The Composer now directed that the new staves to be drawn on the silicon slate should run lengthwise and should cover every page of it. This was done by the editor. Provision was asked for seven measures, to which an eighth was added later.

During the three minutes or so required for writing on the six pages of the slate, the position of the slate, in reference to the editor, was as follows: After considerable moving about beneath the top of the table, during which time it was principally in the hands of the psychic, it approached the writer and remained with him. The under cover of the slate with a bit of slate-pencil tightly enclosed rested on his knee; the upper cover was pressed against the frame of the table. The editor's thumb rested rather lightly on the middle of the nearer Pg 287 half of the upper cover, and his fingers assisted in supporting the nearer half of the under cover. The psychic herself had surrendered the control of the slate to the editor, and could have had no contact with it beyond touching the edge farthest from him. On the second day, Saturday, during which the bass for the last four measures was produced, the slate was in the exclusive control of the editor, the psychic not touching it at all. The progress of the musical writing was both felt and heard; it was a combination of light and rapid scratching, pecking, and twitching, with an occasional slight waving motion up and down.

The score, as first revealed, consisted of open-headed notes with curved stems. They gave no indications of varying values; it was impossible to distinguish quarter-notes from eighth-notes, sixteenth-notes, or grace-notes; and no rests were set down. The notes were placed but approximately as regarded lines and spaces. No stems, save in one or two instances, united the chords, the notes of which were written more or less above one another, yet detached. A few unsatisfactory attempts were made by the Composer to place the bars. These were mostly put in by the editor—sometimes by the direction or with the acquiescence of the Composer—and, when they were drawn in advance of the writing, their presence was always properly observed.

Pg 288

As the revision became more close and careful, the Composer directed that the work be continued down-stairs beside the piano. Here every bar of the treble was played separately as soon as edited, to be pronounced satisfactory by the Composer, or to be modified under his direction. The treble, on its completion—eight measures—was then played over in its entirety and pronounced by the Composer to be correct. He made one or two further emendations, however, on the following day. The eight bars of the bass were gone over in the same fashion. The attempt to play the entire composition, treble and bass, was not satisfactory, partly owing to mechanical difficulties occasioned by the distribution of the matter on the slate and the multiplicity of corrections, and partly from lack of skill in the performer. However, two or three very brief passages were given by both hands and pronounced correct by the Composer, who showed surprise that anything so "*simple*"—as he characterized it—should give so much trouble. In one instance he noted that, while the two parts, treble and bass, were correct separately, they were not played in correct time together. The Composer, throughout, was most patient, persevering, courteous, and encouraging, though toward the end—in the closing measures of the bass—he showed some confusion and uncertainty. "*Wait a moment*," he would say; and once the whisper asked Pg 289 that, as an aid to sight, the editor's hand be spread over that leaf of the slate on which work was in progress. The

Composer had thought, earlier—and so said—that a trained musician could easily supply the bass from the melody. His amanuensis was obliged to acknowledge frankly an inability to cope successfully with so complicated and unusual a matter. The psychic herself, though expressing a fondness for the opera, disclaimed any knowledge of musical notation, and added that never before had she performed such a function as at present.

As the work of correction progressed, the Composer several times asked for opportunity to make the changes himself; whereupon the pencil-tip would be enclosed in the slate and satisfactory emendations be forthcoming. In cases where corrections were made by the writer, the Composer often watched the progress of the slate-pencil a longer one than that which was used between the leaves and gave directions: "*Not there*"; "*Yes, here,*" and the like; and he would often acknowledge a correction with a "*Thank you,*" or meet a suggestion with a "*Yes, if you please.*" On these occasions the slate was some four feet distant from the psychic, and practically out of her sight.

Repeated attempts were made on both sides to get down the name of the composition. Various related versions of the word appeared, none of them quite satisfactory. The Composer seemed Pg 290 to acquiesce in our attempts to relate his title to different Slavic and Italian words for "gypsy," but no importance can be attached, of course, to such a piece of direct suggestion.

The final version of this brief but laborious score has been preserved, and all the stages in its progress have been abundantly annotated. To follow it through in detail, however, would be but weariness. All the salient points in its production fall under one of three heads. There are, first, the passages that seem to have been produced in co-operation with the sitters. There are, second, the passages that seem to have been produced in independence of the sitters. And there are, third, the passages that seem to have been produced in direct opposition to the sitters. Examples of all three classes follow; perhaps only those of the third and last class are really important.

1. The Composer in Co-operation. The piece, in three sharps, opened on the tonic, yet the very first note in the bass was a G-sharp. The following colloquy ensued: Editor: "Does the piece begin with the tonic chord of A?" Composer: "*Yes.*" Editor: "Is the G-sharp, then, to be regarded as a suspension?" Composer: "*Of course. That makes it right. How could it be correct otherwise?*"

Another example. In the second bar a note which the editor had taken for an eighth-note was Pg 291 explained by the Composer as being a grace-note. The editor pointed out that this left only five eighth-notes to fill a six-eight measure. The Composer directed the insertion of an eighth-rest at the beginning of the bar.

In the fourth bar there was a partial chord, E-B—a fifth. The Composer's attention was drawn to this blemish. He requested the insertion of a G-sharp between, thus completing his triad.

But the above examples, and others which might be related, are not without resemblances to thought transference.

2. The Composer in Independence. Under this head may be placed his various instructions relative to tempo, expression, and the like. The signature, three sharps, was set down by the editor, as the result of an answer to his inquiry. But the time—six-eight—was written in on the editor's request by the Composer himself. It was a distinct and separate effort, for which the pencil was put in the slate and the slate placed beneath the table. The time was set down before the notes themselves were secured. The six-eight sign was clearly and neatly written

on the proper staff, in correct relation to the G-clef and to the signature; and the two figures were also in correct relation to each other. The word "Moderato" was written in by the Composer's direction, without any request from the editor. Later, the words "With Pg 292 feeling" and the mark of expression "pp," were obtained in the same way. Ties, grace-notes, and staccato-marks were insisted upon, here and there, with great vigor and earnestness.

Two further examples of the Composer's independence will perhaps suffice. In the sixth measure there was a run of three eighth-notes in the treble, exactly above a corresponding run of three eighth-notes in the bass. In making his revision the Composer directed that each of these three pairs of notes should be joined by stems. This took the treble notes down to the bass, and left the last half of the treble bar empty—a fact unnoticed by the editor and beyond the purview of the psychic. The Composer, however, observed the hiatus, and directed the insertion of two rests.

One other instance: The bar at the end of the first measure, as originally drawn by the Composer, cut off two notes on leger-lines and gave them to the succeeding measure. Another little colloquy: Editor: "Shall I draw the bar where it belongs?" Composer: "*Yes, if you please.*" Editor: "Here?" Composer: "*No.*" Editor: "There?" Composer: "*Yes. Thank you.*"

3. The Composer in Opposition. Numerous interesting cases of cross-purposes between the Composer and the circle developed during these two days. A number of salient examples follow:

On the first opening of the slate, the seventh Pg 293 measure of the treble contained but two notes, which the Composer presently declared to be quarter-notes. This left the first third of the measure vacant; and the Composer, interrogated, directed the insertion of a quarter-rest. The editor objected that this gave the measure a three-quarter look, instead of the proper six-eighth look. "*That is a liberty I take,*" came the answer, like a flash.

At one stage the Composer requested that a certain note should have a "dot" added. The editor placed the dot to the right of the note, thus lengthening its value by one-half. "*No, no,*" objected the Composer; "*put it on top, above the staff.*" His intention had been, once more, to make a note "staccato," and he had been misunderstood.

The editor, in setting down the signature of sharps on the second page of the slate, intentionally placed the last sharp a third below its proper position. He was at once brought to book by "Dr. Cooke," the "control." "*We are being fair by you, and you must be fair by us.*"

In the eighth and last measure, which did not appear to be satisfactorily completed, the Composer called for the insertion of a figure 2. This meant, as became clear enough through a subsequent reference to his published scores, that he wished two quarter-notes to receive the value of three eighth-notes, but was not understood at the time by his helper. "*Never mind,*" said the Pg 294 Composer, graciously, "*I will write it differently.*" He cancelled the figure 2, and completed the measure with a rest.

A similar instance occurred in the fifth measure, where the Composer called insistently for a double sharp × . The editor ventured to object, and the passage was tried on the piano, at the Composer's request. The double sharp was felt by him to be unsatisfactory, and was sacrificed. "*It won't make much difference, anyway,*" was his whispered comment.

A curious point, to finish with: On the first day the editor inquired about doubtful notes by name, as, A, C-sharp, and the like, while the Composer indicated their position by specifying lines and spaces—as, third space, second line, and so on. The next day, when the editor made his inquiries on the basis of lines and spaces, the Composer oftenest named the notes by letter.

Toward the end of the last sitting, "Dr. Cooke" once again came to the fore and hinted that the result of our endeavors might perhaps be not a reproduction of one of the Composer's manuscripts, but of a mental picture in the Composer's mind. The "picture," as secured by us, was not, it must be admitted, without distortion. The Composer himself used the word "scattered" in such a way as to imply that he had sketched out his ideas in life on various detached bits of paper. He added Pg 295 that a certain member of his family "would know." The hopes raised by this declaration have not been realized.

"No more music to-day," whispered "Dr. Cooke"; and the sitting—the sittings—ended.

9 781835 916391